THE MUSICIAN

EMERSON PASS HISTORICALS, BOOK SIX

TESS THOMPSON

PRAISE FOR TESS THOMPSON

"I frequently found myself getting lost in the characters and forgetting that I was reading a book." - *Camille Di Maio, Bestselling author of The Memory of Us.*

"Highly recommended." - *Christine Nolfi, Award winning author of The Sweet Lake Series.*

"I loved this book!" - *Karen McQuestion, Bestselling author of Hello Love and Good Man, Dalton.*

Traded: Brody and Kara:
"I loved the sweetness of Tess Thompson's writing - the camaraderie and long-lasting friendships make you want to move to Cliffside and become one of the gang! Rated Hallmark for romance!" - *Stephanie Little BookPage*

"This story was well written. You felt what the characters were going through. It's one of those "I got to know what happens next" books. So intriguing you won't want to put it down." - *Lena Loves Books*

"This story has so much going on, but it intertwines within itself. You get second chance, lost loves, and new love. I could not put this book down! I am excited to start this series and have love for this little Bayside town that I am now fond off!" - *Crystal's Book World*

"This is a small town romance story at its best and I look forward to the next book in the series." - *Gillek2, Vine Voice*

"This is one of those books that make you love to be a reader and fan of the author." -*Pamela Lunder, Vine Voice*

Blue Midnight:
"This is a beautiful book with an unexpected twist that takes the story from romance to mystery and back again. I've already started the 2nd book in the series!" - *Mama O*

"This beautiful book captured my attention and never let it go. I did not want it to end and so very much look forward to reading the next book." - *Pris Shartle*

"I enjoyed this new book cover to cover. I read it on my long flight home from Ireland and it helped the time fly by, I wish it had been longer so my whole flight could have been lost to this lovely novel about second chances and finding the truth. Written with wisdom and humor this novel shares the raw emotions a new divorce can leave behind." - *J. Sorenson*

"Tess Thompson is definitely one of my auto-buy authors! I love her writing style. Her characters are so real to life that you just can't put the book down once you start! Blue Midnight makes you believe in second chances. It makes you believe that everyone deserves an HEA. I loved the twists and turns in this book, the mystery and suspense, the family dynamics and the restoration of trust and security." - *Angela MacIntyre*

"Tess writes books with real characters in them, characters with flaws and baggage and gives them a second chance. (Real people, some remind me of myself and my girlfriends.) Then she cleverly and thoroughly develops those characters and makes you feel deeply for them. Characters are complex and multifaceted, and the plot seems to unfold naturally, and never feels contrived." - *K. Lescinsky*

Caramel and Magnolias:
"Nobody writes characters like Tess Thompson. It's like she looks into our lives and creates her characters based on our best friends, our lovers, and our neighbors. Caramel and Magnolias, and the authors debut novel Riversong, have some of the best characters I've ever had a chance to fall in love with. I don't like leaving spoilers in reviews so just trust me, Nicholas Sparks has nothing on Tess Thompson, her writing flows so smoothly you can't help but to want to read on!" - *T. M. Frazier*

"I love Tess Thompson's books because I love good writing. Her prose is clean and tight, which are increasingly rare qualities, and manages to evoke a full range of emotions with both subtlety and power. Her fiction goes well beyond art imitating life. Thompson's characters are alive and fully-realized, the action is believable, and the story unfolds with the right balance of tension and exuberance. CARAMEL AND MAGNOLIAS is a pleasure to read." - *Tsuruoka*

"The author has an incredible way of painting an image with her words. Her storytelling is beautiful, and leaves you wanting more! I love that the story is about friendship (2 best friends) and love. The characters are richly drawn and I found myself rooting for them from the very beginning. I think you will, too!"
- *Fogvision*

"I got swept off my feet, my heartstrings were pulled, I held my breath, and tightened my muscles in suspense. Tess paints stunning scenery with her words and draws you in to the lives of her characters."- *T. Bean*

Duet For Three Hands:

"Tears trickled down the side of my face when I reached the end of this road. Not because the story left me feeling sad or disappointed, no. Rather, because I already missed them. My friends. Though it isn't goodbye, but see you later. And so I will sit impatiently waiting, with desperate eagerness to hear where life has taken you, what burdens have you downtrodden, and what triumphs warm your heart. And in the meantime, I will go out and live, keeping your lessons and friendship and love close, the light to guide me through any darkness. And to the author I say thank you. My heart, my soul -all of me - needed these words, these friends, this love. I am forever changed by the beauty of your talent." - *Lisa M.Gott*

"I am a great fan of Tess Thompson's books and this new one definitely shows her branching out with an engaging enjoyable historical drama/love story. She is a true pro in the way she weaves her storyline, develops true to life characters that you love! The background and setting is so picturesque and visible just from her words. Each book shows her expanding, growing and excelling in her art. Yet another one not to miss. Buy it you won't be disappointed. The ONLY disappointment is when it ends!!!" - *Sparky's Last*

"There are some definite villains in this book. Ohhhh, how I loved to hate them. But I have to give Thompson credit because they never came off as caricatures or one dimensional. They all felt authentic to me and (sadly) I could easily picture them. I loved to love some and loved to hate others." - *The Baking Bookworm*

"I stayed up the entire night reading Duet For Three Hands and unbeknownst to myself, I fell asleep in the middle of reading the book. I literally woke up the next morning with Tyler the Kindle beside me (thankfully, still safe and intact) with no ounce of battery left. I shouldn't have worried about deadlines because, guess what? Duet For Three Hands was the epitome of unputdownable." - *The Bookish Owl*

Miller's Secret

"From the very first page, I was captivated by this wonderful tale. The cast of characters amazing - very fleshed out and multi-dimensional. The descriptions were perfect - just enough to make you feel like you were transported back to the 20's and 40's.... This book was the perfect escape, filled with so many twists and turns I was on the edge of my seat for the entire read." - *Hilary Grossman*

"The sad story of a freezing-cold orphan looking out the window at his rich benefactors on Christmas Eve started me off with Horatio-Alger expectations for this book. But I quickly got pulled into a completely different world--the complex five-character braid that the plot weaves. The three men and two women characters are so alive I felt I could walk up and start talking to any one of them, and I'd love to have lunch with Henry. Then the plot quickly turned sinister enough to keep me turning the pages.
Class is set against class, poor and rich struggle for happiness and security, yet it is love all but one of them are hungry for. ......Where does love come from? What do you do about it? The story kept me going, and gave me hope. For a little bonus, there are Thompson's delightful observations, like: "You'd never know we could make something this good out of the milk from an animal who eats hats." A really good read!" - *Kay in Seattle*

"She paints vivid word pictures such that I could smell the

ocean and hear the doves. Then there are the stories within a story that twist and turn until they all come together in the end. I really had a hard time putting it down. Five stars aren't enough!" - **M.R. Williams**

ALSO BY TESS THOMPSON

CLIFFSIDE BAY

Traded: Brody and Kara

Deleted: Jackson and Maggie

Jaded: Zane and Honor

Marred: Kyle and Violet

Tainted: Lance and Mary

Cliffside Bay Christmas, The Season of Cats and Babies (Cliffside Bay Novella to be read after Tainted)

Missed: Rafael and Lisa

Cliffside Bay Christmas Wedding (Cliffside Bay Novella to be read after Missed)

Healed: Stone and Pepper

Chateau Wedding (Cliffside Bay Novella to be read after Healed)

Scarred: Trey and Autumn

Jilted: Nico and Sophie

Kissed (Cliffside Bay Novella to be read after Jilted)

Departed: David and Sara

Cliffside Bay Bundle , Books 1,2,3

BLUE MOUNTAIN SERIES

Blue Mountain Bundle, Books 1,2,3

Blue Midnight

Blue Moon

Blue Ink

THE MUSICIAN

This book is dedicated to the musician, singer/songwriter Nanci Griffith. For over thirty years her music was a light in my darkest moments.

She passed away last summer at the age of sixty-eight. It's customary to say Rest In Peace but somehow that doesn't feel quite right. I have a feeling she's busy in heaven entertaining the crowd with her beautiful voice, as she did here on earth.

1

FIONA

Li returned to me on a chilly day in the deep midwinter of 1928. The Colorado sky, blue against the white backdrop of our mountains, had no cloud layer to shield me from the numbing cold. Just as I had no protection from my own heart. The way it beat for only Li.

Smoke billowed in the air from the steam engine accompanied by the roar and clanging of metal, complaining like a grumpy old man with aches and pains in his joints. It slowed as it came around the bend and came to a stop before me.

I searched for him in the windows. The face I knew as well as my own. And there he was. Centered in a window as if he were a photograph in a crude frame. I lifted my hand in welcome. And he placed his hand against the foggy window.

My stomach fluttered with excitement even as a sense of calm washed over me. He was here. Everything was right in my small world. There would be no one else for me. I'd known it for a while now. I wanted him for all time. Not only as a musical playmate, but as the love of my life. By my side, through seasons and children, joys and sorrows.

By the end of this week, I would be twenty years old. I'd

decided I would tell him, finally, of my feelings. In all the days we'd spent together, I'd searched and searched for hints in that face I loved so. Did he love me too? But I couldn't see it, one way or the other. Li was not like my father or my brother Theo. Everything they felt was portrayed with a nod of the head, twitch of the cheek, or curve of a smile. Not Li. His reticence and caution informed his day-to-day life. Except when he played music. Then, I knew his heart.

And still, I had no idea if he returned my feelings. I'd bided my time, restless and itchy, but knowing it was unlikely. For one thing, he was six years older than me. I might be a silly schoolgirl to him, or the youngest sibling of the original Barnes children. A little girl with black curls and a big bow. I didn't know, and so I waited.

He'd been away in Denver since the new year, performing music in a club. In addition, he'd accompanied a renowned blues singer on the piano for an actual recording. This was utterly too exciting.

For as long as I could remember, my family had departed and returned from the train platform in Emerson Pass. I'd watched with a bittersweet ache as my sisters and brothers left for adventures. Later, I'd waited for them in the same spot I'd said goodbye, delighted to welcome them home. Yet I had no desire to travel myself. Was this a character flaw? This natural contentment and love of home? I've no idea. I was quite simply Fiona Barnes. Sister, friend, daughter, and auntie. My gifts were appreciated. I never had any urge to go myself. Why would I, when everything and everyone I loved was a stone's throw away?

I'd never yearned for travel or new experiences. They came to me in music. I had no ambition or competitiveness in my character, as my siblings did. Unlike my beloved stepmother, who had come out west in a desperate move to save her mother and sister, I had no earthly needs that pushed me forward into difficult things. I was content and happy to be the sister who remained behind and was here to welcome them home again.

Music was the vehicle through which I traveled. My sister Josephine often told me she'd traveled to many places inside the pages of her precious books. "Whole lives are in here," she'd said once, waving a copy of *Heidi* at me. Music was the same for me. Whether singing or playing piano, I journeyed to worlds unknown to me but revealed themselves through the music. If one listened carefully enough, the story of my life was in every note.

Like the river that meandered alongside our little town, I, too, bubbled along happily, expanding and contracting with the seasons and my siblings. I was not the traveler but the one who welcomed the intrepid ones home.

Li stood for a split second on the top step of the train car before disembarking. My body warmed as I took in every detail of the man I loved. He looked good in his dark gray suit with a slightly askew bowler hat pulled low over his forehead.

"Hello, Fiona." He grinned and tipped his hat.

I drew closer, placing my fingers briefly on the lapel of his suit. He smelled of pipe smoke and peppermint. "Welcome home." I held out my hand and he brushed his mouth against my knuckles.

I asked him about his train trip from Denver, and he assured me it was fine. "Your father's first-class ticket was too extravagant, but I enjoyed myself."

"He's very proud of you," I said. "Making a recording with a professional musician. It's perfectly perfect. What was it like to record? Did you get to hear it played back?"

He described in detail the process in a way only another musician would understand. "The blues singers and musicians are just as you imagined them. Crusty, sad, soulful, and so very skilled. My violin may never play another happy tune."

"Oh, don't say such things."

"I'm only teasing you."

He took his suitcase from the porter and asked questions of me. How was Flynn? Were he and Shannon still happily reunited? Would Louisa's baby come soon? Had Josephine gotten the grant for the library expansion? Had Cym and Viktor returned from their competition circuit yet?

I rattled off all our news as we walked to the car. Yes, all was well with Shannon and Flynn. In fact, they'd just shared they were having another baby, due in early fall.

"The reconciliation went well, then?" Li asked, clearly amused.

I flushed at the implication and went on to answer his other questions. Jo had indeed secured the funds for another wing for our library. Cymbeline and Viktor had just returned from a ski-jump competition in Wisconsin where she'd taken first place, beating the man favored to win. "Cym says he was so angry that he hurled his second-place trophy at her head. Fortunately, she's quick, you know, and ducked."

Soon, we were driving along the icy dirt road toward home. It was such a habit to bring him to the estate where he'd lived in our servant quarters with his grandmother and sister for almost all the years of my childhood that I almost missed his driveway. I veered left suddenly, and we brushed shoulders. A spark went through me. Where had it come from, that shot of warmth and excitement?

We bumped along the driveway. Iced-over mud puddles cracked under our tires. On either side of us, trees were covered with frost. A fierce wind had come in the night before, wiping away the layers of snow that had accumulated on bushes and trees. Now they were ice sculptures that sparkled under the sun. After a few minutes, we reached Li's cottage. Built only last summer, it was a similar bungalow style to Viktor and Cym's home.

"Let's get inside where it's warm," he said.

The end of my nose had grown cold enough that I welcomed the idea. Before he got out of the car, however, I reached over and touched his hand briefly. "I missed you."

He turned slightly to look at me. His eyes warmed me as nothing else could. "I missed you, too."

"Did you think about me at all, away in the big city?"

"I thought of you every day and wished you were with me."

"I want to hear all about it, every detail," I said.

"You'll hear everything you need to know when the record is done."

"I will?" I asked.

His mouth lifted into a lazy smile. "You know what I mean. Everything's there in the music. All the love and longing and beauty in the world, right there, in the notes. These musicians, Fi, they were indescribable. For the only time in my life, I didn't feel out of place."

"Why?"

"They're all outcasts, like me. Men and women of color."

"Oh." My heart sank. He'd found new friends, ones perhaps he enjoyed better than me and my family. "Is it lonely for you here?"

"Sometimes. Never with you, of course. But it's hard to be one of the only people in town who looks like me. It's only Fai and Grandmother and me. I have a feeling Fai might not come back to us, so then it will be only two."

Li was a descendant of hopeful Chinese men and women who had come to Emerson Pass before it was a town and merely a destination for the mining of gold. After his parents and grandfather had perished from a terrible illness, he and his sister, Fai, and their grandmother, Mrs. Wu, had come to live with us. Papa had found the three of them living in what remained of the gold mining operation, practically starving as they faced a cold winter. My father had brought them to our house and offered them rooms downstairs in our staff quarters.

He'd insisted Fai and Li attend school with the rest of us. I'd been only three years old that year and couldn't remember a time when they did not live with us. They were as much a fabric of my life as my siblings.

Mrs. Wu had helped Lizzie in the kitchen, adding delightful nuances to our very English culinary menu. As children, we thought nothing of the differences in our appearances from the Wu siblings. They were our friends and classmates, and family, just as Jasper and Lizzie were.

"Was it strange to be away, making music with someone besides me?" I watched him carefully. Had he met someone to replace me? What about women? Had there been any? The thought made my stomach hurt.

"It was strange to be away from you, yes." He smiled at me, fondly, as if I were his little sister, I thought. Not the way Viktor smiled at Cym or Phillip when he looked at Jo.

"Why the sad eyes?" Li asked. "Perhaps you didn't miss me as much as you thought you would and wish I'd go back?"

"That's not what I'm thinking and you know it." I lightly smacked his shoulder. "I was hoping you hadn't replaced me with anyone, that's all."

"Fiona Barnes, you are many things, but replaceable is not one of them."

My stomach fluttered. "I'm glad. I couldn't bear it if you found someone else to make music with."

"I enjoyed my time, but here is my home. In fact, certain aspects of my life became very clear to me while I was away."

I wanted to ask for clarity, but Mrs. Wu, Li's grandmother, appeared on the porch. Li's face lit up at the sight of her. "Let's go see Grandmother."

"You'll tell me more later?" I asked, cringing at the neediness in my voice. Goodness me, I needed to let the poor man breathe. "Or whenever you have a chance."

"I'll tell you everything tonight at the club. Between sets." We were playing at my brother's underground club later. The regulars, of which there were many, had been asking me for a week if Li would be back soon. As much as they enjoyed my singing, the music suffered without Li. He and I were better together, at least when it came to playing jazz and blues. We were a melodious duo, making music together as if one person. I sang while he played various instruments. Sometimes, I would play piano and sing while he accompanied me on the violin. Other times, he would play the violin in the tradition of the fiddle in harmony with my piano and my voice, which could change direction with only a mere nod from my musical partner.

Then, later, when we were older, we began to compose music together. We spent hours together, plucking away at notes until we had a song. Li took it all for granted, the way we could create something beautiful from nothing. He seemed to understand his talent better than I. Or perhaps he accepted it as part of who he was, whereas I thought of it as whispers from the divine. God was good to me. He spoke the notes to me, gave me a voice that people compared to angels, as if they'd ever heard one sing. Once, when I told my sister Cymbeline how grateful I was to God for my voice and musical ability, she'd said, "We're the ones who should thank God, dear sister. For we're the ones who get to listen and dance to the music you make for us."

Cymbeline loved to dance. And ski and run and make trouble for herself. I loved her madly.

I had to tell Li of my feelings. I'd waited for a long time, knowing that he was a man of integrity and conscience. He would not love me until I was old enough. I'd decided I would tell him about my feelings on my twentieth birthday.

I'd told my siblings already. They'd been appalled and worried, made me promise not to tell anyone else. Not even Li himself.

"There's nothing good that can come of it," Jo had said. "You must forget all of this."

7

Theo had nodded, his brow creased with worry. "She's right, Fi. This is just a crush anyway. Once you're older and meet the right man, you'll see this was just a childhood fantasy."

Flynn and Cymbeline had exchanged a look between them. One that said they knew my conservative siblings were incorrect. Growing up, I'd often thought of the four of them divided into two sets: one good, one terrifically wicked. They were like a good and bad angel on my shoulder. I responded better to the naughty devils. As much as I loved Jo and Theo, it was Flynn and especially Cym who helped me make sense of things. They understood my wild heart, my endless capacity for love.

After getting his suitcase from the back, Li took my arm as we walked up the icy steps to his front porch. Mrs. Wu held out her arms to hug her grandson, then stepped back to get a good look at him. "I'm glad to see you."

"I'm glad to see you," Li said. She smiled, sending the lines of her face into a hundred winding roads, before beckoning us inside the house.

The warm air felt like a sudden blast of hot wind. A fire crackled in the hearth and cinnamon scented the air.

Mrs. Wu squeezed my hand and then took my coat to hang in the closet. "You'll stay for tea, won't you?"

"If it's not too much trouble," I said. "I'll help if you need it."

"Nonsense. I'm old but not dead." Mrs. Wu nodded toward the kitchen. "I have the tea already made, and Jasper brought by a box of Lizzie's scones and cakes. She's afraid I'll starve out here all alone."

"Have you been all right?" I asked. "We miss you at the house."

"Oh yes, I'm fine. After Li left I was lonely at first, but then new friends came to keep me company." She pointed toward a basket by the fire.

"Grandmother, are those kittens?" Li shrugged out of his coat and strode across the room to get a better look. I followed him, pretending to be curious but knowing already of the two balls of fluff curled together. They were from a litter from our cat Miss Kitty, named by Delphia. I'd left the basket on the porch the day after Li had left, hoping Mrs. Wu would be delighted by the cats instead of horrified. It was a gamble, but from the look of things, my plan had worked nicely. I peered into the basket. One was an orange tabby and the other black with a white bib and paws. "Where did they come from?"

"They showed up on the porch one day," Mrs. Wu said. "I looked around to see if they had a mother, but it was only the two of them. Someone left them purposefully. They were in that basket. Only smaller. They've grown a lot in one month."

Mrs. Wu's shoulders curled inward. She'd always been small but seemed to have shrunk over the last few years. No one had any idea of her age, not even Li, but we thought she must be in her seventies. My mother had finally persuaded her to retire from our kitchen, where she'd helped Lizzie prepare all our meals. She'd agreed at last and was now settled into the cottage with Li after spending almost twenty years in the downstairs servant quarters at our house.

"Do you think someone chose you specifically?" I asked, feigning innocence.

"I have a feeling someone did," Mrs. Wu said. "Or someones."

It was true. I'd brought Addie and Delphia with me when we delivered the basket. We'd tried to be quiet, leaving the car at the end of the driveway so she didn't hear the hum of the motor. "Are you enjoying them, Mrs. Wu?"

"They like my lap in the evening," Mrs. Wu said. "Poor things have nothing but my bony lap to sit on. It's good Li's home, isn't it?"

"I know I'm happy to see him," I said.

"You're an interfering young lady," Mrs. Wu said to me. "You remind me of your father."

"Thank you," I said, smiling. "I'll take that as a compliment."

"As you should," Mrs. Wu said, returning my smile.

We had our tea and heard stories about Li's trip. His eyes sparkled as he described the recording event and all of the characters he'd met during the process. "It was a good thing to do. One of the most rewarding of my life."

"Are you sad to return to life as usual?" I asked.

"Not at all. I'm glad to be home." He smiled at me, and my stomach did a sudden double-time twist, as if I'd lost the right beat.

I thanked them for the tea and told them I needed to get home but would swing by to get him later for our gig at the club.

"I'll drive myself tonight," Li said.

"Oh, all right then." Why did this hurt? It was silly. He often drove himself. I'd hoped for a little more time alone with him.

He walked me out to the porch. I told him not to come out to the car. "I've had to take care of myself these last few weeks. Without you to keep an eye on me. My brothers seem to think I'm a helpless child. I don't need you to always be by my side, you know." I wanted him next to me but not to save me or keep me safe. Just to be.

"Miss Fiona, all grown up." He smirked, teasing me.

"I am, you know. If you haven't noticed." I lifted my eyes to look at him before stepping away. Halfway down the steps, I heard him utter something under his breath. "What did you say?" I called out to him from the car. Had he said, "I noticed?" No, surely not?

"Nothing, just that I'll see you later." He gestured for me to get in the car. "It's cold. Get home."

"Yes, yes." Someone in my life was always telling me what to do. I didn't mind, really. It's just sometimes I wondered if everyone thought me incompetent. That wasn't the truth, and they would know that if they ever really analyzed things.

As I drove away, he remained on the porch, watching me.

2

LI

I NEVER IMAGINED IT WOULD HAPPEN IN EMERSON PASS. NOT after my years in Chicago, where I lived in the shadows, eyes cast downward and my steps as careful as a stray cat, hoping no one noticed me. Here in my hometown, I felt safe, even loved. If not for my music or my close friendships with the Barnes siblings, it might have happened sooner. I'd become complacent, walking as bold as I pleased and playing music with Fiona Barnes almost every night at her brother's club.

That's when they got me.

I'd only been home for less than twenty-four hours. It was nearly 3:00 a.m. The club had closed at half-past two, but it had taken me a few minutes to pack up my instruments and count the tips left in the jar on top of the piano. Fiona had gone home with Cymbeline and Viktor, but I'd stayed behind to lock up. Flynn and Phillip had gone home to their wives hours before this.

My car was around back where Flynn asked the employees to park if the club was busy. The club was always crowded these days, thanks to Fiona and me and the cheap booze. Fiona and I made music almost as scandalous as the illegal gin. Not the same music we made on Sundays at church. But close to God just the same.

I walked in the footsteps left behind since the last snowfall. My legs were long and I had to pull back my usual stride to fit my feet in the tracks. When I got to my car, I'd already started to shiver and buttoned up my long wool coat. These clear nights were so pretty they'd take your breath away, but they'd also freeze a man or woman without a blink.

The door to my car was frozen so I had to tug extra hard. I'd just opened it when something yanked me backward and into a snowdrift. Then they were there, hovering over me. I'd seen them earlier in the club, sitting at a table in the corner, tossing back gins all night. Their breath came in clouds, obscuring their faces. Wool hats pulled to their eyebrows. Eyes hidden in the shadows. Bulks of darkness in the dark.

One of them kicked me in the stomach with the tip of his boot. Pain. Another kick, harder this time.

"What are you doing, slant eyes? Where's your friends, huh? Nobody to protect you now, is there?"

A different voice, slurred from drink. "You think you're such a fancy man, don't you? Acting like you belong with Fiona Barnes."

One of them dropped to the snow and pummeled my face with his fist while the other one kicked me repeatedly in the back. They could break me in half. Or make it so I couldn't walk again.

He was up again now and kicked me in the shin. I yelped in pain and instinctively curled into a ball to protect my most vulnerable area. What about my hands? Would they break my fingers? Anything but that.

"Let's finish him off," one of them said. "So he can't identify us."

"He shouldn't even be here."

"You should have gone home where you belong. We don't want you here." He backed up his comment with a kick to my head. The pain exploded behind my eyes.

"Stop," I whispered. "Please stop."

"Shut up." Another racial slur. One I'd heard often in Chicago.

"Let's get out of here before someone sees us."

I covered my face and waited for death to come. This was the way it would end, out here under the moon with the snow to numb my wounds. In that moment, my life was as clear as the sky. It was the people who mattered. The kindness shown to me. And Fiona. Her lovely slender fingers poised above the piano keys. The sound of her soprano voice. The way her black curls fell over one eye when she was at the keyboard.

Fiona. If I died, Grandmother would find the letter in my pocket. At least Fiona would know how much I'd loved her.

A kick in the back made me cry out in pain. My vision clouded. I would pass out soon, I thought. And I'd welcome it. From afar, I heard a shout, followed by a gunshot. And then they were gone. Flynn and Phillip appeared, kneeling by my side. Where had they come from? Hadn't they already gone home? Was I hallucinating?

"Are you all right?" Flynn's voice was hoarse and scared.

"Who was it?" Phillip asked. "Who did this to you?"

I peered up at them, my vision blurry. "I saw them in the lounge earlier," I muttered before groaning in pain. "But I don't know them. Too many new people here." They were the ones who should go back to where they came from.

"Can you stand, or should we lift you?" Flynn asked.

"It's only my middle," I said. It was hard to breathe. They might have cracked a rib with their boots. I kept that to myself.

They helped me up. My legs felt as though they had no bones or muscles with which to hold me up. I slumped against Flynn. "What are you doing here?" I asked.

"We had to finish up our inventory," Phillip said.

"I don't think I can drive," I said.

"Do you want us to call Theo?" Phillip asked.

Theo was one of our town doctors and the other half of the Barnes twins. Flynn and Theo. Good friends. Their father was the reason my grandmother, Fai, and I had survived way back when. Now here I was again, fighting against the snow.

They led me over to Flynn's car. I hadn't noticed it parked down at the other end of the employee lot. They helped me into the back seat and Flynn took a flask from his pocket. "Take a nip of this. It'll help with the pain."

He would know, I thought. He'd almost lost his life when a bullet had torn into his chest. Before Christmas. It was now February.

"Who would do this?" Phillip asked as he climbed into the driver's seat.

Flynn had already settled into the passenger seat by then. "And why? Do you have enemies like I do?" He turned around to look at me. I could only see through one eye. The right was swollen almost shut.

"Not that I know of," I said. "But one called me a name. For being Chinese."

Flynn cursed. "We'll find them and make sure they don't ever do something like this again."

"I didn't fight for freedom to have this happen in our town," Phillip said.

But this was their town, not mine. I could pretend that I belonged like these two fair-skinned, Irish- and English-descended men, but when it came down to it, I did not. I was not welcome in America. Or pretty much anywhere except China. But that was no longer an option. I'd lost that chance when my father and grandfather left it all behind in search of gold.

I groaned when we hit a pothole.

"Sorry," Phillip said.

I closed the other eye and leaned my head against the side of the car. There had been a few times in my life when an unwanted truth had come to me, swept in like an unexpected snowstorm. Once had been when I was in Chicago after an audition for the symphony. I'd known it as I tucked my bow into my violin case. They would not offer me a position. Not because I wasn't as good as the others. Or even better. The color of my skin and the shape of my eyes made sure of that.

And as we pulled down the driveway to my newly finished cottage on the Barneses' property, another truth came to me. One that left me breathless and sick. I could not have Fiona. She would be in danger next to me. Her life of laughter and love would be extinguished if she was married to me. She'd have to live in fear and worry. Our children would be shunned. That was not the life I wanted for her. Not Fiona, so pure of heart. A woman who loved the Lord and her family and the flowers that peppered the meadows in spring and making music. She was safe and well taken care of. She would not be with me. All the efforts I'd made to make it so were a joke.

We pulled up to my house, and Phillip turned off the car. "We'll help you inside and make sure you're all right before we go."

"I'm fine." I opened my door and set one foot into the snow before looking back at my friends. "Grandmother's here if I need anything. She'll be forcing one of her teas on me by morning."

They helped me to the door, and Flynn gave me another pull from his flask. "Try to get some sleep," Flynn said. "This'll help."

"Listen to me, brother," Phillip said. "We'll figure out who they were, and they'll be sorry they ever came to Emerson Pass."

"There will always be more," I said.

"And we'll run them out too," Flynn said. "You're ours, you know. Family. Same with your grandmother and Fai."

We weren't family. In fact, my grandmother had worked in the Barnes kitchen with the family cook for most of my life. Lord Barnes had taken us in, having found us living in the old office down at the abandoned gold mine. They'd sent Fai and me to school with the rest of the Barneses. Lord Barnes had arranged for me to go to university in Chicago to study music. He'd not expected me to come home. It had nearly killed me to disappoint him, but when I explained how things were, that no one would hire me, he understood. "You're home now, and we need music as much as the chaps in the city," he'd said in his British accent.

Now I thanked the boys and went into the house, careful to close and lock the door behind me. Stifling moans of pain, I walked down the short hallway to my bedroom. Grandmother's soft snores told me I hadn't awakened her. Fai was away at school, thank God. She would have a fit if she saw me right now.

I lay on my bed with my clothes still on, too shocked and hurt to think about taking off my suit. I'd be better in the morning. Grandmother would help me.

Gingerly I put my head on the pillow and prayed for sleep. The letter I'd written to Fiona lay against my chest, tucked away inside the pocket of my jacket. I'd written it to her that morning but had not had the courage to give it to her tonight as I'd promised myself.

It had become unbearable not to tell her my feelings. My love for her had only deepened over time. She was now twenty, not quite old enough to marry but close enough. By this time next year, I hoped she'd be my wife. If my suspicions were correct. I'd carried my secret around for months, never allowing myself any leniency. It must stay hidden. But then, tonight, I'd glanced over after a song and met her eyes. Love. That's what I'd seen shining back at me from those deep blue pools of light.

Given my differences from all the other men in Emerson

Pass, I wanted to tell her first before asking her father for his permission to officially court her. We were together all the time anyway, but this would be different. Lord Barnes trusted me to look after his daughter but sharing my intentions with her was quite another story.

I'd carried the first version of my letter around in my pocket for days, thinking that at any moment, I'd give it to her. But my reticent and careful nature held me back from making a move. What would Lord Barnes and his wife think of my request? Would they grant permission for a Chinese immigrant to court and subsequently marry their precious Fiona? Only time would tell. However, I wanted her to know my intentions first. If I were wrong and I was the only one of the two of us in love, then I would not bother Lord Barnes.

The letter rested in the inside pocket of my wool coat. It was still the deep midwinter here in the mountains of Colorado. I would give it to her after tomorrow's show. Otherwise, it would truly burn a hole through my jacket.

Dear Fiona,

I will attempt to put it simply in a letter, these feelings that are strong and complicated, but feel I will fail in my attempt. How does one tell someone the contents of their heart? So many times I've wanted to broach the subject but my cautious nature has made it impossible without knowing your feelings. Since I returned a few years ago from my time at university, my feelings for you have changed from a sense of friendship and protection to something much deeper.

I've not wanted to tell you until you were old enough to give me a chance. I know I have a lot against me, many reasons why you wouldn't consider me. However, I have to try. If being around your family has taught me anything it is to pursue dreams, no matter how outlandish they may seem to others.

So, that's it, dear Fiona. I have loved you for at least a year now and can no longer hold it in. I'd like to ask your father for permission to court you, but only if you wish it to be so. If you do not have the

17

same feelings for me or if you think everyone, including your family, would be against us, I'll never mention it again. But if there's even a small chance that you could love me, please let me know.

Yours forever,

Li

3

FIONA

The day after Li came home, I'd spent the morning with Shannon, helping with the babies. Cymbeline met me as I walked in the door.

She was already dressed for dinner in a short gown made of purple material that shimmered under the overhead light of the foyer. "There you are," Cym said, grabbing my hands and swinging me around. "Papa has a surprise for you."

What had happened? She seemed different, with a glow that made her even more beautiful than usual. "What kind of surprise?"

"Mama and Papa are in the sitting room with their tea. They want you to come in when you're ready."

I slipped out of my coat and hung it in the closet. What could they have to surprise me? I already had everything I wanted. Except for Li. Still, I had hope. The way he'd looked at me yesterday, a stirring of surety had simmered inside me.

A fire warmed the room. Papa and Mama sat near the fireplace. The light from the fire cast the room in a gauzy orange hue.

Cym dragged me over to the couch to sit opposite our

parents. Mama's cheeks were pink. She held a letter in her hands.

"Ah, there you are, sweetheart," Papa said. "We've been waiting for you."

"I'll get you a cup of tea," Cym said as she leaned forward to pour from the silver pitcher.

"What is it?" My stomach turned over. "You're all very mysterious."

"This is a letter from an old friend of mine." Papa gestured toward Mama, prompting her to hand me the envelope.

The postmark was from Paris. Who did we know in Paris?

Papa continued, as if it were the most ordinary news in the world. "He's connected in the music world over in Paris, and he's secured you a mentorship with a Mr. Pierre Basset."

"He's supposed to be the best voice teacher in the world," Cym blurted out.

"A stretch perhaps," Papa said. "But he *is* supposed to be quite talented at bringing out the best in his young protégés."

"Many have gone on to careers singing in the opera or theater in Paris and London," Mama said.

What had any of that to do with me? I waited to hear more.

"This Mr. Basset has been persuaded to teach you for a period of time. If you prove to be as talented as we know you are, he can arrange for other opportunities. He's well connected in the art community."

"A real career," Cym said. "Not singing at church or the club like you're doing now."

"But I like singing at church," I said. "Nothing makes me feel closer to God."

"Yes, but darling, this is a chance to study with one of the great teachers," Mama said. "This kind of chance doesn't come often."

"When is he arriving?" I asked, succumbing to my fate. I

wasn't ambitious, but if they all wanted me to have the opportunity for further study, then I would go along with it.

"No, sweetheart, you would go to Paris," Papa said. "We'll rent an apartment for you and hire a maid."

Mama clasped her hands above her chest. "Isn't it exciting?" In the next moment, her face fell. "But, darling girl, I'll miss you very much. You'll be gone for such a long time and far away."

"If I go," I said, voice as shaky as the rest of me. "What if Cym needs me? She's going to have a baby."

"Not for ages," Cym said. "You'll be back by then."

"You want to go, don't you?" Papa asked.

"I suppose." I avoided Cymbeline's gaze. She would be disappointed in me if I refused to go, my sister who craved adventure. "I quite like it here, playing music for people I know."

Mama studied me, her brown eyes indulgent. Of all of my siblings, it was me she most often looked at in this way. Even my youngest sisters, who were her own blood children, didn't invoke the same tolerance. I'd been only three when Mama came to us. We were as bonded as if I'd come from her womb. There was something special between Mama and me, a quality I couldn't quite put my finger on. Two souls so alike that when we were together, they seemed to call out to each other—*ah yes, it's you.*

"If you don't want to go, we will not force you," Mama said. "However, I've learned from my own experiences that doing something somewhat terrifying can lead to one's true destiny."

"Perhaps that's what I'm frightened of," I said. What if my destiny took me far away from my family and the mountains of Colorado? What if my destiny was not Li?

"It's only natural, love," Papa said in his British cadence, still very evident despite his many years in America. "To be afraid, that is. Courage is not the lack of fear, you know."

"But the ability to do whatever it is that scares us anyway," I said. Papa had told us this many times. I wanted to be brave, but not as much as I wanted to run up to my bedroom and bury my head under one of our soft pillows.

Mama clapped her hands in her lap and spoke excitedly. "They're much more progressive in France than we are in America. You'll learn a lot about art and culture."

"I'll have to go on the ship all by myself?" I asked, not nearly as excited by the prospect of exchanging a Colorado spring with all our wildflowers and birds and walks along the river. Wasn't that nature's art? The next thoughts came fast. What would it be like to be all alone? With Cym, I could do it. The thought of sleeping all alone in a cabin sounded terrible. And an apartment in Paris with a stranger as a maid? It was unthinkable.

"How would I get there?" I asked. "I'd need someone to accompany me."

"Yes, unlike your mother, who came out here alone all those years ago." Papa's gaze flickered to her, and they exchanged a knowing smile. Too poor to secure a chaperone, she'd come alone from Boston to become Emerson Pass's first school-teacher. But she'd met Papa and all of us and was never alone again, whether she wished for peace and quiet or not. "It would be good to send a companion with you."

"But who? Cymbeline's married now." I looked over at her. "Viktor wouldn't be able to come with us, and it would be wrong of me to ask you to be away from your new husband for such a long time."

"Two of my girls in Paris alone isn't my idea of a chaperone," Papa said. "Especially if one of them is Cymbeline."

"Very funny, Papa." Cymbeline's eyes shone as bright as jewels. "I can't go anyway, even if Viktor wouldn't mind." Her hand rested on her flat stomach. "It wouldn't be wise for me to be that far away from home or Theo."

"Yes, of course," I said, feeling selfish for wishing it other-wise. I was happy for her. I was. But this would all take some time to adjust to.

"I believe he or she comes in the fall if my calculations are correct." Cymbeline beamed. "Me, a mother! What is the world to think? Viktor's thrilled, as I knew he would be. He's already building a cradle. I am too, of course. It'll mean no jumping for a while, but you'll be surprised to hear I don't care one bit. A baby, Fiona. Can you imagine? I'm going to have a baby."

"You'll be a wonderful mother." I hugged her. But the world seemed wrong just then. Cym with a baby and me going off to Paris. This wasn't how it was supposed to go. The idea of leaving Cym in her time of need made me light-headed.

"I must be here for Cymbeline. I can't be gallivanting around Paris," I said.

"You'll be back before he or she comes," Cym said. "Don't worry, goose. It's your time to have all the attention on you for once. I won't be there to be demanding your attention or Jo telling you what to do. You'll be studying music in Paris with only yourself to please."

"Paris is a large city," I said. "I don't know if I could live there alone without anyone from home. What if I can't find my way around?"

"Don't be silly," Cym said. "You'll be fine. Viktor and I found our way around after only a few days." I'd heard so many tales from Cym's honeymoon that I felt as if I'd been there myself. But Cym and Viktor were courageous souls, unafraid of change or the unknown. They'd had each other, too.

"Emerson Pass is enough for me," I said under my breath. "It pleases me to be here."

Either they didn't hear or were ignoring me because Mama agreed, reiterating that it would be a special time for me and how much I deserved it after being such a good friend to my siblings.

"So, if not me, then who?" Cym asked, casually, as if she'd only just thought of the idea. "Perhaps Li Wu could go with her?

Oh, my sister was wicked. I loved her so.

She knew my feelings for Li. All my sisters and brothers knew. Even if I'd wanted to keep any, there were no secrets among the five of us older siblings. After Flynn's secret led to so much chaos, we'd all vowed to never again keep something from one another.

"If Li can come with me, then it sounds more palatable," I said, imitating Cym's casual tone.

"Li? I don't know," Papa said. "He has his grandmother to take care of now. It would be a burden if we asked him, and he wouldn't be able to say no. He's always going on about how much I've done for him. I'd hate for him to agree only to please me." Papa had given Li and his sister and grandmother a place to be warm and well-fed when he found them living in the old mining office. Li's parents and grandfather had come to Colorado in search of gold, like so many in the heady days of the gold rush. Sadly, they'd perished, leaving behind two young children with only their elderly grandmother to care for them.

"Papa, it's a trip to Paris," Cym said. "He'd be foolish to say no."

"Yes, indeed." Papa's brow creased. "Perhaps we should take her." He looked over at Mama, clearly thinking out loud. "The little girls are old enough to stay without us for a few months, especially with Lizzie and Jasper here to look after them. We could have that honeymoon we've always been too busy for. I could show you England."

Mama put her hands to her cheeks. "Alexander, really? Could we?"

"Why not? There's peace throughout all of Europe now. There would be no danger. I could see my brother. It might be time to mend our relationship." I'd never really known why Papa and his brother didn't get along but knew it pained him.

"But first, Fiona, you'll have to decide if this is what you want to do," Papa said. "It's a considerable expense, so I want you to be sure."

How could I say no? Not after seeing the excitement on Mama's face. If they went, would Li be able to come too? What about the money? Wouldn't it all be terribly expensive?

"Is it too much?" I asked in one last attempt at persuading them to keep me home. "Papa, you must tell me if it is. I shan't care to spend all your money." *Please say it's too much.*

"The expense is not a problem," Papa said softly. "But only if you truly want to go."

"I'm afraid my voice isn't good enough," I said. "And what will I do with all that training anyway? It's not as if I want to tour the world stage or whatever it is famous people do."

"You can bring it home to Emerson Pass," Mama said. "To delight the rest of us born without your talent. Music is the food of the soul, darling."

I smiled. "Yes, it is."

"Why don't you want to go?" Mama asked simply.

I looked into the orange and blue flames of the fire, hoping she couldn't see the deception that draped over me as ugly as a dust cloth. "I don't feel the need for an adventure as Cym did. Nor am I as clever as Jo or as ambitious as the twins. I'm only Fiona. Who am I to go to Paris and act otherwise?"

"You're an extremely talented young lady," Papa said. "Just as your siblings are. But no one has your musical ability or the voice of an angel. We want you to study with the best."

"And Pierre Basset. The chance to study with him is a chance of a lifetime," Mama said. "He's trained some of the finest voices in the world. And think of it, darling—time in Paris when you're young."

"But you're going to leave me there alone?" I asked, feeling teary. "All by myself. And what do we know about Mr. Basset?" Was he kind in addition to being a good teacher? "Does he know I don't want to be an opera singer?" The shrill tones didn't appeal to me. If it made me uncivilized, I didn't care.

25

Blues, jazz, and popular music made me happy. "Do you think he'll want me to?"

"He understands you're not that kind of singer," Papa said. "I made sure of that."

I thought for a moment about how this had come to be. Papa had circumvented me in this decision. Shouldn't I be the one to decide with whom and where I studied? Even as I thought this, a thick fog of guilt engulfed me. Papa wanted only the best for me. He'd assumed I'd be happy to go. Paris in the spring and summer. Studying with a world-renowned teacher? Who wouldn't want this?

Me.

However, if Li could accompany me, then I would be fine. Would it be a chance for us? Perhaps he would come to see me differently if we were somewhere new without the influences of my family and the close-knit community of Emerson Pass.

"Yes, thank you, Papa. I'd like to go, but only if you send Li with me." Lying made my stomach hurt, but there were times it was necessary. I could do anything for a few months, I told myself. In addition, I should be happy for the chance to grow as a singer. There were things I didn't even know I didn't know. I would have to be brave. "He could look after me, as he does here."

"I agree that it's a good idea," Mama said. "Alexander? Will he be safe there? What if he runs into the trouble he had in Chicago?"

I burned with anger thinking of what Li had to endure during his time at university in Chicago. The awful people who had mocked him and worse, abused him, for his Chinese ancestry. He was an American, just like any of the immigrants who had arrived here from Europe not so very long ago. Like Papa, Lizzie, and Jasper, who had come from England.

"He would certainly benefit from Paris," Papa said. "He does a superb job of looking after you here during your nights at the club. If he would like to go, I would be happy to pay his way in exchange for keeping you safe."

It didn't occur to them that Li was a man. A young man. One my siblings and I considered a contemporary. Was it because of his ethnicity? Would he feel the same way about some of the other young men in our set? I hated to admit it, but I didn't think so. He would not think of Li as a threat to my virtue because he was of Chinese descent.

"There will be parties and young men," Mama said. "It would do my heart good to know Li was there to watch out for you. I'll be nervous for you, but you must not let this opportunity pass you by. Step off the train," Mama said this last part under her breath.

"Step off the train?" I asked.

"Pay me no mind. It's only a sentimental notion of mine." Mama brushed her hands together. "Now, have some tea. We'll start to make arrangements tomorrow."

Please, God, let Li say yes.

4

FIONA

MY BIRTHDAY PARTY HAD CONSISTED OF A FAMILY DINNER AND
then games afterward. I'd told Li earlier that I had something
exciting to share with him. He'd promised we could sneak away
for a talk later, but then he and my brothers and brothers-in-
law had disappeared into the sitting room for brandy and
cigars. Now everyone was inside playing games or talking
together in various corners of the formal sitting room. I'd
declined an offer to play another card game to follow Li out to
the back porch. I found him on the steps. He startled as I swept
through the screen door of our enclosed porch to join him.
"Hello."

"Fiona, you scared me."

"I'm sorry. I wondered where you'd gone off to." I sat next to
him on the second step, careful to keep my boots out of the
snow. "What are you doing out here? It's freezing."

"I needed a little air. Your brother gave me a draw from his
flask, and it made me a little dizzy."

"You should stay away from whatever's in Flynn's flask," I
said, laughing. "Whatever it is, it's probably enough to eat away
the lining of your stomach."

28

"Are you enjoying your birthday party?" Li asked, turning to look at me. In the light from the house, I could see purple shadows under his eyes that matched the bruises on his face. Had he not slept well? Although he was dressed impeccably, he seemed a bit tattered, not refreshed as he'd appeared when I picked him up at the train just days before. "Are you all right? You're not feeling poorly, are you?"

"No. A little tired, that's all. Nothing to worry about."

"I am." I smiled as I searched his face for clues to what troubled him. We knew each other very well. Something was worrying him. "Thank you for coming."

"I wouldn't miss your birthday party," Li said.

"Now that I'm twenty, you no longer have to look after me."

"Or perhaps you'll need someone with an even keener eye? The young men of Emerson Pass hover about like locusts."

"Locusts isn't right. They haven't devoured me yet."

"True. But they could."

"With you and my brothers, there's not much chance of anyone making a meal of me." I nudged him with my elbow. He sucked in a breath as if I'd hurt him. "Are you hurt?" I asked. Was that why he hadn't slept well?

He let out a long sigh. "I didn't want to tell you and spoil your birthday, but I might as well. Last night, after you left the club, I was jumped by two men as I walked to my car. They beat me up."

I couldn't believe what I was hearing. Jumped? Beat up? "Here, in Emerson Pass? Outside the club?"

"Yes, in our own town." He bent over, wrapping his arms around his knees. "It can happen here, too, I guess. The attack was remarkably similar to what I've come to expect from other places, actually."

He'd hinted before about the times he'd been harassed in Chicago but never told me details. "How badly did they hurt you?"

"I'm all right. A little sore around the ribs, that's all. They didn't touch my hands, thank goodness."

"Do you know who they were?"

"I'd not seen them before, no. They seemed to think they belonged here and I didn't. They told me to go home."

"Home? This is your home." Rage coursed through me. I clenched my fists, wishing the cowards were in front of me right this instant.

"They meant China."

"How stupid," I said, hot. "You've lived here all your life. Your family belongs here. You're part of our family, for goodness' sake. Who are these men? Papa wouldn't stand for it. Not in his town."

"Maybe they moved in while I was away? I don't know." He sighed and then drew in a ragged breath. "Never mind all that. This is your birthday party."

"Li, we can't simply ignore it. Have you told Papa? He'll make sure it never happens again. Or we can put Cym and her pistol on the job."

He shook his head, not even smiling at my joke about Cymbeline. "It's not that simple. These types of men are everywhere. They don't like my kind. If it were up to them, no one like me would live here in America."

"This is America. People have come here from all over." I stopped myself before I went on and on when it was clearly only upsetting him further. "I'm sorry that happened to you." I didn't know what else to say. My news about Paris and my hope that he would join me there seemed stupid now. This was reality. Here in our own town, men had hurt Li. A member of our family. There would be payment extracted from these men, whoever they were. I'd make sure of it.

He straightened and adjusted my cap by sliding his thumb under the brim. "It's all right. Tell me your news. You were about to burst with it a minute ago."

"It's nothing that important, not really. Not compared to what happened to you."

"Tell me what it is."

"I do have news." First, I would tell him about Paris and then finally confess my feelings. I reached into the pocket of my wool coat I wore over my evening dress. "Papa wants me to go to Paris to study with a Mr. Basset. Supposedly, he's one of the best voice teachers in the world. Papa arranged it as a surprise, along with an apartment in Paris."

"Fi, that's wonderful. I'm happy for you."

"I'd have to be gone for months, and I'm not entirely certain I want to go. Everyone keeps telling me I should be excited, but I hate to miss the spring flowers." I paused, about to explain that flowers were only a symbol of everything here at home. He knew, though. Li understood me. We could have entire conversations without words. Music was our language but even without it, we understood each other.

"All of this." He waved his hand to indicate the house and yard. "It will all be here when you return."

"Yes. Perhaps." I drew in a deep breath, inhaling the scent of fir and pine needles. From inside came the raucous laughter of my siblings and their spouses. They'd started a game of gin as well as gotten into the gin. "There's more. I'd like you to come with me. Papa said he'd pay your way. You'd be my chaperone."

He recoiled a bit as he had when we were kids and he'd been the first to spot a snake. "Come with you? To Paris?" His eyes narrowed, examining me closely with a dark, serious expression. "I'd like to, but I can't. I have responsibilities here."

"Your grandmother?"

"Yes, I couldn't leave her. She's frail these days."

My heart sank. I'd have to go alone. I'd be away from him for what would feel like a hundred years. "I understand, but I'll miss you terribly."

"You'll be better off going without me. Much safer."

"Why would you say that?" I asked. "You always make sure I'm safe."

"I can't keep you safe. Look what happened to me in our own town. In Paris, it would be worse. I'm not welcome here or there or anywhere."

I didn't want it to be true, but the men attacking him in the parking lot had shaken me. I'd thought it was different here, but maybe I was wrong. Emerson Pass was growing larger. New residents arrived at least once a month. People who didn't understand the principles my father had instilled here. "Cym said Paris is very progressive. They don't treat people badly who look different or have different tastes in…things…that we do here in America."

He tapped his foot against mine. "It's all right. You'll do fine on your own. You don't need me."

"I'll miss you too much to go," I said. "I'll tell Papa no."

"Don't be ridiculous." His voice was as soft as the breeze that tousled my curls. "You must go."

"I'll stay here with you. I don't want to go, but I feel guilty thinking otherwise. Why can't anyone see that I'm perfectly content right here at home?"

He'd gone still and quiet, as he did sometimes, as if he lived in another world for moments at a time, only to return to me reluctantly.

"You will go," he said. "To give up the opportunity would be…" He shook his head.

"What?"

"It would be a travesty. This is a chance of a lifetime. Especially for a young woman. You must take it. Even though I'll be lost without you."

"I don't want to be away from you," I said.

"You'll have such a grand time that you'll forget all about me."

My heart ached at the wistful tone in his voice. "I wish you could come with me. You could take classes, too, if you wanted. Cym says jazz clubs are all over Paris."

He spread his hands over his knees. "I can't go. That's all there is to it. You understand about family, Fiona. I know you do."

A flicker of bitterness made me want to strike out at him. I snuffed it out before I said anything hurtful. Li *was* needed here. His grandmother relied on him. I was selfish to think he could just up and leave simply because I wanted him to join me. "I'm a brat. I shouldn't have asked." No one understood about familial loyalty more than me. "I'll not say another word about it. It was unfair of me to ask."

"I hate to disappoint you. It's my least favorite thing in the world."

"Don't. You're always good and loyal, looking after me and your grandmother. You never complain, even though I've probably been a burden to you." I was feeling worse by the second, wallowing in my despair and unrequited feelings, like picking at a scab better left alone. "How could I blame you for wanting me to go just to get rid of me for a while?" I said this lightly, as if my heart weren't breaking.

He spoke slowly, as if speaking to a dim-witted pet. "Fiona, I want you to go because it's a wonderful opportunity for you, not because I want to be rid of you. What a thing to say. Looking after you is my privilege."

I leapt up and turned on him, glaring at him from the bottom step. "I'm not a child or a pet. It's not *looking after* that I need from you. It's companionship and understanding and… and—" I cut myself off before I said anything more to embarrass myself.

His expression of befuddlement might have tickled me had I not been so miserable. "What in the dickens has gotten into you? I *do* understand you. I'm right here—where I've always been and always will be."

"I'm in love with you." I spat the words out as if they were bullets from a gun. "That's what's gotten into me." Tears flowed down my cheeks, probably ruining my powder and rouge, but I didn't care. Nothing mattered without Li. "I've loved you for years now. I do everything I can to draw your attention—to make you fall in love with me—but still you think of me as a child, or maybe I'm unlovable."

He continued to stare at me, motionless and quiet during my unhinged diatribe. His skin glowed under the moon. His dear, dear face. How I wanted to take it into my hands and feel the fine bones, memorize them with my musical fingers as I did the keys on a piano.

Finally, he spoke, slowly, seeming to deliberate over every word. "I do not think of you as a child. Contrary to your thinking, I find you to be the wisest among us most of the time. You're special, not only to me but to everyone you know. But you must forget about this idea of us as anything other than best friends."

"But why?" I hiccupped, trying to get control of my embarrassing sobs. What was wrong with me? If he'd had any romantic inclination toward me, I was surely ruining it by acting unstable and emotional.

He took his handkerchief from his pocket and handed it to me. "Because it's best for you. You've not yet been exposed to the type of men who would be a good match—men who would make a proper husband. Which I'm not and will never be. I'm your musical partner, and we're lucky to have that."

"Lucky? How are we lucky?" I dabbed at my cheeks, but the gesture was useless. The tears kept coming. For so long I'd held in my feelings, and now they erupted from me without ceasing.

"Because in many places in the world we would not be allowed to perform together, let alone be friends. This notion of yours is simply that. A notion."

"It's not an idea. It's a feeling. One inside here." I tapped my chest. "One that can't be pushed aside. Not when you feel things as I do." The world wasn't made for me. I was too much. Too sensitive, too full of love. It was only my family whom I could love like this. No man would ever know what to do with me. I'd have to pour it all into my music for the rest of my life. I would go to Paris and make a new life. Maybe I would never come back. Even as the thought came to me, I dismissed it. I could never leave my family. Not for long, anyway. But going away might be the best thing I could do now.

His expression softened. "You deserve a man of your own kind. Not one like me, who would put you in danger merely by being your husband. Have you told anyone about your feelings for me?" He tented his hands under his chin.

"Yes." Another sob rose up from my chest. "My brothers and sisters. No one else."

He bowed his head. Glossy black hair fell over his forehead, covering his face.

"I'm sorry," I whispered. "But I have no secrets from them."

"Perhaps you should." He spit this out in small, nasty bites. I'd obviously made him very angry. "Honestly, you're going to get yourself in trouble. Promise me you'll say nothing about this to anyone else. Go to Paris. Go live the life you're supposed to have, and put me out of your mind."

I was crying so hard now that I could scarcely breathe. "Is there nothing in your heart for me?"

"I can never allow myself to entertain any such thing. Don't you see? There are certain things I cannot have. You're at the top of that list." His voice cracked. "Please, let this go. It's what's best for both of us."

With that, he rose to his feet and stood with his hands at his side. "I'm sorry you're hurting, However, this will go away when you're in Paris. Soon I'll be a distant memory. I'll be someone you had a girlish crush on—you'll laugh at yourself later. We both will. When you come home and we resume playing music together and you're married to a count or lord or whomever, you'll know I was right." He trailed off, obviously unsure what to say next. "Please, Fiona, I'm not worth crying over. I'm nothing."

"Don't ever say that again. You're everything to me."

"I'd never forgive myself if anything were to happen to you because of me." He brushed strands of my hair from my damp cheek. "All I want in the world, more than anything else, is for you to have a good life. That would not be possible with me."

"If you loved me, you wouldn't care. You'd find the risk worth it."

"If only things were as simple as that." Even in the dim light, I could see how his eyes had dulled. He loosened his tie and unbuttoned his shirt. "Do you see this?" His collarbone was bruised an ugly purple. "This is from a man's boot. They kept kicking me even though I was on the ground, defenseless. Do you understand that if I were to have the audacity to love you I'd put you in danger of the same thing? I cannot live with that. If anyone were to hurt you—I'd rather die."

"Oh, Li." Who was I to know what it was like to live in his body, to feel fear wherever I went? "I'm sorry."

"Go to Paris, Fi. Have the time of your life. Don't look back for me. There's no reason to do so. Only misery would come to you. Take it all. Take everything this life has to offer you. No one deserves it more than you."

My throat ached; I could barely swallow. Hot tears melted into my cheeks. His face swam before me. "I'll do my best." I wanted Cym suddenly. She would let me cry for as long as I wanted.

"Goodnight, Fiona. Happy birthday." Li disappeared into the darkness, his feet crunching the frozen snow until I could no longer hear him. I sat on the steps and wept, sure my heart would break into two right then and there.

5

LI

I HAD TO FORCE MYSELF NOT TO RUN AS FAST AS I COULD. AWAY
from Fiona. The one and only woman who would ever pene-
trate my heart. The only woman I would ever love. As long as I
lived, there would never be another.

It nearly killed me to walk away. She loved me. I'd suspected
her feelings had grown and changed since my return from
Chicago, but I'd not been sure. I'd hoped she didn't care for me
as I cared for her. Now that I knew the truth, it made me feel
more despair instead of less. She would now suffer as I did.

Grandmother waited for me in the kitchen. We'd only
moved into our new house six months previously. I don't know
how she felt, but I still found it strange to take her home when
our home had been here for most of my life.

My chest ached at the sight of her hunched over at the table
where the staff ate most of their meals. Small and frail, her
shoulders had started to curl inward as if she were slowly
creating a shell around herself. Grandmother had always been a
small woman. However, her strength physically and mentally
had never made her seem such. She was a giant in my eyes.

Seeing her this way did not diminish that view but did remind me of the transient nature of this life.

She looked up as I approached. "You smell of the outside air."

I put my hand on her bony shoulder. "I was sitting outside for a few minutes, enjoying the quiet." Knowing she would approve, I added this last part. Grandmother was one who encouraged the noting and enjoyment of the smallest of pleasures. I'd never asked her why. I assumed it was because of her meager beginnings. Near starvation has a way of putting all of life's woes into perspective.

"I'm ready to go now." She rose to her feet. I could almost hear the creaking of her bones as she straightened as best she could and linked her arm with mine.

"Did you enjoy the evening?" I asked as I escorted her across the kitchen to the door. It would take a while to climb the stairs, and I wanted to give her the impression we had all the time in the world. Even though I wished I were already home in bed. The darkness would have to be my friend. Without Fiona, night and day would be equally dark. I yearned for my bed where I could wallow in my misery without the fear of watchful eyes. My grandmother and Fiona had eyes that saw all of me. They were hungry for the view of me, too. Not in a way that made me feel as if my bone marrow had been sucked dry but in the way that fed me, filled me with purpose. The two of them were the notes to the everyday music of my life. Without them to anchor the melody, I wasn't sure how I could survive.

I needed to, though. Grandmother was almost eighty years old. She would be leaving me soon. Fiona would go to Paris. She would come back, I both feared and hoped, with plans to marry a nobleman. Don't ask me why I thought this. But I knew somehow. I should have been preparing for the time when Fiona no longer needed me, no longer looked at me with eyes that shone with love, that longed to remain upon me. I should never have entertained the idea that we could be together. What was I thinking?

Grandmother and I made our way through the snow to my car. The car I'd been so keen to buy, only to find out all the wealth in the world didn't make up for the absence of love.

I held open the door and aided her into the passenger seat. Once I had a blanket covering Grandmother's legs, I jogged around the car, anxious to get away before anyone could waylay me. No such luck. Cymbeline Barnes, on the arm of her husband, called out to me. "Goodnight, Li."

As Grandmother lowered her window, I lifted a hand to wave. She was Cymbeline Olofsson now, I reminded myself. The happy wife of one of the finest men I'd ever known. Their union had made us all happy. Spirited Cymbeline with steady Viktor. The perfect match.

"Goodnight, Mrs. Wu." Cym broke free from Viktor's arm to crouch near the car's window, speaking to my grandmother. "Thank you for coming. It wouldn't have been right without you."

"Thank you, Miss Cym. It was my pleasure." Grandmother's weathered hand patted Cym's soft skin, milky white under the moon.

"Lizzie and Mama miss you terribly at the house," Cym said. "But we're all happy to see you resting more."

"I hate resting." Grandmother lifted one shoulder in a shrug. "But these old bones tell me otherwise."

Cym rose tall and looked at me over the top of the car. "Li, the new song was beautiful. Perhaps my new favorite."

"Thank you." I'd written it for Fiona's birthday present and had played it for her tonight on the piano in their sitting room. No words, just music.

"However, the music made me sad, so forlorn. Not for dancing." Cym watched me with eyes so like her sister's. Only they were the eyes of a competitor. A woman who would catch the world by the tail and swing it for as long as she wished. Not like Fiona, who would take the world into her lap and love it with her soft musical hands.

"I could write dancing songs, too. One for your birthday, I suppose."

Cym laughed that throaty laugh that made most of the men in Emerson Pass weak in the knees and wishing they could murder Viktor in his sleep. "I'd be honored. Remember my affection for the Charleston."

"I'll keep that in mind," I said.

Viktor, who had stood behind his wife, stepped forward. "Goodnight, Li." To his wife, he said, "Darling, we must let Li take his grandmother home. It's late."

"Yes, of course." Cym lifted one hand and placed it on top of the car. "Li, now is the time. If you're to keep her here, you must tell her."

"Tell her what?" My stomach fluttered with nervousness. Were my feelings so obvious?

"Tell her you want her to stay," Cym said.

"We mustn't interfere," Viktor said, a gentle warning in his tone.

"This is my baby sister's happiness. If there were a time to interfere, it is now." Cym turned back to me. "Did she tell you about Paris?"

"Yes. I'm happy for her," I said.

Two full beat notes passed before she spoke further. "Is that the way it is, then?"

"It's the way it has to be," I said. "You know that to be true. You all do."

"The rest might believe that to be true," Cym said. "But not me. Not Fiona."

"If only we ruled the world, then," I said. "Goodnight, Cym. Viktor."

She stepped away from the car. Viktor wrapped his arm

around her narrow shoulders. Deceivingly narrow. I'd seen her jump off the side of a mountain with skis attached to her boots.

I got into the car. The engine roared to life and brought the scent of gasoline. I backed up, careful of the fence, and pulled out to the dirt driveway that would lead us home.

LATER, AT HOME, I WARMED WATER ON THE STOVE FOR Grandmother's nighttime tea. She made it from a concoction of dandelion leaves, mint, and rosemary, claiming it gave sweet dreams to all who drank a cup before bedtime.

Grandmother, to my surprise, had not retired to her bedroom when I brought the tea out to her. Instead, she sat in her favorite chair by the fire with a kitten on her lap. I'd put a few logs on the fire when we returned, hoping to warm the house a little before we went to sleep.

"Grandmother, would you like your tea here?"

"Yes, please. My little friend is cozy." She stroked the kitten's head with the pad of her thumb.

I placed it on the small table next to the chair. "Can I get you anything else? A cookie?"

"No, thank you. I had quite enough at the party." She lifted the cup to her lips. A slight tremor in her hands caught my eye. Time robbed us of too much. Youth gobbled us up in ferocious bites until one day wrinkles and age spots covered hands that shook during the simplest of tasks.

"Come sit with me for a moment," Grandmother said.

I did as she asked, lowering myself into the chair next to her.

"Tell me, love, what troubles you tonight?" Grandmother asked, before taking a sip of her tea.

"Nothing at all."

We sat in silence, other than the sound of the wind against

the outside of the house. The room's hushed light hid many things, but not my grandmother's all-knowing eyes.

"There's Fiona and Paris, of course," Grandmother said. "The inevitable."

"Yes." I closed my eyes for a moment against the crushing pain. "She's going soon."

"She'll be back. Like you, she has her chance for studying and experience, and then she will return to her family."

"Yes, it's quite nice for her, isn't it? Such an opportunity."

I leaned my head against the back of the chair and examined the ceiling. My eyes ached from the unshed tears. An image of Fiona's lovely face as she cried came before me. I'd have taken her in my arms if I could. However, not doing so was what she actually needed. Not tonight but later, when she came to her senses and realized how futile her adolescent feelings were for me.

"Lizzie doesn't want her to go," Grandmother said. "She's afraid of the debauchery of Paris. Is that the right word?"

"Yes, that's a good one." My grandmother had learned English from working beside Lizzie for the last several decades. Her accent remained thick, but all of us in the household could understand her perfectly.

"They all underestimate her," Grandmother said. "Her docile nature hides a great strength. She will be fine."

"Yes, I'm sure."

"Perhaps she'll find a man of noble birth to marry."

"He'll have to fall in love with Colorado if he wants Fiona." I said this with more than a hint of bitterness. My Fiona. That's what I wanted to say tonight and every night. *My Fiona. My love. My wife.*

We sat in silence as she finished her tea. When she was done, I helped her to her feet and into her room.

Instead of going to bed, I sat by the fire until it was nothing but embers, contemplating my future. But all I could see was an empty wall, devoid of Fiona. Devoid of joy.

"YOU LOOK AS IF YOU DIDN'T SLEEP AT ALL LAST NIGHT," Grandmother said the next morning as she nibbled on a piece of toast.

"It wasn't the most rest of I've ever had, that's for certain." I spread a generous amount of strawberry preserves over my piece of toast.

A knock on the door drew us from our breakfast. "I'll be right back," I said, getting up from the table while wiping my mouth with a napkin.

Fiona stood there, dressed in a light blue dress and wool hat with a sassy blue feather that wobbled in the wind. She looked tired and drawn. Dark smudges under her eyes told me of a hard night.

"I'm sorry to come by without an invitation," Fiona said.

"No apology necessary." She'd never apologized before. We came and went from each other's homes as easy as a summer's breeze. There was an awkwardness between us now, as I'd worried there would be if one of us confessed our feelings. I was right.

"I came by to tell you how sorry I am for my behavior last night. I'm sorry I made you uncomfortable."

"It's nothing. Forget it."

"Yes, isn't that what you'd have me do?" Her pink mouth twisted and twitched, as if the muscles couldn't decide which way to go.

"What else is there?"

"To do? Or why did I come?" Tears glistened in her eyes. She pressed her lips together for a moment before speaking. "Never mind, I came by to tell you I'm leaving early next week for New York and then taking the ship to Europe."

"You're going then?"

"Yes, I've decided to go. Papa's decided he'd like to take Mama and me. I wanted to say goodbye, obviously. But also, I wanted to remind you that I'll not be available for the dance this weekend."

We were supposed to play at the dance in town. I had forgotten. I'd forgotten everything in my grief.

"That's all right," I said. "I'll think of something." What would it be? Without Fiona, I was only half of a duo, a melody without a chorus. A band without its singer.

"Well, anyway, goodbye, Li. I'll see you when I return."

"When will that be?"

"I'm not sure. Six months? A year? It will depend."

On what? I didn't ask. My chest hurt so badly that my next breath pained me. "You'll do very well. I'm proud of you."

"I'll do my best, as I always do." This time a real smile lifted her mouth but did not change the dullness in her eyes.

"I'm in awe of you, as I've always been." If it had not been for Fiona, so much younger than I, would I be the musician I was today? From the start, she'd been disciplined and loyal to the piano as one would be to a dear friend. Her practice regimen had inspired me and yes, triggered a competitive streak in me. Although she would never admit it, her singing ability made her so much more of a sought-after commodity. The good people of America loved their popular songs with all the words and music flowing together into a story. My voice was terrible.

"Papa's wanted to visit England for some time now. It's a good reason to make the long trek."

"Yes, and the little girls are old enough to stay with Lizzie now," I said. I was babbling, buying time. If my yearning for her to stay had power over ugly reality, she would be beside me, clinging to me as I clung to her. Not parted. Not ever. "It's good you've decided to go," I said. "You'll be safe traveling with your parents, so I shall not worry." I gripped the edge of the door.

"Well, I must go. I've loads to do before leaving."

A prickle of panic swept along my scalp. "Of course."

She turned to go but seemed to change her mind at the last second. "You must think me a silly little fool to have believed you might love me." Her voice, usually robust and resonant, was breathy and childlike. An image of her as a little girl with her big bow tied in her dark curls came to me. She'd once been just that, little Fiona. But now, God, she was my whole world.

I loved her with every part of my soul, for all time. Not saying so was proof how much. "You'll meet someone wonderful."

"I don't care if I do. I'll have music and my family. It will be enough." She lifted her chin, bravely. My Fiona. My heart. She held out her hand. "Goodbye, Li."

I shook her small delicate hand and took one last look into her blue eyes. "Best of luck."

She nodded. "Please say goodbye to Mrs. Wu for me."

"I'll do that."

She touched the brim of her hat and then turned to go. Her skirts rustled ever so slightly, and then she was crossing over the snowy yard to her car in short, graceful strides. For a second, I rested my forehead against the doorframe.

But no, I couldn't watch her drive away. I went back into the house, afraid I might be sick. Leaning against the closed door, I drew in deep breaths to steady myself.

"If you love her, then pray for her." Grandmother stood in the doorway between the kitchen and sitting room. "You're doing the right thing—letting her go. There are certain times in our lives when we must sacrifice for those we love. Unselfish love is perhaps the deepest kind. She'll return soon enough anyway."

"Yes, Grandmother. Thank you."

She turned away, hobbling back to the kitchen table.

I knelt on my knees in front of the fireplace and whispered a prayer. "Please keep Fiona safe from harm. Please send her the man who will make her forget all about me. And please, I humbly ask, take away this pain in my chest. Give me strength to find my way without her."

6

FIONA

When I arrived home from Li's, Papa and Mama were in the study across from our sitting room. My father had his head in the newspaper, nodding in agreement with whatever he was reading. Mama, uncharacteristically, stared into the fire. An open novel rested on her lap.

I knocked on the doorframe. "May I have a word, please?"

The paper came down onto Papa's lap, making that delightful crinkling sound I associated with him and mornings. Mama looked over at me and then beckoned me into the room with a wave of her hand.

"Fiona, where have you come from?" Mama asked.

"I went to see Li," I said. "I wanted him to know we're leaving sooner than expected." At breakfast this morning, I'd told them he'd declined my invitation and asked that we consider going as soon as travel could be arranged. Mama had promised to put the travel arrangements together as quickly as possible.

"It's such a shame he won't consider accompanying you," Mama said. "However, I understand his worries about Mrs.

Wu's health. He wouldn't want to be so far away, especially with Fai being at school."

I stood before them, with the roaring fire at my back. They sat in twin leather chairs separated by a small table between them. Oh, how the cheery little fire tried to warm my cold bones and blood, but to no avail. I shivered and wrapped my arms around my middle.

Mama raised one eyebrow. "Fiona, are you sure you want to go?"

"Yes, I want to." A lie. But a necessary one, whether it was to myself or others. I must go. It was the only hope I had of forgetting Li.

"Only good comes from courage," Mama said. "You'll see."

Papa stood, pulling me into an embrace. "It will only be for a short time, and then you'll come back home."

I buried my face in the rough fabric of his tweed jacket. He smelled of pipe smoke, coffee, and the spicy scent of the pomade he used for his hair. I looked up at the fine lines that were etched upon his face from a life of smiling and laughter. Time had been kind, creating a map on his face that told the story of a life devoted to love and family.

I would do this brave thing, to honor everything he'd done for me. All the ways he'd tossed kindness about as if it cost him nothing. And Mama? She'd come here to Emerson Pass when she'd never been parted from her mother and sister simply because she had to.

And here I was, sniveling about spending time in Paris with one of the finest teachers in Europe. I was a spoiled, petulant brat. But no, this was not the end of my tale. This was only the beginning. I would do this. I would be the woman everyone already thought I was.

Step off the train, dear one. Your life awaits.

THAT EVENING BEFORE DINNER, I STOOD IN MY SLIP BEFORE MY wardrobe. Dresses hung obediently, waiting for their turn. I'd take them all with me to Paris. Ones for day and afternoon teas and evenings out. While there, I'd have more made. Lucky, I thought. Blessed.

Then why did I feel as if a claw had scraped out my insides? *Because there is no substitute for love, silly girl.* All the riches of the world couldn't cure a broken heart.

A sob rose from deep inside me. *Please don't cry*, I begged myself. *Be like Josephine and Cymbeline, stoic or obstinate, respectively, during times of trouble.*

The tears came anyway. I lay across my bed sideways, crying as if I would never stop. A soft knock on the door roused me from my misery. I lifted my head. "Who is it?"

"It's Cym and Jo." Cymbeline's voice. My sisters.

I wept harder, barely conscious that they'd come into my room.

"Oh, pet, what is it?" Jo asked as she sat next to me on the bed.

"I'm utterly wretched." I sobbed as I rose to throw myself into her lap. "My heart's broken."

Cym came to sit on the other side of me. "What's happened?"

"I told Li my feelings, and he doesn't love me. He told me to go to Paris and marry a nobleman."

"Oh, dear," Jo said.

Cym's face went from concerned to angry in an instant. "You're too good for him. The louse. The sniveling little rodent."

"Cym, really?" Jo said. "We mustn't be unkind."

"Why not?" Cym asked. "He's hurt our Fiona."

"Are you sure he doesn't return your feelings?" Jo asked. "I find that hard to believe. I've seen the way he looks at you."

"Yes, he was quite firm about it," I said. "It was humiliating. I don't know why I told him. Now I have to live with his pity the rest of my life."

"If he doesn't want you, then there's something the matter with him," Cym said. "You're the best of us. The best there is."

"What did he say *exactly?*" Jo asked. She liked to know the precise words people said and what order they were in so that she could understand the full story. What she seemed to often forget is that life was not as neatly packaged as a novel. There were no satisfying endings. At least not for me.

I told them as best I could the entire conversation, ending with our awkward goodbye this morning. "I went over there like an idiot. To tell him I was going, as if he cares."

"I think it's good you told him," Cym said. "Now you know. Now you can go to Paris and dance with a thousand young men if you want."

"It's not a contest about how many young men she can dance with," Jo said. "She needs just one. The right one."

"I'll never marry." I buried my face in my hands. "Li's my one true love. There's no one else for me. I'll be an old maid who teaches piano to children. Soon, I'll be that old lady everyone's afraid of, even my own nieces and nephews."

"You could never be scary," Cym said. "Even if you wanted to."

"He can't be your one true love if it's unrequited," Jo said.

"Is that true?" Cym asked. "How do you know?"

Jo let out an exasperated sigh. "Because it's not true love if the love is one-sided, for one thing. For another, who wants to waste their devotion to a man who doesn't love her back, thus taking the spot of the man who should be in her heart?" She raised her eyebrows. "Did that make sense? I lost the thread in the middle there."

Cym caressed my arm with her fingers. Despite my misery, her touch felt good on my skin. I rose from Jo's lap to rest my weight against the solidness that was Cymbeline. She was strong, all muscles and brain combined with a giant heart. There was nothing she couldn't do.

"Will it always feel this way?" I asked. "Like I want to die?"

"No, it won't," Jo said. "I know a little about this, if you recall. I thought I'd lost my true love in the war only to find out he was a lying cheat."

"But then Phillip came," I said, wiping my face with a lace handkerchief. "Handsome, sweet Phillip."

"That's right," Jo said as she took my other hand and pressed it gently to her chest. "You're going to be fine. This time next year you'll have had so many experiences and perhaps even a courtship with a man who loves you, and you'll not remember a thing about how you're feeling right now."

I desperately wanted her to be correct, but right about then peace and comfort felt impossible to ever achieve again.

"Now, we have to get you put together before we go down for dinner," Jo said. "You're as wrinkled and wet as a newborn pig."

That made us all laugh. I clutched Cym for what felt like dear life. She and Jo were always here for me. Nothing could change that. Love between us was a given yet I never took it for granted.

"Do you promise someday I'll feel better?" I asked them.

"Yes, because you're good," Cym said. "There's no way God isn't planning many wonderful things for you."

"I don't feel good," I said. "I'm spoiled and ridiculous."

"You're not either of those things." Cym turned to take both my shoulders in her strong hands. "You're heartbroken right now but later, when you look back on this time, you'll see how it shaped you into the woman you wanted to be. Jo and I have both had these moments of despair, and we lived through them to be better."

"And we had you there for all of it," Jo said. "Encouraging us, loving us. Just as we will do for you."

"Sisters are forever," Cym said. "Good Lord, I sound like a bad poet. But you understand what I'm saying."

"We do," I said, swiping more tears as they burned hot trails down the thin skin of my cheeks.

"Now let's finish getting you ready for dinner," Jo said. "We should celebrate your upcoming trip. We're all so proud of you."

I touched my fingers under my eyes; my skin looked like puffed pastry dough. "All right. Here we go then."

Then, as women had done for centuries, despite broken hearts, losses, uncertainty, ailments, and even soul-destroying poverty, I placed both feet on the floor and got on with it.

THE MORNING WE LEFT, MAMA AND PAPA AND I STOOD WITH THE entire family on the platform of our train station. We would take the train to Denver and then all the way to New York City, where we would board a ship to France.

There were hugs from my sisters and brothers and all the spouses. My little sisters, both crying, hugged me, then did the same to Mama and Papa. Delphia, her golden hair shining under the sun, whispered in my ear. "I'll be marking the days off the calendar, one by one, until you come home to us." I knelt to give her kisses on both cheeks. She was nine now, but looked younger, as she was small and lithe. A baby tiger, I often thought —beautiful, strong, and ferocious. She sometimes scared her peers because of the fire in her eyes and the way she pounced on every aspect of her life. Not me. I was used to it. I'd grown up next to Cymbeline. They shared the same fire.

Addie, who was now fifteen, shared Delphia's coloring, which they'd gotten from Mama. However, she was tall and as slender as an aspen sapling, standing taller than any of our sisters. Despite her illness as a child, she now glowed with pink-tinged health. Each day after Theo had discovered her allergy to anything with flour, she'd grown lovelier. Now she stood before us a great beauty. A sparkle in her blue eyes was not fiery like

Cym's and Delphia's but more like Josephine's, serene and intelligent and perhaps even omnipresent. She'd recently confessed to me that she would like to be a writer, which had surprised no one. She was always scribbling away in her journal. I often wondered what she wrote within the pages but suspected I would never know. Until her book was published, that is. I felt certain there would be something of great worth that arose from the tender thoughts of my sapling sister.

I hugged Addie tightly and whispered in her ear to be sure to write. "I will," she said. "But I'll leave the boring parts out."

"Like all good storytellers," I said.

Theo and Flynn and Jo's husband, Phillip, were talking with Papa about business. He'd left the three of them in charge of his affairs for the months he and Mama would be away. He seemed remarkably untroubled. If it were Flynn leaving, there would be pages of instructions about what should be done and how. Perhaps one grew mellower about all things, even money, as we aged?

I'd already said goodbye to Lizzie, Jasper, and their daughter, Florence, back at the house. Lizzie hated goodbyes. She'd said one to her mother years ago when Lizzie had come to America with Papa and had never been able to return to say a final one before her mother passed away. This made her loathe any kind of farewells, even from those who promised to return.

So I was surprised when I saw, out of the corner of my eye, Mrs. Wu and Li approaching our loud and ever-stretching family.

"I'm sorry," Li said close to my ear. "She insisted on coming to say goodbye. She had some kind of dream and said she must see you one more time."

A shiver went through me. "Was it a premonition of my death?"

Li blinked, his straight eyelashes like small combs made of silk. "No, I don't think so. I hope not."

I smiled at him, hoping to convince him how fine I was now, as if I'd already forgotten my foolish and youthful claims of love. If only it were true.

Mrs. Wu approached. She pressed a sachet of spicy cloves, cinnamon, and nutmeg into my hand. "To ward off any evil spirits."

"Will there be some?" I asked.

"You're going to Paris, so yes. There are temptations and charlatans. I dreamt of a man who would bring great sorrow upon your family. Be careful. Do not trust anyone." Mrs. Wu's eyes were like flint, dark and serious. I'd never seen or heard her say anything in jest, now that I thought about it. Li was also serious of nature. I would find a man who said clever and witty things and told funny stories at parties. Then I wouldn't remember Li or long for him ever again. I'd be fine. Glorious even.

"I'll be sure to be careful," I said.

She squeezed my shoulder with her gnarled hand. "Good girl."

I glanced over to see Li watching me. He averted his gaze before I could get a good reading on him.

"We've already said goodbye," I said to him. "I'll see you in six months."

He bobbed his head. "Yes."

Write to me. I wanted to shout it, demand it. But that would be the last thing he or I needed.

The porter shouted instead, something about last call.

"Shall we?" Papa asked.

I tucked my arm into Mama's.

"Don't forget that Jo's in charge of you two," Papa said to my youngest sisters.

"We know," Delphia said, mischief rolling over her face like a brightly colored scarf in the wind.

And then we walked up the steps of the first-class car and took our seats.

"Came in on the third-class car and leaving on the first," Mama said to Papa. "What a life I've had."

"What a life you've given me," Papa said as his gloved hand covered hers.

The massive engine puffed and chugged as we slowly made our way out of the station, the great love between my parents a balm to my broken heart as I pressed my face against the glass for one last wave to my family.

Li was no longer standing with them. I saw a flash of his black coat headed through the double doors of the station. He didn't even wait to see my train leave. Well, that was that. Soon, I would no longer care.

Please God, let that be sooner than later, because right now I feel as if I'm dying.

7

LI

I WOKE THE MORNING AFTER FIONA LEFT TOWN AS DESOLATE AS I'd ever been. I'd tossed and turned all night and finally fell asleep in the early hours of the morning. The sound of a neighboring rooster woke me just after sunrise. I lay on my side watching the light seep between the curtains and decided I felt about a hundred years old. The idea of existing without Fiona by my side day in and day out was nearly unbearable.

I finally dragged myself out of bed to put coffee on for Grandmother and make a little breakfast. She was still sleeping and would start in the kitchen if I didn't have something ready before she woke. I'd told her when she moved in here with me that she would not be expected to cook and clean for me. She'd done enough of that in the twenty years we were with the Barnes family.

Grandmother had worked in the kitchen at the big house until last summer when I had my house finished. Lizzie and I had to convince her that it was time to retire. She didn't speak to me for weeks after I finally got her to agree. Now, however, she seemed to have embraced her new lifestyle, sleeping later, allowing me to cook for her, and spending hours reading on the porch.

I'd just finished boiling eggs and cutting thick slices of bread when Grandmother came in with a letter in her hand. "This is for you to send for me if you go into town," she said.

A quick glance at the address told me it was to my sister. "I'll be in later this morning. I have three lessons to teach at the schoolhouse, and then I'm going over to the church for choir practice." Usually Fiona and I led the choir together, but I would have to do it alone today. "Is there anything else you need?"

"I could use a new library book. I'm finished with the one you brought me last week."

"I'll drop in and get you one," I said. "Any requests?"

"Whatever Josephine tells you to get is fine with me."

I set a plate of eggs and toast on the table in front of her and then joined her with my own breakfast. We ate without speaking, both in our own thoughts. The Wu family was not like the Barneses, always talking over one another and teasing one another without mercy. When I'd been with them, I was one of the family, subject to the same arrows as the rest of them. I loved every second of it.

I asked about breakfast and if she'd like another cup of coffee, everything as normal as could be. Only it wasn't. Fiona was on her way halfway around the world to begin what would be an exciting life.

In juxtaposition to my sad mood, the weather was unusually warm. I went through the rest of the day in a fog—lessons, church choir, post office. By the time I arrived home, it was nearly time for dinner. When I walked into the cottage, the scent of freshly baked biscuits and a savory stew greeted me.

Grandmother had already set out a small kitchen table for two. "I could have made something for us," I said.

"Nonsense. I'm full of energy, and you've been working." She gestured for me to sit and then poured me a glass of water from the pitcher. "Lizzie came by earlier. She told me you were asked to join Fiona in Paris." She sat across from me and looked at me with an unflinching gaze.

I lifted my fork and held it aloft, wondering what to say. "Yes, but as you can imagine, I couldn't possibly accept."

"Why?"

"Because I didn't want to leave you here alone," I said.

"Was that really the reason?" Grandmother looked across the table at me, steam from her stew curling around her face.

"What other reason would there be? She has the opportunity to study in Paris. Who was I to keep her here simply to play music? The church choir will still be here when she gets back."

"I could have stayed back in my old room at the house. What's the real reason you didn't want to go with her? That you gave up the chance of a lifetime?"

I poked my fork into one of the creamy potatoes. "It would have been wrong of me to go. She doesn't need me, Grandmother. In fact, I make things worse for her."

"How so?"

"I put her in danger. A man like me with a girl like her? You know why it doesn't add up to a joyful life for her."

"Is it so impossible?" Grandmother asked. "For you to make her happy? Lizzie says she loves you."

"How does Lizzie know that?" I sat forward, alarmed.

"She simply knows," Grandmother said. "The way women do. The same way I know you love Fiona but have decided to torture yourself by sending her away."

I closed my eyes as a dart of pain took my breath away. "I do love her. But to love her well means I cannot have her. I must stay away from her and let her find the right type of man to spend her life with. Even if she thinks all would be well, soon enough she would know the truth. Our marriage would lead to discontent. Soon, she would learn to resent me for ruining her life. Or, God forbid, something could happen to her because of me. It's bad enough that we perform together as we do. There are dangerous men who do not want us together."

"Not here."

Those two words hung between us in the air until I answered. "Here too. It's there, in the underbelly of a place. Even Emerson Pass." I'd lied about what happened the other night to my grandmother, saying I'd run into a door at the club. She would worry and fret, and I couldn't have that.

I thought of Lord Barnes and his wife. They were the finest of people. However, they would not want their precious Fiona with the likes of me. Even they would see that love between us would not work. "Do her parents know?"

"Lizzie says they do not. It may not have occurred to them. They see you as an older brother, a protector."

"That's just it. I'm not. I'm what she needs protection from."

"I do not agree." Grandmother buttered a piece of the thick wheat bread with precise and deliberate strokes of the knife. "But if you're not willing to fight for her, then perhaps you don't deserve her after all."

I wanted to retort with my reasons for staying away from her and for letting her go—that it was my expression of love for her. Letting her go *was* fighting for her. However, I kept it all inside. For what good would it do to reiterate that which Grandmother would never understand? She saw me as weak. As unwilling to fight. How could she not? After the life she'd lived, the sacrifices she'd made to keep us safe after the men in her life had dragged her across the world for a misguided dream.

That was just it, though. She'd had to suffer because of her husband and son's quest for gold. I would not do the same to Fiona. As much as I wanted her for myself, it was better for her to marry a man who would not be beaten up outside her brother's club and left to die. I could only love her from afar. The sooner I accepted this, the better.

Ah, but you can't, my heart whispered in silent reprimand.

I WAS OUT WALKING IN THE WOODS ABOUT TWO WEEKS AFTER Fiona left for Europe when I came upon Delphia. The youngest of the Barnes clan, she was only nine years old but had the countenance of a sophisticated, if rebellious, young woman. There was something about her pointy chin and fierce blue eyes that seemed both wise and impish all at the same time. Unlike her other sisters, who wore their thoughts and feelings on their faces, Delphia was a bit of an enigma.

At the moment, she was kicking a stump with the tip of her boot. She turned to look at me. "Oh, it's you. What are you doing?"

"Taking a walk. What are you doing?"

"Kicking this stump."

"May I ask why?"

"Because I'm mad. Very, very mad."

"About what?" I asked. We were having one of our unusually warm days. Snow that had come only yesterday and covered trees and shrubs softened. Clumps slid from the branches to pile around trees. Tracks from bunnies or squirrels had left patterns in the snow between trees. I cleared a spot on the stump and sat.

"Well, first of all, they've all left me and Addie."

"You mean your parents and Fiona?" I asked.

"Who else would I be talking about?" She scowled at me from under the brim of her red knit cap. "They've gone off and left me during my time of need. Addie's too, for that matter. It's not just myself I'm troubled about."

"Right. I'm sorry their leaving has angered you. Did something in particular happen today?"

She crossed her arms. "Now that you ask, yes indeed, it has. I've gotten into trouble from Lizzie and it's not fair. Not one bit. I'm innocent of all wrongdoing."

"What are you accused of?"

"It's what Lizzie calls my smart mouth. Apparently, it's inappropriate for a child my age to have any opinions whatsoever."

I hid a smile behind my hand until I composed myself. "What opinions have caused offense?"

"Well, I don't understand why we have to go to church without Mama and Papa. They're not at church. Fiona's not at church. Thus, we too should have a hiatus."

"Hiatus?" Where had she learned that word?

"A break from our usual routine. If they can go off and leave us, then I think we should get something out of it."

"And that something should be staying home from church?"

"Among others. For example, it's fine for us to eat every meal downstairs with Lizzie, Florence, Jasper, and the rest of the staff, but we still have to go to church. Do you see the hypocrisy in that?"

I didn't exactly follow, but I nodded. "You think it should be all or nothing?"

She sighed. "Finally, someone who understands."

"Could it be that you're missing your parents and Fiona and that's what you're really angry about?" I smoothed away the snow to make room for her on the stump. "They've gone for a long time. Surely that must be hard for you."

"It's harder for Addie. She's tender, you know." The forlorn way she spoke gave me the distinct impression that it was not only Addie who was tender.

"They'll be back before you know it," I said gently.

"No, they won't. It feels like forever." She pointed to the snow. "Do you know how long it will be until this snow is melted?" Her voice wavered. "It's too long for them to have left us. I don't know what made them do it. Unless…"

"Unless what?"

"Unless it's because I'm so awful that I drove them away.

What if they never come back and Addie and I are orphans forever?"

I chose my words carefully. "They're coming back. Your parents could never stay away from you forever. I know this might seem odd to you, but your mother's never been able to go anywhere or see much of anything but this town and the inside of her own home. She's spent all of her adult life looking after others, and this was a chance for her to enjoy herself. See some of the world and meet your father's family."

"What about me? Why couldn't they take me?"

"You have school. Would you want to miss months and months and have to repeat it all again next year?"

She picked up a wad of snow and hurled it at an unsuspecting tree. "I'm already too smart for my grade. I heard our teacher say something about it to my sister Jo the other day. So getting behind would not be ideal."

"In addition, you wouldn't want to leave Addie here all alone, would you?"

"I suppose not. If I were to go, she would have to go too. We stick together. We have to. The rest of them all knew one another before we were even born."

"Once you're all grown up, you can go on traveling excursions of your own."

She ground the heels of her boots into the snow. "I suppose."

"Until then, what can you do to get yourself back into Lizzie's good graces?"

"I don't know. Act more like Fiona and Addie?"

"That might help. Although it's best to be yourself."

"Not according to Lizzie," Delphia said.

I stood and offered her my hand. "Come along, I'll walk you back to the house."

"Fine. It's best to get my punishment over with, isn't it? Lizzie will make me stay in my room for the rest of the day. And it's such good weather. I'm feeling all together bitter about it, Li." She put her mittened hand into mine.

"I can understand."

"Why didn't you go with Fiona? I heard her talking about it with Cymbeline, and she said she wanted you to go with her."

"I have responsibilities here."

"Like your grandmother?" Delphia asked.

"Primarily, yes."

We walked together through the woods until we saw the big house through a thicket of trees.

"Li?"

"Yes?" I picked her up to carry her over a skinny part of the creek and set her back down on the other side.

"You do think they'll come back?" Delphia looked up at me with her bright blue eyes.

"Your parents will come back." Fiona? I wasn't so sure. She could be meeting a count or lord at this very moment.

"Did you know Fiona's in love with you?"

We walked in the slushy tracks left by a car up the Barneses' driveway. What did I say to that question?

"She was crying a lot before she left," Delphia said. "Which made me not like you very much, but now I do."

"I'm glad I've redeemed myself in your eyes."

"Don't you think Fiona's pretty?"

"Who wouldn't?" I asked.

"Only a fool."

Fortunately, we were at the house by then. Addie came running out of the front door just as we came through the gate.

"Delphia, where have you been? We've been worried sick."

"I went for a walk." Delphia lifted her pointy chin, reminding me a lot of Cymbeline.

"Lizzie's fit to be tied," Addie whispered. "You should just head right up to your room. Lizzie's downstairs for a couple of minutes. She had to check on something or it would burn, which made her even madder at you. I'll sneak you up something to eat."

"Good, I'm starving." Delphia scampered inside the house and closed the door behind her.

Addie, who had grown into a ravishing young lady, gave me a shy smile. It was hard to believe that just a few years back she'd been terribly ill with stomach issues. Now she glowed with health and although not exactly robust, she was no longer painfully thin. "Thanks for bringing her back."

I explained that I'd found her kicking a stump.

"She'll have bruised toes again," Addie said with a sigh.

Again?

"She's having a hard time with Mama gone. Lizzie's kept a tighter leash on her than we're used to."

"How are you doing?" I asked.

"I'm fine. Very busy. I'm working on a new novel, so I have no time to miss Mama and Papa or Fiona."

"New novel?" I asked. "You have a first one?" She was only fifteen.

"This is my third one," Addie said. "The first two are rubbish, but I may be onto something with this one."

"Well, that's good to hear. I wish you luck." I turned to go. The sound of a car coming down the driveway diverted my attention.

Addie and I both turned our gaze toward the vehicle.

"It's Cym," Addie said. "Back from her errand. Those two men won't be bothering you again."

"Wh-what did you say?" I stared at her.

"The ones who beat you up. Fiona asked my brothers to take care of them, but Cym insisted on going with them. She had her pistol with her, so God only knows what happened."

My feet tingled at all the ways that could have and perhaps did go wrong.

Cymbeline parked and came barreling out from behind the

driver's seat. "Li, just the man I wanted to see. I just went by your place and your grandmother said you were on a walk. Lo and behold, here you are."

I looked at her warily. "What did you need?"

"I wanted to tell you that we took care of those two men who bothered you." Leave it to Cymbeline to use the word *bothered* instead of *beat*. She would not want me to feel embarrassed. Pride was her biggest weakness. I was grateful for it.

"What did you all do?" I asked.

"We politely asked them to leave town." She grinned and lifted her arm. Blood stained the sleeve of her wool jacket. "It was a lot of fun."

"Oh, Cym," I said. "You didn't have to do that."

"Let me tell you something," Cym said. "You're one of us, and when anything happens to one of us, we take care of it. Simple as that."

"We don't want men like that in our town," Addie said softly.

"That's right. And anyone else who thinks they can give you trouble will get the same treatment. I mean, most people prefer it if their noses aren't broken."

"Cymbeline, you didn't?" I asked, secretly pleased.

"It might have been me. It might have been Flynn. Who knows?" She gave us one more mischievous grin. "Anyway, I need to go inside and see Jasper about getting the blood out of this jacket. My husband won't be pleased to see me ruin another coat."

Another one?

8

FIONA

By the end of my first week in Paris, Papa had managed to find an apartment with two bedrooms in the Fourth Arrondissement. From the window of the small sitting room, we could see the Notre Dame cathedral as well as the two islands in the Seine River, which separated the right and left banks. My first meeting with Mr. Basset was still a week away, so Papa, Mama, and I spent our time visiting museums and parks. We'd spent an entire day in the Louvre, with Mama staring at paintings for long moments of time. I enjoyed watching her reaction to the biblical scenes more than the paintings themselves. She'd spent at least an hour gazing at *Mona Lisa* and then all of lunch afterward exclaiming about how small the painting was. "I had no idea it would be so tiny," she said, eyes sparkling. "And her smile. It's as charming as they say, isn't it? I fully expected her to start talking to me."

We had lunch and dinners in the street cafés, sharing bottles of French wine and watching the Parisians. I'd never seen Mama more exhilarated than she was in those weeks we spent exploring Paris together. At mealtimes, she wrote notes in her journal with details and descriptions of places we visited and the people we saw. "I want to remember it all for later," she said to me one day at lunch. "To tell your sisters and brothers but also for myself. A trip of a lifetime, isn't it, darling?"

Papa had nodded in agreement and they'd stared into each other's eyes as if they were young lovers instead of the parents of seven.

We were at dinner the night before they were to leave for England. Papa had suggested a fancier restaurant, but Mama and I both wanted to go to the corner bistro where we'd shared at least a half dozen dinners. The waiters knew us there by then and showed us to our favorite table.

I thought about her as I sat there sneaking glances at my beautiful stepmother. She was many years younger than Papa. Regardless, years had not stolen the bloom of her beauty. Her brown eyes remained bright and her skin unlined. She wore her hair short now, as most of us did, and it suited her small heart-shaped face. For the first time, I wondered what it would have been like for her to have an opportunity such as this, instead of coming to Emerson Pass to teach in a rustic schoolhouse to the dozen or so of us who were her first pupils.

Sitting here now, I had to wonder—were there any regrets? Would she have liked to study art or literature here in Paris? Or was her simple life satisfying enough?

"Mama, have you ever felt as if you missed out on your youth by marrying Papa and taking on all five of his mischievous children?"

She gazed at me for a moment, clearly surprised by the question. Then she darted a glance at Papa, who watched her bemused and smitten, as he always was in her presence. A soft smile lifted the corners of her mouth. "No, I've never regretted one moment. It was my privilege to take care of my mother and sister and then you children and your papa. There were no choices, really. I did what I had to do. And it has all given me the most satisfying life. It's the small and mundane moments in life

—ones we are too busy to notice—they are the ones we look back upon with the most affection. The sound of my children's footsteps in the foyer as they tumble in from school, for example. I've treasured each one, each day." She swept her hand through the air to indicate the café. "And now look at me. Dining in a bistro in Paris. I've been here many times, you know, in the pages of a book. It's just as I imagined."

"Do you have any regrets?" I asked them. "Anything you wish you'd done differently?"

"Not me," Papa said. "Everything that came before led me to this exact moment. Which I wouldn't change for all the world."

"Believe it or not," Mama said, "going out to Colorado was terrifying. I had no idea what to expect the day I stepped off the train in 1910."

"I can't imagine if you hadn't come to us," Papa said to her. "What would have become of our family?"

"Or of me," Mama asked softly. "Fiona, my wish for you is simple. I hope you find your North Star as I did. Adventures are good, but home is the most important aspect of life. And home is simply where the people you love live. However, that doesn't mean you shouldn't do all kinds of interesting things. To have the opportunity to do so before you marry and have children is a gift. We're glad to provide this for you."

"I'm grateful." I looked down at my lap. My dropped shirt-waist dress was made of the finest material and with great care, thanks to Mr. Olofsson's stellar craftsmanship. I would have to tell him when I got home how it rivaled the dresses of the elegant Parisian women. "I am." My voice wavered. "But I'll miss you all very much."

"It's all right to miss us," Mama said. "As long as you don't let it keep you from living every moment here. Life goes so fast, my darling. You won't believe it, truly, how the days seem to evaporate. Perhaps faster when you've been as happy as I've been. I want to hold on to you children with all my might, to go back and do it all again. But mother time keeps moving, and so must we."

"Thank you for everything you've done for me." I teared up and took a moment before I could speak again. "I've been such a lucky girl."

"You've always been a joy, love," Papa said. "From the very first. Of all of our children, you've worried us the least. You've always been my sweet little Fiona."

"Do you know what you said the first time you saw me?" Mama asked.

"No, what?" I asked.

"You thought she was dead," Papa said. "And that she was a princess. A dead princess." He laughed. "Can you imagine?"

"Mama, you're still as beautiful as a princess," I said. "I'm glad you were only knocked out."

Mama flushed at my compliment. "I never thought of myself as pretty. I was always skinny and pale. I never felt pretty until I saw how your father looked at me. I want that for you. For a man to look at you that way and for your heart to feel as if it might explode with joy."

"I want that too," I said.

"But for now you have your music," Papa said.

"And Paris." Mama beamed at me.

If they only knew how I felt, how broken I was. *No, no,* I chided myself. They didn't need to know. It would ruin the illusion of this great gift they'd given me. They should think of me as grateful and inspired.

I glanced around the bistro, taking in the artistic and eccentric crowd. Many of the women wore trousers, wide-legged and sophisticated.

Henri, our waiter, brought our steak tartare, setting it in front of us with his usual flourish. "Madam and mademoiselle, good evening. Monsieur, the gentleman at the table in the corner would like to send over a bottle of champagne."

"Really?" Papa asked. "Which one?"

"There is only one champagne," Henri said.

"No, I mean, which man," Papa said, chuckling.

"Oh yes. The one with hair like pig bristles. Crumpled and worn suit," Henri said, sounding delightfully haughty with his thick accent. "He is enamored with the young mademoiselle." Henri discreetly placed a small calling card next to my plate.

"Oh dear, you have an admirer." Mama gestured with a quick tilt of her head toward a table where a dashing young man sat with a group of people. He had hints of copper in his dark blond hair and friendly, lively eyes. The women were dressed in the suits so popular here in Paris. Coco Chanel's influence, they'd told us in the shops.

I glanced down at the card. James West.

"Not French, then?" I asked Henri.

"Oh, no, mademoiselle. Very English."

"A proper Englishman," Papa said, with emphatic enthusiasm. "Excellent."

"He's a very poor Englishman." Henri didn't lower his voice. In fact, his resonant tone seemed to rise to a new decibel. Could my admirer hear him? "And he cannot afford to send over champagne. A book editor." His tone dipped drily. Apparently, Henri didn't hold editors in high esteem. "He can barely afford his own dinner. They're celebrating. One of the others has published a book, in *America*."

"Would you please thank Mr. West for us?" Papa asked. "Tell him we couldn't possibly accept. Instead, send a bottle to their table from me." He reached into his coat and pulled out one of his own calling cards and gave it to Henri.

"So many lords," Henri said, as if we weren't sitting within earshot.

Mama's eyes sparkled. She scooted to the edge of her chair and straightened her posture. "He's an editor? How exciting. I wonder what book and who the author is?"

"We can invite them up to the apartment," Papa said. "And find out for ourselves."

"Oh, Alexander, could we?" Mama asked. "I've always wanted to know a real author and editor."

As if he could say no to that.

MY APARTMENT WAS LIGHT AND AIRY WITH TALL CEILINGS AND ornate carvings in the fireplace mantel as well as arches over doorways. It had come furnished with brightly colored sofas and chairs and intricately designed tables. Everything very French, Papa had commented when we first arrived. He'd also made sure the flat had a piano, a baby grand that took up a large portion of the sitting room.

Our merry group of artists gladly accepted our offer of drinks and dessert upstairs.

"Tell me, Miss Barnes, do you plan to stay here all by yourself for the entirety of your stay here in gay Paris?" Mr. West asked.

"We've hired a maid. Gabriella," Papa said, gruffly. "I have several good friends who live here as well, who've promised to look in on my daughter several times a week." This was not true, but Papa wanted it to seem as if I were well looked after.

"I'd be honored to provide my services," Mr. West said. "In any way needed. And please, call me James. All my friends do."

James West's friends consisted of the author Sebastian Cooper and his wife, Paula, as well as an artist who called herself Saffron Pierce. Saffron wore baggy trousers splattered with paint and a man's shirt with a tie loosely knotted around her neck. Her companion, a slight man who appeared to speak only Spanish, lurked nearby like a shadow. A young American woman with blond curls, red-stained lips, and a dress with rows of fringes that Jo had told me were only worn by dance-hall

71

girls rounded out the group. She introduced herself as Sandwich, a nickname presumably given to her by the friends now gathered in my Parisian flat. As thin as a whippet, with skin so white I imagined her as nothing more than a moonbeam.

To my surprise, Papa and Mama seemed to take them all in stride, without an iota of disruption in their manners. We must have seemed quite provincial to them. Mama with her silk and pearls and me with my conservative drop-waist dress. Papa wore a perfectly tailored dark suit that hung just right from his slender frame. *Thank you, Mr. Olofsson,* I thought again. For the first time in my life, I could see the "Lord" in Papa's title. He commanded the group into submission, insisting on opening wine and suggesting a board of cheese for our dessert. Cheese, which he pronounced *fromage* in a decent French pronunciation.

Mama and I escaped to the small kitchen to prepare our offering of cheeses. Papa stayed behind with our guests to open wine.

"We need Lizzie here to tell us how to arrange these attractively, but we'll do our best." Mama unwrapped one of the soft cheeses and placed it on the wooden board we'd found in the cupboard. "Such a lot of different cheeses here in France. I had no idea of all the varieties. Had you?"

"Certainly not." I'd never heard any word for cheese other than our very American one and felt quite out of my element. How would a girl from a frontier town in Colorado survive in Paris with these sophisticates? *If only Cym were here,* I thought. *Then I could bear it.* She would lift her haughty chin and give them that look that silenced all critics.

Fortunately, we'd shopped that afternoon for what Papa called essentials, including soft cheeses named Brie and Camembert and a hard cheese he called Cantal, but that looked exactly like our cheddar cheese from home. In addition, there was another hard cheese the clerk had described as the French cousin to the Swiss gruyere called Comté. Lastly, Papa had purchased a cheese that smelled of my brother's boots. Blue cheese, he'd called it. *More like stinky cheese*, I thought now as I unwrapped it. "Mama, is it supposed to have these strange blue lines?" I held my breath as I bent closer to inspect.

"Yes, that's why they call it blue, I suppose," Mama said.

Papa had had several cases of wine delivered to the apartment as well, saying I would need them for entertaining. I'm not sure how he knew this would be essential or that we'd have guests that very night, but he seemed in his element here in Paris.

"It's unfortunate we gave Gabriella the night off," Mama said.

"No, we don't need her," I said, stepping back to admire our work.

A burst of laughter drifted in from the other room, followed by Papa's smooth voice. I glanced at Mama. She looked pretty in the orange light of the kitchen. The sun had disappeared already, leaving behind orange and pink stripes in the sky.

"Mama, I don't know if this was a good idea," I said. "We don't know these people." I thought about Lizzie's worry about the debauchery of Paris.

"Not to worry. Cheese after dinner never hurt anyone."

"Not that. I mean, leaving me here in Paris. I don't want you to go. I can't do it."

She drew me to her. "Listen closely. None of the people here are any better than you. You're as talented as any of them, if not more so. You remember this—you're a Barnes. Do you see your Papa out there? He's not intimidated."

"He's from this world."

"Yes, and we're not, but you will be soon. This new world will shape your thoughts and make you see everything differently. You'll learn many new lessons, from the different cheeses to meeting interesting people."

I'd have to trust her on that. Right now, I longed for the

comfort of my sisters and brothers. And a very Lizzie meal of chicken stew and her fresh bread.

When we returned to the sitting room, the guests all had glasses of wine. Smoke from cigarettes gathered near the ceiling and scented the room with an unpleasant odor. I opened several more windows to bring in fresh air. I'd found a stack of plates that could almost fit in the palm of my hand in the cupboard as well as appetizer forks that we would have used at home for our first course but were for hard cheeses here.

Most of the evening passed in a blur. The novelist, Sebastian, was not only a pontificator but also quite full of himself and his talent. He spoke with an affected accent with elongated vowels and nary an *r* sound to be heard. An accent I'd never heard anywhere in the States and suspected didn't exist. His athletic wife, who wore no makeup and had her nondescript brown hair cut into a boyish bob, seemed like a nice Midwestern girl, quick to laugh and seemingly oblivious to her husband's ridiculousness. Oh and that husband! I began to count every time he took a drink of wine but stopped when I reached the count of twenty.

Mr. West was my favorite of them. He *was* dashing, as Mama had pointed out. His hair, wiry in texture, hung in waves over his forehead. A slightly bent nose in no way detracted from his handsomeness. His smile, however, took him from ordinarily nice-looking to devastatingly so. I was fascinated by the way his unlined face transformed into three arcs from his chin to his eyes. His laugh was like a tickle. One couldn't help but laugh with him.

After drinking a glass of Bordeaux, I found that instead of listening to what everyone else seemed to find dazzling and riveting conversation, I drifted away. I imagined Cym or Jo here with me and what they would say about the gathering. Would they begin to compare each of them to farm animals as I did now? James West was a russet-colored retriever, enthusiastic and friendly, and really nice to have to curl up next to on the couch. Sebastian was even easier to cast. A rooster, even though his coloring was more of a brown hen. Paula was a racehorse, well-bred and monstrously strong yet fated to be put out to pasture. The girl who referred to herself as Sandwich, which by this time I'd learned was a nickname for Sandra, seemed like a socialite from New York City or Boston, and, as I'd thought earlier, was a whippet or greyhound, thin and white. And the artist Saffron and her companion? In her messy clothes and cropped hair that sprang out of her head in coiled-back springs, Saffron was a fat and satisfied barn cat, in contrast to her lithe, slick Spanish husband, who reminded me of a ferret.

It was nearing midnight, and I yawned as if my head might split in two. The cigarette smoke had made my eyes scratchy, and I longed for bed. Fortunately, James noticed my weariness and rose to his feet. "We mustn't keep you any longer. This was most generous, Lord Barnes."

Everyone got up then, in various states of drunkenness. I moved to stand next to Papa and Mama at the door to say good-night to our guests. James West was last to go, lifting my gloved hand to his mouth for a kiss. "May I call on you, Miss Barnes?"

"You may call me Fiona," I said. Did I want him to call upon me? No, I wanted Li. The comfort of his familiar face. However, he didn't want me. I was here to begin a new part of my life. "That would be lovely, thank you."

He turned to Papa and held out his hand. "Lord Barnes, thank you again. I'm one of the titled poor, left over from another time; however, it would be a great honor for me to look after Fiona while she's here. You can leave tomorrow knowing she's safe and well-cared for."

"I'm much obliged," Papa said. "Thank you."

I collapsed against Papa's side the moment they were gone. "I thought they'd never leave," I said quietly.

"It's the French way," Mama said. "Staying up until after midnight and rising long after sunrise."

Papa gave my shoulders a squeeze. "Off to bed, love. Do sleep late tomorrow. We don't have to be to the train station until the afternoon."

I kissed and hugged them both, all the while fighting the lump in my throat. I didn't want tomorrow to come. Would I be frightened all alone in this apartment? "This place will seem big and dark without you."

"You'll have the piano to keep you company," Mama said. "And remember, it's not for long. You'll be home before you know it."

"We'll be back for another visit in only a few months," Papa said. "Time will fly."

From his mouth to God's ears.

ON A MORNING A FEW DAYS AFTER MAMA AND PAPA HAD departed, I was playing piano and practicing my vocal scales when a knock on the door distracted me. Gabriella scurried out of the kitchen to answer. I heard her soft voice speaking French and then the voice of a man.

James West. He'd come to visit as promised. Would he expect anything from me? Other than friendship? I hoped not.

I walked out to the foyer, tidying my hair. He stood there with his hat in his hand. "Hello, Mr. West."

He bobbed his head. "Please, call me James."

"Hello, James."

"I wondered if I might ask for the pleasure of dining with you this evening?"

I remembered what Henri had said about James's financial situation. Perhaps it would be better if he were to dine here with me?

"I'd not like to cause you distress," I said.

"Distress?"

"Of a financial nature."

The flush of his cheeks matched the copper tones in his hair. "You mustn't worry about that. I always find a way."

"Would you rather dine here with me? Gabriella can fix us something simple. She's a very good cook. Before we dine, we could take a walk along the river. You'd be doing me a favor to walk with me, as I'm too nervous to do so by myself.'

"It would be my honor."

"Come around five? I have my first lesson with Mr. Basset this morning."

A shadow passed over his face. "Yes, Mr. Basset. He has quite the reputation."

"He does?" I squeaked. What did *reputation* mean? Would he be an ogre or tyrant?

"Yes, it's another reason I wanted to stop by this morning. I didn't want to say it in front of your parents, for fear they'd worry."

"Worry?"

"I asked around about Mr. Basset. He's gossiped to be a ladies' man."

I waited, hoping for more explanation.

An expression crossed over his even features that I couldn't read, somewhere between embarrassed and reluctant. "That's one of the reasons I wanted to come today. You must be prepared to discourage his advances. Given your appearance and the fact that you're here alone without a chaperone, they will no doubt come."

"Advances?"

"Of a romantic nature," he said. "I'm mortified to have to bring it up, but I don't want you surprised. From what I hear, he can be quite insistent."

"I don't know what you mean by insistent."

"He does as he pleases, whether the woman welcomes it."

I gasped, horrified. "But why would he do that? It's most ungentlemanly."

He would no longer meet my gaze. The flush of his cheeks had now moved to his neck just above his collar. "Because powerful men are accustomed to getting what they want. He's known for making careers." He coughed. "In exchange for their affections, that is."

"I see." My stomach roiled, queasy. If only Papa hadn't left already. This would be reason enough to cancel my lessons with the acclaimed Mr. Basset. I dipped my gaze, examining the tips of my shoes. Why had I come to Paris? This had been a mistake, and now I was stuck here. "Gabriella will be here at the apartment. Will that provide some protection?"

"I'm not sure. I would be happy to offer my assistance and be here during the lessons."

"That's too much to ask," I said. "You have business of your own to attend to, surely?"

"I am at your service," James said. "Perhaps see how he conducts himself today and we can discuss it tonight?"

"Yes, that's fine." I paused, searching for the right words. "Do his pupils mind these unwanted advances?" How dare the older Mr. Basset put young women in this position?

"Again, I'm not sure. They might want to further their career and see it as part of the cost. Or they might not be able to ward off his...overtures."

"If my father had known this, he wouldn't have sent me over here." I didn't need a career. Singing at church was all the work I needed.

"Maybe I should have said something to him? I wasn't sure what to do."

"No, you've done nothing wrong," I said. "I'm indebted to you. If I'd not been warned, I might not have understood."

"Please, be cautious." He backed toward the door. "I'll see you at five."

"Yes, I'll look forward to it."

After I closed the door behind me, I realized Gabriella was standing there, tugging on her yellow braid. "Gabriella, is everything all right?"

"*Oui, oui*. It is that I now worry over Monsieur Basset."

"Do not worry, please. I'll be fine."

"This Monsieur West is very handsome, yes?" She gave me a shy smile. "And good, no?"

"I suppose he is." I smiled. "But he's not for me."

"Because he is poor?"

A burst of laughter escaped before I squelched it. Gabrielle's clear green eyes were earnest, and I didn't want to hurt her feelings. "No, because I love someone else. It wouldn't be fair to Mr. West if I were to pretend otherwise."

"This is too bad. I should like for you to like Monsieur West." *Me too*, I thought.

"Would you like your lunch before Monsieur Basset arrives?"

"I suppose I should, even though my stomach is in knots."

"Knots?" Gabriella's brow wrinkled.

"Nervous," I said.

"Oh, yes, very good." She did a small curtsy before heading off to the kitchen. I went back to the piano but didn't play. Instead, I looked out the window at a fat cloud that moved across the sky. Would it cover the sun and shower rain over the city? Shivering, I felt a bit like an unexpected rainstorm had soaked through my clothes. What would be would be. Regardless, I would have to have courage. When Mama spoke of an adventure, I felt certain she didn't mean of this nature.

9

FIONA

Mr. Pierre Basset was late by almost thirty minutes. While I'd waited, I paced around the apartment, so nervous I knocked over a vase. Somehow, it landed on the rug and didn't break. I had no idea if it was worth anything but wouldn't have liked to have had to pay for damages.

I'd dressed modestly in a dark blue dress that hung loosely over my small frame. The apartment was warm, so I opened all of the windows in the front room.

The sounds from the street were loud with cars honking, engines revving, and the shouts and laughter of pedestrians. I'd been here without my parents for only three days, and the loneliness made my bones ache. Gabriella was sweet and seemed keen to please, but the language barrier between us kept us from any meaningful conversation. She was a round-shouldered young woman with a golden braid down her back and had managed to tell me that she'd come from a village in the Loire Valley, just outside of a castle. I'd wanted to know more, but that was all I could understand.

Now a knock on the door drew me away from the window. I yanked open the door. A man around Papa's age stood before me. Like my father, he was handsome, with one of those faces that had probably aged well, making him as good-looking as he'd been in his youth if not more so. Did he use this to his advantage when it came to preying on women?

"Miss Barnes, I presume?" A clipped, posh accent. London society, like Papa. I shivered.

He had thick salt-and-pepper hair that sat on top of his head in waves. A trim mustache gave him a sinister look. Or was I just reading too much into it?

I said a silent prayer, asking God to look after me, as I opened the door to let him come into my sitting room.

Gabriella appeared, taken aback that I'd opened the door myself. She recovered quickly, taking Mr. Basset's thin overcoat and hanging it in the skinny closet.

Mr. Basset lifted my hand to his mouth to brush it against his mustache. "It's a pleasure to meet you finally, Miss Barnes. Your father's friends were quite persuasive and effusive about your talent. I hope I'll not be disappointed."

"I hope that as well," I said.

"Your father knows a lot of powerful people." His fat tongue flicked over his top lip.

I led him over to the piano. "Yes, sir. He left England and a title to move to America."

"What would possess a man with 'Lord' in his title to do such a thing?" he asked this while taking in the piano with what seemed to be irritation.

"My father has the heart of an American," I said. "He wanted adventure and control of his own destiny. That was more important to him than a title."

"Only a man with a title would think such a thing. It's as absurd as abdicating a crown, which we'll never see. Not in our lifetime, anyway."

I thought this a strange thing to say, but the English were taken with their monarch.

Mr. Basset took off his suit jacket and draped it over the back of the chair. "Warm today, isn't it?"

"I've opened the windows. Will it be too noisy?"

"Yes, we'd better close those so I can hear your voice without the background of Parisian drivers. Nasty business, cars."

I shut all three of the windows, all the while feeling the stare of Mr. Basset on my backside. By the time I turned around to face him, sweat dribbled down the small of my back.

"They didn't mention your comeliness," he said.

"Photographs were not part of the application process," I said, feeling for a moment as sassy as Cymbeline. I'd taken an immediate dislike to the man.

"Perhaps they should be. You'd have gone to the top of the list."

"What do we do first?" The sooner we started, the sooner we could be done.

"Let's see what you can do, my little songbird from the American frontier."

I bristled with irritation at his condescension. He knew nothing of where I came from or how hard I'd studied. Regardless, I succumbed to his authority, running through scales and other exercises.

At the end of the hour, he came to a stop at the end of the piano bench. "We have a lot of work to do. However, it's not an impossible task to make you good enough that you won't embarrass yourself or me at the recital."

"Recital?" I gulped in air, hot and perspiring, and wished I could open the window.

"Yes, we'll arrange for a showcase at the end of our time together. This will be a chance for you to demonstrate what you can do. Directors and nightclub owners will be there. Often my girls will be offered contracts afterward. If I deem you ready, of course."

"What would I need to be ready?"

He sighed, as if I presented a great burden. "My dear girl, I shall not overwhelm you with that rather tedious list at this time. I'll not have you discouraged before we even begin."

Without asking permission and as slippery as a snake, he sat on the piano bench next to me. "We must begin with breathing. You've the technique of a peasant calling in her sheep." He placed his hand on my back. "Now, breathe into your stomach. All the way."

My breath was shallow from nervousness. I could barely gather a regular breath, let alone one that would allow me to hold a note for any extended period.

I didn't want his hands touching me, but I didn't know what else to do. Was this what a teacher of his caliber did?

"Do it again." His hand crept around the front of me and to my horror pressed into my belly.

I held my breath but not before I got an unwelcome sniff of his odor—onions and stale cigarette smoke. "*Now*, please, not next week."

I drew in a breath that felt as if it brought poison air into my lungs.

"Don't waste my time," he said, barking like a mean dog. "You must move my hand when you breathe into your belly. That's how I know your breathing's correct."

I had no idea what he meant, and I was terrified having him this close to me. In all the years Li and I had collaborated together, he'd never touched me. Hoping to get his hand off me, I sucked in the deepest breath I could. His hand didn't move.

"Don't you know at all what I'm speaking of?" Basset asked. He removed his hand and put it on his own stomach. "Watch closely." He drew in a breath and as he did so, his stomach seemed to expand several inches, thus pushing his hand out toward the piano keys. "Do you see now? The breath, in order for it to be properly sustained for long notes, must come into the diaphragm. In this way, you'll be able to hold long notes.

83

And, perhaps as importantly, not distract the listener with your ugly breaths while singing a refrain." Back went his hand to my stomach. Bile rose to my throat. Did he do this to all of his students? Was this the first step in coercing them into his bed? *Stay calm,* I told myself. *Get through this first lesson and then I can go home.* This treatment was not worth all the singing skills in the world. Oh, how I longed for home and my sisters.

"What is it?" Basset asked sharply. "Do you want to remain a peasant?"

My bottom lip trembled as I tried to control my emotions. I wanted so badly to let loose the flood of tears that were just below the surface. I would not give him the pleasure of seeing how scared I was. No, I would give him his stupid stomach breath.

I breathed in, focusing on moving the air into my belly as instructed. His hand moved out and then in again.

"Better." He seemed pleased with himself. "Do you feel what it is I want?"

I nodded, not trusting myself to speak.

"Good," Basset said. "Between now and our next lesson, I'd like you to practice this breathing technique. I have another for you as well. Do you have candles?"

"Yes, I believe so."

He rose from the bench, his forehead furrowing with irritation. "Have the maid bring them."

"Now?"

"Yes, now."

I scooted to the end of the piano bench, happy to leave his presence for a moment. Gabriella was in the kitchen, putting together several sandwiches for lunch. She jumped when I spoke.

"Mademoiselle, you scared me. I didn't hear you."

"I'm sorry. Could you bring several lit candles out to the piano? I don't know why, but Mr. Basset wants them."

"Yes, I'll bring them right away."

I thanked her and returned to the sitting room. Mr. Basset had arranged himself on the chaise, draping one arm along the back and crossing one leg over the other. A lit cigarette dangled from his mouth. Smoke clouded around his head.

"She's bringing them," I said.

"Good. While we wait, tell me more about yourself, Miss Barnes. What truly brings you to Paris? Surely it's not only to study with me but to enjoy the rich, uninhibited culture?"

"Mostly to study, Mr. Basset."

"All work and no play makes for a dull girl." He took a drag from his cigarette and then blew smoke rings, as if that would entertain me. I wasn't a child, even if he thought of me as one.

"I'm not here for long," I said.

"All the more reason to play." He took another puff from his cigarette before offering it to me.

"No, thank you. I don't smoke."

"All the better for your voice," he said. "May I trouble you for a drink? I had a late, rather raucous evening."

A drink? It wasn't yet noon. Did I have anything to offer him? Was it wine he wanted or something stronger? "What do you prefer?"

"Do you have a brandy?" He stretched his legs out long on the chaise. Was it my imagination or did it seem like he'd positioned himself to display the front of his hips? I flushed at the very thought of what lay beneath the fabric of his trousers.

"Yes, I believe my father left brandy. Let me look." I hurried over to the liquor cabinet and opened the double doors to peer at my supplies. Fortunately, Papa had known to order it for me. Was it common for people like Mr. Basset to drink brandy in the middle of the day? Papa had only ever had a small glass of whiskey in the evenings.

I'm such a lost girl here, I thought as I poured him a glass of what I thought was the brandy. There were four liquors in glass decanters.

"Is this what you want?" I asked, setting it on the table nearest the chaise.

He picked it up and gave it a good whiff. "Yes, brilliant. Thank you." He tipped the glass back and the amber liquid disappeared.

Gabriella appeared with two long candles inserted into silver holders. "Sorry for the delay, mademoiselle. I had to search for them in the pantry."

"Put them here." Mr. Basset pointed to the table that now held his empty glass. "And can you get another brandy, please?"

Gabriella froze, clearly unsure if he'd asked her or me. I gave her a faint nod to let her know she should do it before returning my gaze to Mr. Basset.

He swung his legs from the chaise and set them firmly on the rug before turning to light the candles from the flame of a silver lighter.

Gabriella delivered his drink, setting it near the candles. "Will there be anything else, miss?" Miss instead of mademoiselle? Was it a code for something? As in, let me know if you want to run and I'm right behind you.

"No, thank you, Gabriella. We're almost through here."

She darted away. I wish I could as well.

"All right, now, what we're going to do is teach you a little more about breath control." Basset patted the spot beside him. "You'll need to get closer, though. Even I don't expect my pupils to blow out a candle from that far away."

Sit next to him? No, I wouldn't. I marched over to the piano bench and brought it over to the spot next to the table. "I'll do it from here."

He watched me with eyes the color of a muddy field, brown mixed with trampled green grass. "I don't bite, Miss Barnes." His voice had lowered in volume and tone. Was that supposed to seduce me?

"Don't you though?" I'd not meant to fight back, but it was as if Cym and Jo were with me, whispering in my ear what to do, what to say. "Bite, that is?"

His dark eyebrows rose and remained there for a moment. "Do you like biting, Miss Barnes?"

My stomach turned with repulsion. Did young women fall for this, or was it simply that they were desperate for his introduction into the art world? I didn't need him. I was fine with or without his offerings. I was Fiona Barnes, daughter of Colorado and Alexander and Quinn Barnes. His carrot had no appeal to me. I was not a hungry bunny.

"Mr. Basset, perhaps we should get something straight. I'm not charmed by you. I'm not taken in by your lewd comments. If they're meant to be a threat or an invitation matters not to me. My father hired you at great expense. I'm halfway around the world, away from my family, and perhaps seem vulnerable to you. However, I can assure you I am not. You have no power over me because I don't want anything from you. Those other girls, the ones you make mistresses in exchange for jobs, are not like me. They don't have the backing of parents or even homes. I'm assuming so, anyway. You take advantage of them. You should be deeply ashamed. God watches, no matter where you are."

He chuckled, clearly amused by my little speech. "You have fire in you. I'm surprised."

"Why should that surprise you?"

"An American heiress, spoiled and soft," he said. "These are the qualities I expected."

"You know nothing about me or my family," I said. "We're proud and ethical and not swayed by treachery, threats, or promises."

"This only makes me want you more," he said. "But I shall

refrain." His smile broke over his face. To others, he might seem attractive, but to me, he looked like a fox. "Do you have any idea of the doors I could open for you?" He asked this casually and in that same low tone that was supposed to be seductive but instead made me nauseous.

"Do you have any idea how little I care?"

"Then what are you doing here? What's a little mouse doing in the cat's city, hmm? A tiny girl such as yourself in mean old Paris? What else would bring you here, other than ambition?"

"A man like you wouldn't understand my motivations. But I can assure you I have no need for your introductions."

"Try me."

"Pardon?"

"Tell me what brought you here," he said.

"The chance to learn from a man reputed to be one of the best teachers in Europe. An opportunity to see a little more of the world. But both of those are really of no consequence to me. Unlike your other pupils, Mr. Basset, I'm fine with or without you. As much as I'd like to improve my craft, it's not worth compromising my principles."

"What a lovely orator you are, Miss Barnes. Such a lot of American pluck. Isn't that what makes you Americans drool?"

"Drooling is what dogs do," I said, as haughtily as I could.

"Keep in mind I can make you into the singer you'd like to be. You have a lot of work to do, but there's potential. A lot of potential. I shall behave myself, act like a priest around you." He laughed as he raised his hands in the air. "Don't look so suspicious. I'll be the model teacher. You can't judge a man for trying."

"You're the age of my father."

"You wound me, Miss Barnes." He tapped one finger on the top button of his shirt.

I glared at him, pretending I was Cymbeline. "I doubt that, but I'd like to."

"I surrender. I'll be good." He didn't smile this time but instead looked almost sincere. "I'd like to teach you, if you're still interested."

"I'll not allow you to touch me. Not anywhere, no matter what. Do you understand?"

"Your wish is my command."

"And now I should like you to go," I said.

He got up from the chaise slowly, as if his knees ached. I hoped they did. "I'll see you on Thursday, same time."

"Thank you." I gestured toward the door. "You may let yourself out."

I thought for a moment that he would refuse to leave, but thankfully he dipped his head in a respectful manner. With one hand on the piano, as if it were a friend and protector, I watched him walk toward the door. He grabbed his overcoat and hat before turning back to me with that practiced smile of his. "Good day, Miss Barnes."

The moment he was gone, I ran and locked the door. Although relieved to have him out of my apartment, I shook from head to toe. I sank into the comfort of a sofa cushion and buried my face in my hands.

What had I gotten myself into?

SEVERAL DAYS AFTER MY FIRST LESSON WITH MR. BASSET, I TOOK a trip to the post office, hoping for letters from home. I had three letters, one from Mama, another from Josephine, and the other from Cymbeline. I waited until I was home and sitting comfortably before opening them. I read Mama's letter first.

Dearest Fiona,

I hope this letter finds you well. We arrived in London with no mishaps and then went north to the place of your father's birth and upbringing. We've spent a wonderful visit with his brother and sister-

in-law. *The years have a way of soothing old wounds. Your father and his brother seem to have forgotten whatever disagreements they once had. Robert and his wife, Cassandra, have talked about coming to Colorado for a visit. She's scared of bears and coyotes but I assured her she would be fine in Emerson Pass. Gossip was more likely to nip you than a bear. I chuckled when I said it, but she merely looked at me with wide eyes. I must seem like a wild woman to her.*

You have been on my mind, dearest. Leaving you in Paris had seemed right up until the time we got there and I actually had to say goodbye to you. I hope the esteemed Mr. Basset is what we imagined and that you're enjoying working on your craft without interruption. I felt certain that your merry band of artist friends would keep you entertained. Have they?

I wonder, too, about the handsome Mr. West. Have you seen him since that night? I had a good feeling about him. He is the kind of man who would make an excellent husband and father. Perhaps I was more taken with him than you? I mention it only to say that I don't want you to feel any pressure when it comes to him or any man. There is a lot of time for you to find the right mate.

A letter from Josephine was waiting here for us. She wrote that our boys had taken it upon themselves to avenge Li after the attack. She didn't give many details, for which I was thankful. Suffice it to say, the men will no longer be bothering Li or anyone else in Emerson Pass. They've been not-so-politely asked to leave town. Jo hinted that Cymbeline might have partaken in the scheme to escort them out of town. I can only imagine what trouble she's flirting with since she's been home and without her beloved sport to focus her energy upon. Josephine says everything is going well with Cym's confinement. I am grateful for that. Between you and me, I was a tad worried she wouldn't take Theo's medical advice to take it a little easier than usual.

Speaking of Li, Jo said he has not been himself since you left. He won't admit to it, of course, but she said he seems very low. She and Cymbeline have asked him and Mrs. Wu to dinner several times, but he's declined with one excuse or the other. I do believe those horrid men have shaken his faith in our community. To be frank, I'm shaken myself. Your father has devoted his life to building a haven for anyone who wishes to comply with the unspoken laws of decency and kindness. These days it seems harder and harder to maintain the standards we once had. With growth comes advantages but also setbacks.

I will close now as your father has come to gather me for tea. As you know, the English take their tea quite seriously, and I mustn't be late. I love you, dearest girl.

Yours,

Mama

I opened Cymbeline's next.

Dearest Sister,

You won't believe the nonsense that's happened since you left. Firstly, Viktor won't let me out of his sight. Other than when he leaves for work (thank God he has a job) or has to run an errand, he's here with me, watching me like a hawk with its baby. I don't know what he thinks will happen to me without his keen gaze. I shan't fall over just from walking from one room to the other. He's forbidden me to conduct my usual exercise, saying it might harm the baby. I spoke with Louisa, and she's in agreement, that a baby is nestled inside my womb like she's sleeping between the softest yet safest pillows. Thus, I have been doing my usual exercises, invented by him I might add, while Viktor is at the bank working. We've hired a girl to help around the house, and I've bought her silence with a few extra coins a week. She has to help me with the washing, otherwise Viktor will see my clothes stained with perspiration and know right away.

You're probably shaking your head right now, worried too. You shouldn't worry. My body needs to be strong for the baby and my sport. I refuse to give up everything I enjoy just because I will have a son or daughter. The men in our lives don't have to, so why should we? I want to be in good physical condition afterward so that I can begin training for the next competition.

Anyway, enough about that. Without you here to talk with, I have no one to tell my secrets to. No one understands me as you do. Well, perhaps Viktor, which is why I have to hide things from him. He understands me but doesn't always agree, which poses a problem.

I've been thinking a lot about you and Li since you left. He's been moping about town like a sad child of late. I feel sorry for him, if you want to know the truth. I've decided that he's a man who will be perpetually unhappy. Why, you wonder? Because he has such high-minded principles that he cannot get out of his own way. I believe if he allowed himself to, he would see that he does indeed love you. The more he protests, the more suspicious I get. Who does that sound like, after all? Me, of course. How many times did I tell you I hated Viktor when truly, if I'd been honest with myself, I would have known how deeply I love him. What evidence of this do I have in regard to Li, you ask? Don't deny it, I can see you frowning as you read this letter. Teehee!

Anyway, about Li. Please refer to the abovementioned moping. He's sad without you, Fiona. Miserable, in fact. I know it. If only he could see that allowing himself to feel what he feels will set him free. He has high moral principles. That's the trouble right there. He sees you as untouchable and thus has entrenched himself in the belief.

However, I digress. I miss you and cannot wait until you return to me. I know it's selfish but I'm so very glad you'll be back before this baby comes. I'm absolutely, utterly terrified of its arrival. What kind of mother will I be? Don't answer that. But I'll have you and Jo and Mama to help me, so perhaps the child will be all right despite her mother's lack of skill. Do you know I can't even figure out how to make bread? Mine comes out flat as a pancake. We can talk about that when you get home. But seriously, what's the bakery for anyway? They do it better than I can, so why shouldn't I just buy a loaf of bread? I digress...

I love you more than I could say, dearest sister. I count the days until your return.

Love,

Cymbeline Olofsson. (I can't get enough of writing my new name.)

I opened Josephine's next.

Dear Fiona,

My little sister, I miss you dearly. It's as if the sun went behind a cloud here without you and Mama. I cannot wait until you return. Thinking of how long it will be gives me a panicky feeling in my stomach. Perhaps it's having lost our mother when I was so young, but I hate the idea of anyone I love being too far away.

There's not much news to report from here. The girls are keeping me busy. Phillip and Flynn are working hard to prepare the new ski run for next season. They've been out with the crews every day taking down trees. I fret until they return, worried something will happen to them. The saws terrify me.

Cymbeline is looking very well, so please don't worry about her. I believe she's been sneaking around, however, and doing those strange exercise routines when Viktor's at work. One day when the girls and I were out for a walk to gather wildflowers, we saw her through the trees. She was in a plank position and was passing a bag full of rice from one hand to the other. Little Quinn was quite interested, unfortunately. We might have another one in the family.

I ran into Li outside the Johnsons' shop the other day. He was walking with his head down, obviously thinking about something, and ran right into the new streetlamp. I happened to be near him when he did it and I'm embarrassed to say, burst out laughing. He laughed as well but not in a way that reflected in his eyes. He seemed thinner, too. I hope he's not ill. Cymbeline said he's suffering from the Fiona Blues. We both think he misses you.

Speaking of Li, I should not have reacted so negatively to your confession about your feelings for him. I hope you know it's out of love, not any attempt to control you or sway you away from whatever it is that's in your heart. Who we love is not always something we choose— perhaps it never is. We love who we love. I only wish he felt the same way. As someone who knows the sting of rejection, I am sympathetic as well as empathetic. I hope you meet someone soon, as I did, who takes away all thoughts of him. Unless, of course, he comes to his senses and realizes that you're the best woman in the world.

I should close. I have to supervise dinner and bath times for the girls. You're on my mind so often. I love you, little sister. Please take care and write me soon if you have time between your lessons and drinking all that French wine.

All my love,

Josephine

I stared, unfocused, at the letters in my lap. Thoughts jumbled around in my mind. Everything from Li to Cymbeline and what the boys had done to run the men out of town. Funny that Cym hadn't mentioned that at all. What had they done? The image of Li running into the streetlamp worried me. Was he ill? What if something was wrong with his sight? Or what if Mrs. Wu was sick and he was in such a fretful state that he ran into the lamp?

Cymbeline and her exercises troubled me as well. Was she right or was her delicate condition truly that?

My thoughts returned to Li. The ache of missing him never ceased. I sighed and closed my eyes, and wave after wave of homesickness washed over me. I would be home again soon, I reminded myself. For now, I would take comfort in the letters from my beloved family.

I went to the desk to write return letters to each of them. I described as best I could the fun I was having, leaving the part about Mr. Basset out in the letters to my sisters and Mama. They would only worry, and there was nothing they could do to help anyway. When that was done, I thought about Li some more. Then I picked up the pen and wrote:

Dear Li...

10

LI

I'D NOT HEARD FROM FIONA IN THE TWO MONTHS SHE'D BEEN
away, so it was with great surprise that I found a letter in the
post. The sun was hot and bright overhead as I walked to the car
with the letter safely in my pocket. Although spring was officially still weeks away, the weather had turned warm. I
perspired in my dark suit and under the brim of my hat. I went
to sit on a bench under a shade tree, holding the letter in both
hands. Should I open it here or wait until I got home? Did I
want to read the contents? No one had heard from her thus far.
I knew from Cymbeline that she and her parents had arrived
safely in Paris but other than that, I knew nothing. I'd tried to
convince myself this was for the best. I hadn't had much luck
thus far.

The leaves above me quivered in a breeze that didn't seem to
reach my overheated skin. *Fine,* I thought. *Open it and get it over
with.* I slid my finger under the seal and pulled up the flap, then
the letter itself.

Dear Li,

*I've written at least a dozen first sentences before tearing up the
paper, only to try again the next day. I'm regretful I poured my heart*

out to you like a little fool and hope you'll forgive me. I'm sick that I've perhaps ruined our friendship forever. Please say I haven't.

I decided this morning that I would write to you as if I hadn't acted so rashly and all was normal between us. So, here it goes...

I've been busy training with Mr. Pierre Basset. Papa rented a nice apartment for me, with two bedrooms, a maid's quarters, and a piano. The view looks out to Notre Dame and the River Seine. All quite scenic and inspiring. I've been composing like mad and have a few new tunes to share with you upon my return.

Apparently, Pierre Basset has a reputation as a ladies' man. He has numerous mistresses, all of whom were or are his female students. I hate to admit how shocked I was by this. Living in Emerson Pass didn't prepare me for the French culture in that regard. Not only does he turn his voice students into mistresses, but he asks for their favors in exchange for assistance furthering their musical careers. Can you believe that? According to Mr. West, most of Mr. Basset's students are only too happy to give their virtue to him.

I have my own thoughts about how "happy" they are to do so. Unlike me, many of his students don't have a family as I have and are unprotected against men like Mr. Basset. They must feel as though they have no choice but to do as he wishes. I suppose this is the way of the world, though? Women without means must survive somehow. Perhaps they see it as a small price to pay? Or perhaps it is a large price and they have to do it anyway.

For his part, Mr. Basset does do what he says he will and helps these women go on to singing careers. The venues and opera houses he has access to throughout Europe make him a powerful man. I couldn't care less, of course. I'd sooner sell my soul to the devil than play Mr. Basset's game. Anyway, I don't want to tour Europe. I'll be happy to return home to sing at church and our club. Again, I have Papa to keep me from such a fate. I've always known it to be true but since I've been here, I see clearly how lucky I am.

During my very first lesson, Mr. Basset suggested one of his sala-cious rendezvous. Fortunately, Mr. West had warned me that he might do so, or I might not have understood the gestures. I told him in no uncertain terms that I would not be the type of woman he could coerce into his bed (shudder) and if he wanted to have that kind of relationship, he would have to find another student. He laughed at me, as if I were a silly child. It was maddening!

Regardless of Mr. Basset's unwanted overtures, I'm learning a lot from him. As hateful as he is under all that charm and French cologne, he's taught me more in our first several weeks of lessons than I've learned my entire life. The exercises he's tasked me with have strengthened my voice considerably. For my part, I have dutifully practiced. I've found it helps to keep a regimented routine here in Paris or I might fall into a life of ill repute. I'm only joking. It would take more than a few outings to a Parisian café to change me.

In other news, I've become acquainted with a Mr. James West. We met him before Mama and Papa left for England. They quite approved of him, even though he's an impoverished lord without a penny to his name. He's become a good friend and buffer to Mr. Basset's advances. I've met others, too, all colorful characters. I wish you could meet them. I'll tell you all about them when I get home. There's an author, an artist, and their partners. I still haven't discerned who is married and who lives out of wedlock in the same apartment. It shouldn't matter to me. In fact, it's none of my business whatsoever. I must remember that.

But, oh my, Paris! You won't believe all that I've seen and done. I know it's best you've stayed with your grandmother and it's very selfish of me to wish you were here, but I cannot help it. We would have such fun visiting the jazz clubs and walking in the scenic parks. The museums, too! Such beauty. The River Seine—how would I describe its power and allure in musical terms? It would be a great opera perhaps?

I should close, as it's quite late. I'm quite embarrassed about my behavior. I cringe every time I think of it. I hope you'll forgive me and upon my return we can go back to our easy friendship. I hope, too, that you and Mrs. Wu are well. I miss you all very much.

With affection,

Fiona

I read the letter through a second time before bringing it to my nose to see if Fiona's scent had been caught in the paper. It smelled only of emptiness.

I folded the letter and put it back in the envelope. Fiona alone in Paris with the likes of Mr. Basset made me shake with fury. And her new friend, Mr. James West? Had she mentioned him to let me know she had moved on as I'd asked her to? Was she allowing him to court her? Her parents "quite approved" of him. Of course, they would. Impoverished or not, he was English aristocracy. He was exactly what she needed. Or was he?

My insides burned at the thought of her going about Paris on this man's arm. Who was he *really*? Was he impoverished because his family was corrupt or incompetent? Was he good or bad? Trustworthy? A gold digger? There were many questions and concerns. Perhaps it wasn't only this Pierre Basset who threatened the well-being of my dearest friend. Was she safe from James West?

I was helpless to assist her. I knew this. However, the urge to drop everything and go to her was as powerful as the hunger I could still remember from before our time at the Barnes estate.

I drove home with the windows down. The warm air ruffling my hair smelled of wildflowers. I stuck my left elbow out the window and let the sun shine down on my bare skin.

Put this out of your mind, I told myself. *You did the right thing.* She would come home with this James West and marry him in the very church where she loved to sing. Or maybe she would stay in Europe and never return to Emerson Pass? At that thought, I veered off the road and corrected only at the last moment or I would have landed in the ditch. I pounded the steering wheel with the heel of my left hand. What kind of man was I? She had gone and done exactly as I told her and now I was angry? It was too late anyway. I'd done what I'd done. For that matter, it would never have been the right time for Fiona and me. Why must this be so hard to remember?

Grandmother was out back watering the spring vegetable garden when I arrived home. She knelt on her walking stick for support as she let the water trickle from the can over the small shoots of my carrots and lettuce.

I unlatched the garden gate and called out to her. She looked up, squinting under the brim of her wide garden hat. "Did you bring me a new book?"

"Yes, I did. Josephine wasn't there, but one of the other librarians helped me. It's another mystery."

"Good. I'll look forward to reading tonight." Grandmother put more weight on her stick. Her eyes were shadowed under the brim of her hat, but they watched me with that same discerning way they always did. "What's happened?"

"Happened? Nothing." The letter burned through the fabric of my trousers pocket. *Only my life is over.*

She stepped closer and gestured toward the back door with her stick. "Let's go inside. I'm thirsty."

I turned and held open the gate for her and followed behind her across our patch of grass until we reached the stone walkway I'd laid last summer. Grandmother took this section carefully, as the stones were uneven.

The house felt cool after the warmth of the late-afternoon sun. While Grandmother took off her hat to hang on the rack by the back door, I poured her a cold glass of water. She sat at the table and thanked me. "It's warmer than I thought it would be today."

"Spring is here," I said, putting false enthusiasm into my tone.

"The tomatoes will be good this year." Grandmother set aside her glass and smacked her lips.

"I hope so. We could use some jars in our pantry for next winter." This would be my life from now on, pretending I cared about tomatoes or spring. I mustn't let Grandmother know how my insides bled.

I helped myself to a glass of water and joined her at the table. "I got a letter from Fiona."

"Ah, I see."

I looked away from her scrutiny. The crisp curtains that hung over the kitchen window flapped in the welcome breeze. Birds called to one another from the trees surrounding the yard. Love songs. Nature's music.

Grandmother rubbed her thumb absently on her glass. The warmth in the kitchen had caused the glass to sweat and drip onto the surface of our pine table. I got up to grab a towel, then swiped up the dampness.

"May I read the letter?" Grandmother asked.

"Yes, if you want." I tugged it from my pocket and set it near the glass.

Grandmother took it from the envelope and read it, her eyes traveling slowly across the page. When she was done, she put it back into the envelope and pushed it over to my place at the table. She didn't speak, tracing a knot in the wood with her finger. The second hand on our clock ticked away happily.

I folded the towel and placed it back on the counter. *The windows could use washing*, I thought. And the garden needed more water. Grandmother's attempts with the watering can were not enough. I would haul buckets from the well after dinner to thoroughly soak the dirt.

"Li, look at me."

I did so, bracing myself for whatever she would say next.

"Fiona is brave, but she's in danger. This Mr. Basset is a bad man. Who knows about Mr. West? She's living alone there with a maid who is perhaps as innocent as she is. She's defenseless. She doesn't know the language. Your French would help her."

"My French?" I'd taken several years at college but hadn't spoken it much since.

"Yes, your French. You've said yourself you have a knack for languages." She brought her age-spotted hands together in her lap. "Yes, you must go. If Lord Barnes were home, he would want you to go. He might even ask you. If he knew what was going on over there."

I leaned against the rim of the sink and stared at her. "All of this is impossible."

"She needs you. I should have insisted you go when they asked you the first time. We've left her all alone in that city with these strange men. You're the only one who can go. Her sisters and brothers are too busy."

"It's not practical," I said. "The trip is expensive. The boat takes weeks to get there. By then, she could be married to Mr. West."

"That's right. Which is why you must go and see for yourself this Mr. West." Grandmother squinted at me, then dabbed at her face with a handkerchief she'd pulled from her pocket.

"I have responsibilities here. She's doing fine without me." I plunged my hands into the pockets of my trousers. Something small and hard was in the seam of one pocket. I pulled it loose, expecting it to be a pebble, but instead it was a carrot seed, flat and rectangular in nature. I'd worn these pants when I was planting the spring garden. They'd been washed since then, but the seed must have burrowed into the seam.

A seed, I thought. A symbol of the dormancy of my life, hiding away in the shadows without any hope of bursting into life.

"You *will* go," Grandmother said. "She needs you. She's too polite to ask, but that's why she's written all of this to you. We owe it to that family. You know that."

"I built this house for us. For you to have a place to rest your head that belongs to our family. Finally. You sacrificed everything for Fai and me. It's important that I take care of you now." I swept both our glasses into the sink, avoiding her gaze.

"You must listen to me." Her voice, soft but poignant, pulled at me, turning me around to look at her. "You've always been a good boy, doing everything you're supposed to, taking care of me and Fai. Is it possible that you could go and enjoy yourself while helping Fiona? What harm can come from you going to Paris? I will be fine here."

I ran a hand through my hair, feeling it fall right back into place over my forehead. "She has James West now. What if I were in the way? What if I ruined all her chances for happiness? He's an Englishman, probably made from the same mold as her father. Isn't that what she should have?"

"Do you think that's what she wants?" Grandmother asked.

"I don't know, but I think it's what she needs." I examined my hands and my long, slender fingers made for making music. "But it doesn't matter. I love her and cannot have her. Going to Paris and seeing her as the light of someone else's eyes—I don't know if I'm strong enough. I might crack in two."

"You must go. You're all she has. All she needs. Her father trusts you."

"I'm weak, Grandmother. You know I am. When it comes to Fiona, I can't think logically."

"We're both strong, my boy. Do you know what we've survived already in this lifetime?"

I closed my eyes, remembering the cold, dark mining shaft where we'd huddled, homeless and starving, those weeks before Lord Barnes found us and brought us home. We'd buried my mother and father in the spring, after they'd died within weeks of each other. My grandmother had been left all alone with two little children in a country she didn't speak the language of. There had been no gold in that rush my parents had risked it all for. Grandmother had fed us berries and bunnies she managed to trap. Until winter had nearly wiped us away. And then Lord Barnes had come.

"You're right," I said. "We owe Lord Barnes a great debt. But is this what's right for Fiona or me?"

"Go to Paris." Grandmother folded her hands on top of the table. "I didn't raise you to shirk your responsibilities. Fiona's without—" She interrupted herself and looked up at the ceiling. "What's the English word?"

"Without guile? Compassionate to a fault?" The list of adjectives for Fiona was long. I stopped before I embarrassed myself.

"Yes. You must see this Mr. West with your own eyes. You should be there when she has lessons from the terrible man. I'll return to my room at the big house. Lizzie might need my help anyway. She has no idea how to make my herbal teas."

We talked no more about it that night, going about our usual routine. However, before bed, I sat down to write a letter to Fiona.

Dear Fiona,

Thank you for writing to me. There's no reason for you to apologize about the incident before you left. I am truly sorry I hurt you. I wish things were different, but wishing so doesn't make them so.

I'm writing to let you know I will be headed your way on the first train and then boat out of America. Although I know you're quite capable of looking after yourself, as demonstrated by the way you put him in his place straight away, I will not rest knowing you're in danger. I have chosen not to share your predicament with your siblings. As I'm sure you agree, telling them would lead to one of them disrupting their life to go to you. I have the least to disrupt, so it should be me. In fact, I should have come with you when you first asked. I'd feel terribly guilty if anything should happen to you when all would have been well had I just agreed to be your chaperone.

If you're wondering about Grandmother, she feels strongly I should join you. She's offered to move back into her room at the big house while I'm away. She hasn't said but I think she might miss it there. Regardless, I am going to do as she's asked. Everything will be here when we return.

Given my calculations, I should be there at the end of June. I'll not wait to hear from you, as the letters take such a long time to arrive.

If Basset does anything else, there's no reason you have to continue studying with him. No voice lesson is worth compromising one's integrity or most of all, safety. He may seem all-powerful but remember who you are. You're Fiona Barnes, the best person in the world.

I paused to nibble on the end of my quill. Best person in the world? It was a little much, but I would leave it. Rewriting wasn't necessary when time was of the essence. I finished the letter simply.

I will see you soon.

With love,

Li

11

FIONA

I WAS AT THE PIANO PRACTICING MY SCALES WHEN GABRIELLA came in from running errands. Her cheeks flushed from the heat and her hair in disarray, she started speaking in rapid French the moment she entered the room. I didn't get most of it but from what I could gather, she'd picked up cheese and bread and it was hot outside.

"And here is a letter to you from Colorado." She placed it on top of the piano.

"Thank you." My stomach lurched at the handwriting. A letter from Li. He must have gotten my letter. Hopefully I hadn't worried him. After I sent it, I thought about how it might alarm him and wished I hadn't mentioned Mr. Basset. Weeks had passed since I put it in the post. Thus far, Mr. Basset had complicd with my request. He hadn't touched me. However, that didn't mean he didn't make not-so-subtle innuendoes. For the most part, I ignored them and focused on his instruction. Sadly, it was very good. I was making marked improvement in my breath control and power. As much as I despised him, I had to admit he was good at what he did.

I opened the letter with trembling fingers and read through

105

it twice. Was it possible? He was coming here? I was heavy with guilt and sank into one of the leather chairs. I should never have said anything about Mr. Basset. Had I done it purposely? To draw him here?

I got up and paced from one end of the room to the other and back again. What did all this mean? Was my safety the real reason he was leaving everything? Did it matter? He was coming to me. He was already on his way. I held the letter against my chest before bringing it to my nose to smell for Li's scent. Nothing. But what did I think it would smell like after weeks on a ship?

A ship. He was probably on the ship over the ocean at this very moment. Two more weeks and he could be sitting right here in front of me.

"Gabriella," I called out.

She scurried in from the kitchen, her face tense. I'd frightened her with my shouting. "Are you in need of me?"

"I'm sorry," I said, laughing. "I didn't mean to scare you." I waved the letter at her. "My friend is coming. We must get the room ready for him."

"This is friend of your heart?"

"Yes, but you mustn't let on that you know," I said. "He doesn't feel the same way."

She looked at me blankly. I grabbed the English-to-French dictionary and looked up *unrequited*. "*Sans réciprocité*," I said to her.

"Ah, *vous devez être très triste*." She wiped under her eyes as if she were crying.

Whatever she'd said, she had the idea. I flipped to *sadness* to find the French word. "*Oui, tristesse*."

"*Il doit vous aimer, pour faire tout ce chemin*." Gabriella gave me a knowing nod.

"I don't know what you said."

She waved her hand dismissively and then grinned. "He will

like French food. My food, yes?"

"I know he will." Spontaneously, I grabbed her into a quick hug. "I can't wait for you to meet him."

THAT NIGHT JAMES AND I SAT OUTSIDE UNDER AN AWNING AT the café below my apartment. The night was warm and muggy and smelled of perspiration, red wine, and the aromas from the kitchen of garlic, onions, and butter. James, handsome in a summer suit, had been entertaining me with stories from his youth, spent mostly in the English countryside. As I listened to tales of traipsing through meadows playing games with his friends, catching frogs and frolicking with his dogs, it became evident that our childhoods were not that different.

Since our first meeting, James and I had spent many evenings together, eating or on evenings when the weather was nice, walking along the river.

"Someday I hope to repay you for your kindness," James had said one night.

"You will," I'd said. "These things have a way of coming back around." I had a running tab with Henri and an understanding with James that I could not allow him to suffer when I had enough to feed us both.

"Fiona, have I lost you with my boring stories?" James asked now as I set my water glass aside.

I straightened and smiled at him from across the table. "Not at all. I was thinking how similar our childhoods were, despite the miles between us. My brothers were fond of searching for frogs, and we all ran around outside playing games. There were sleigh rides in the winters and ice-skating on our pond in town." A wistful tone had come into my voice.

"You're homesick," James said.

"I shouldn't be, but I am, even though I'm having a lovely time. Do you ever want to go home to England? At some point?"

"Well, the weather sounds better than the dreary rain that colored my youth in gray." James nodded at the waiter who had come with our second course.

I'd ordered a chicken dish made with white wine, carrots, potatoes, and onions. Steam rose from the plate, bringing the scent of rosemary to my nose, which reminded me of home. I could see Lizzie in the kitchen chopping vegetables, taking me away from Paris for a moment. Smells of home.

James's steak came with a dollop of herb butter that melted over the meat and formed pools on his plate.

He cut into his steak. Blood rushed from the sides, meeting the butter but not merging. Like oil and water, butter and blood don't quite mix.

"I don't know. There wasn't much there for me. My parents would like me to come home and make a good match. One that would save us. But I would like to go to America."

America? I set that aside to think about in a moment. I watched him as he ducked his chin and cut another piece from his meat. "I don't understand. What do you mean by a good match?"

"If I were to marry into a family with money, then I would be able to save our estate. As you know, my family has titles but our money's dried up and we're hanging on by the grace of God. For centuries, the men in my family have not worked or done anything useful. Without income, money dwindles until there's nothing left." He looked up, eyes twinkling. "There's your economic lesson for today."

I smiled back at him, but my heart felt heavy. What would his family do if he did not find a good match? "Will you marry only for money? What of love?"

"I'd like it if those two qualities aligned in the same woman, but I'm not entirely hopeful."

"Have you ever loved anyone before?" I asked.

"Other than heroines in books, no."

"Is that why you're interested in me? Because of Papa's money? Answer honestly. I can't blame you for self-preservation." I wouldn't be hurt if the answer was yes. But if so, then perhaps that would explain why there were no sparks between us.

"Absolutely not. I enjoy your company." His eyes crinkled at the corners when he smiled at me without a hint of cunning.

I nodded. "I enjoy yours as well."

He met my gaze for a second or two longer than one would expect. "But there's nothing here, is there? Nothing but friendship?"

I touched my fingers to his shoulder. "Friendship isn't such a bad thing. One can never have too many friends. Anyway, it's best not to confuse ourselves with hope of falling in love. It's not meant to be, is it?"

"I suppose not. Still, I'm at your disposal. However I can be of service, I am here." He cut another section off his steak and stabbed a slice of potato to go with it but didn't lift the fork to his mouth. "What about you? Have you loved anyone?"

I glanced out to the street. During this time of the evening, the street was quiet, free of cars and delivery trucks. Across from our building were several more cafés, a bakery storefront, a bookseller closed for the day, and a market with various meats and cheeses displayed in the windows.

"I have loved someone. But it's hopeless. He doesn't love me back." I squished a soft carrot between the tines of my fork.

"Is that one of the reasons you're here in Paris? Running away from some heartless American bloke who has broken your heart?"

"Partly, yes." I lifted my gaze to meet his kind eyes and softened, safe to speak the truth without fear of judgment. That was the thing with James West, I decided. He was easy to be with and talk to, perhaps because tension between us did not exist. It might be simply him, though. His unguarded and sincere way of speaking about himself made it possible for others to do as well. "Everyone seems to think that Paris was what I needed. I'm not so sure. Love doesn't vanish because of a trip overseas."

"Do you want to tell me about him?" James's hair rustled in a sudden breeze, causing several strands to catch in his long eyelashes. I'd wondered since meeting him who he reminded me of, and in that moment I knew exactly. He was like my brother Theo, quiet, reticent, deeply intelligent. Perhaps that's why I felt so comfortable with him?

For the next few minutes, I described how the Wu family had come to live with us as well as Papa's insistence that all children go to school. "We didn't think anything was different between us and any of the other children in town. They were our friends. But we didn't understand what it was like to be Fai and Li—how their differences were always forefront in their minds. I was insensitive and naive not to see how it affected him."

"The world can be cruel," James said. "Especially to those who are different."

I nodded, describing the way Li was attacked outside the club. "I didn't think anyone in our town would do such a thing. Sadly, I was wrong."

"And you're sure he's aware of your feelings?" James asked.

"I told him, yes. Before I came here and just after he was hurt by those men. It didn't go well." I flushed in remembrance of my humiliation. "I don't know why I assumed he would feel the same way. There are too many differences between us. Our ages and backgrounds make it impossible for us to ever be together."

"It's possible that he can't allow himself to feel any other way," James said. "We do that, you know. Deny ourselves what we can't have, as if we had any control either way. We're born into a set of circumstances and there's not much we can do to get out of them. He might have felt that even more keenly after being beaten up in a place he'd felt safe. It may have emphasized how hard it would be for you and him if you were to marry."

I nodded, miserable. "Yes, and he's right, of course. It's only that I wish it were all different but even if it was—Li wouldn't love me. He sees me as a child. Someone to take care of, not love."

"Those are not mutually exclusive, are they?" James asked softly.

"I don't know." I pushed a chunk of chicken around my plate. "I don't know anything about love, other than my heart feels shattered and I wish I could wake up tomorrow without the heaviness of unrequited love."

"I'd like that for you too," James said. "But love doesn't always behave as it should."

"In America, we see circumstances as something we can overcome through hard work or cleverness. Love is not one of them. Hard work or cleverness or even how good you are means nothing when it comes to romance. Our hearts choose from an entirely different set of things. One can't make another love them by sheer will."

"True," James said. "It's not only romantic relationships. My mother and father are abysmal at showing affection. Very English, you know."

I didn't know but nodded, as if I did. Parents who withheld affection were as foreign to me as the streets of Paris.

"It might be difficult to believe this, but I think coming to Paris was the right thing. You're away from everything you've known, including Li. Give it a little more time. I think you'll soon find that your heart has mended. Maybe you'll find a nice man here to fall in love with. Not me, obviously."

We laughed together and clasped hands on the top of the table.

"It's easier to be friends. There's no possibility of separation."

I ate some of my dinner, forcing myself to take bites, knowing that it was good for me to eat. "There's something else."

"What's that?" James lifted his glass and looked at me as he took a drink of his wine.

"I've received a letter from Li. He's coming to Paris to make sure I'm all right. It's all my fault." I explained about my letter telling Li too much about my experiences here. "I shouldn't have said anything about Mr. Basset. Now he's leaving everything to come take care of me." And what had I expected? Knowing Li as I did, what did I think he would do if he thought I was in peril? "I've disrupted his life by behaving like a child." For that matter, when had I ever taken care of myself? I'd been the pet of my entire family. Sweet little Fiona, who needed looking after. Even after my little sisters came, I still remained the youngest of the original five of us. The moment I had trouble, I'd written to Li. No wonder he couldn't see me as anything but a burden.

"When will he arrive?" James asked, clearly untroubled by my consternation.

"He'll be here in a few weeks. Right now, he's on the ship. I'm assuming, anyway."

"Good, I'd like to get a good look at him." James grinned before stabbing another bite of steak.

"He's purely good," I said. "His only fault is that he doesn't love me."

"He must love you a little to come halfway across the world."

"As a friend, like you. Isn't it strange, James, the way I can welcome friendship from you and wish it were otherwise with Li?"

"The ways of the heart are mysterious." His gaze flickered to the setting sun, peeking through the upstairs windows of the building across from us. "Still, I wonder about this visit. It's quite something to come across the world to ensure your well-being."

"Wouldn't you do that for me?" I asked, teasing.

"That's just the thing. I'm not sure a man would do that for anyone he didn't have deep feelings for."

Despite my attempts at the contrary, a trifle of hope arose in me. "Guilt, maybe? Because of my father's aid all those years ago?"

"He turned down Paris the first time, didn't he? I think there's more to Li's motivations than guilt. But we'll see, won't we? I'm going to do a thorough investigation when he arrives."

I laughed when he wriggled his eyebrows. "Until then, I'm glad to be here with you."

"Likewise, dear lady."

1 2

FIONA

S<small>EVERAL NIGHTS LATER</small>, I <small>SAT ON MY TERRACE WITH</small> S<small>ANDWICH</small> and Saffron. Sandwich was in the process of rolling flecks of tobacco into a thin piece of paper, then licking it with the tip of her tongue. She did it with a grace I found captivating. Saffron puffed on a previously rolled cigarette, plumes of smoke encircling her like the flowers of wild grasses back home.

Inside, James and Reynaldo were discussing politics and drinking wine. The glittering lights of Paris decorated the summer night. From downstairs came the noise from the café as well as the pub we could hear but not see. We all had wine glasses in our hands. I sat on one of the two chairs with Saffron beside me. Sandwich leaned against the railing, looking slim enough she might fall right through the bars if she wasn't careful.

"Tell us how you're doing here all on your own," Saffron said. "My first few months here were dreadful. I didn't know a soul nor speak a bit of French."

"They've been fine. A little lonely," I said. "I'm homesick."

Saffron crossed one leg over the other and gave me a good hard look. She wore wide-legged pin-striped trousers and a boxy blouse made of white cotton. Her fancy clothes, according to her, as they were not splattered with paint. "Only the best for you, darling," she'd said when she came in, before kissing me on both cheeks and calling me delicious.

"You need to get out more," Saffron said. "I could take you a few places so interesting you'd forget all about home."

"No, thank you," I said. "I like to be up early to practice."

"Practice what?" Sandwich asked, looking interested before lighting her cigarette.

"Music, dirty girl," Saffron said. "You have a singular and infuriating focus on sex."

I flushed and looked toward the lights of Notre Dame. It wasn't the first time I'd been embarrassed that evening, and I had a feeling it wouldn't be the last. Spending time with these two women was like holding on to a sleek, sharp slope with my fingernails. I never knew what was coming and could fall off at any moment.

"James should take you out more," Sandwich said. "He'll protect your innocence."

"He's noble. We can say that, can't we?" Saffron asked.

"I prefer to stay in," I said. "Anyway, I have enough trouble right here in the apartment."

Both women whipped their heads around to look at me. "Whatever do you mean?" Sandwich asked.

"Do either of you know Pierre Basset?"

"Sure, we've heard of him. Sandwich here knew a girl he—" She cut herself off. "You know, a girl who was friendly with him."

"Have you heard anything about him?" I asked.

"Other than he's a terrific womanizer, not really," Sandwich said. "My friend had to give him the goods when she couldn't pay her bill."

Goods? I assumed that meant sex. "She was studying with him?" I asked.

"Yes, he told her she had potential, which I didn't hear myself." Sandwich inhaled from her cigarette and blew the smoke out in a quick puff before continuing. "I don't know much about music, but she sounded like a caterwauling cat to me."

"She wasn't that bad," Saffron said.

"You liked her because she's pretty," Sandwich said. "You weren't listening with your ears."

Saffron thought she was pretty? But what did that have to do with the woman's singing ability? Why would it distract Saffron? An idea came to me. Did she like women? No, that couldn't be it. She was married to Reynaldo.

Saffron laughed. "Perhaps it was that. Regardless, he billed her for a lesson she never had with him. She met him at some party and he invited her to stop by his studio to audition for his master class. He didn't allow her into the class. Instead, he presented her with an unexpected bill for his time."

"Auditions are not lessons," I murmured under my breath.

"Correct," Sandwich said. "Thus, my friend's confusion about what exactly she was being billed for. She had no money."

"And she had to pay one way or the other," Saffron said, completing Sandwich's story.

I tucked all this away to think about later. Now they started asking me all kinds of questions. How did I come to study with him? Had I heard of his reputation before coming here?

I answered honestly. "My father arranged for me to study with him. He got the recommendation from an old school friend of his. Papa had no idea what he was sending me into."

"The lion's den," Saffron said in her monotone way. It was hard to imagine her excited about anything.

"You be careful," Sandwich said. "I'd hate to see you get in any kind of trouble because of him."

"Listen to her," Saffron said. "She's been through a lot herself. Until she found us, she was a lost little puppy."

"Not entirely true." Sandwich took one last drag of her cigarette before putting it out in the ashtray I'd found in a closet. The balcony was skinny with only a small metal table and two uncomfortable hard-backed chairs. I'd taken my breakfast out here several days in a row. I loved to watch Paris in the morning, waking like a party girl after a late night. Before nine, the streets were quiet with only the bakery workers up and about, the street cleaners and maids heading to work. Tonight, it was a lovely place from which to watch people.

"However, I'm quite familiar with men like Basset," Sandwich said. "Sometimes the poor fools even fall in love with him."

Saffron shuddered. "You women and your men, always looking for someone worthy when I'm available, free of charge."

Sandwich raised one thin eyebrow and brought a finger to her mouth to shush her friend. "The youngster's not ready for all of that. We must let her in on our secrets slowly."

I could feel myself slipping off the slope. What did they mean exactly?

"It's hardly a secret," Saffron said, drily. "Perhaps Fiona is like me. You can't know just by looking at a woman."

Like her? What did that mean? "I've worn trousers back home when I had to help in the barn or garden," I said.

Saffron laughed, deep and throaty. "See there, Sandy, we've got ourselves a real revolutionary here."

I smiled politely.

"People like me," Saffron said, "don't have the luxury of being with the normals. They know right away I'm different."

"What do you mean?" My curiosity got the better of me. I had to ask. "Do you prefer women?"

"Nothing, sweet little thing." Saffron glared at Sandwich. "Tell us more about this place of barns and gardens."

"It's beautiful there." I described our mountains and the wildflowers that decorated the meadows with vibrant colors. I told them about our vegetable garden and that we grew a lot of what we ate. "Lizzie cans a lot to put away for the cold months. There's Mrs. Wu too. She makes special teas that will cure almost anything."

"I could have used one this morning for my hangover," Sandwich said.

"I don't know if she has one for that," I said.

We chatted for a few more minutes about our backgrounds and what had brought us to Paris. I was surprised to learn that Sandwich was from Ohio.

She rolled her eyes. "Born and raised. I couldn't wait to get out of there. When I graduated from high school, I used every bit of my savings and bought a ticket to New York. I'd planned on staying there but I met a man who was on his way to Paris and before I knew it I was tucked into his cabin and on my way too."

Tucked away in his cabin? I tried to hide my shock, but I must not have done a good job because they both laughed.

"Not everyone has a rich daddy," Sandwich said. "A girl has to make choices, and sometimes that means sharing a cabin with a gentleman old enough to be her father. One way or the other it comes back to a daddy of some kind."

"Or mother," Saffron said, with a mischievous grin.

"Are you and Reynaldo married?" I asked. The minute it was out of my mouth, I felt stupid.

"Reynaldo and I live together," Saffron said. "He's not my husband."

She and Reynaldo lived together without being married? Until recently, I'd never heard of such a thing. My cheeks flamed.

"Do you love each other?" I asked, inwardly cringing at how childlike I sounded in front of these two women of the world.

"Sure, we do. We care about each other very much without having to change ourselves or pretend to be something we're not." The women exchanged a look between them. I was embarrassed but didn't know exactly why. "Let's just say we have a symbiotic relationship. One that allows me to do as I please and the same for him."

"Men always do as they please," Sandwich said.

"You know what I mean." Saffron flicked the end of her cigarette into the ashtray.

I didn't but decided to keep quiet. Listening to these two gave me a lot to think about later.

"You're not in that little mountain town of yours any longer," Sandwich said. "People like us belong in Paris."

People like us? Did she mean me too?

"Do you want to fall in love and get married?" I asked Sandwich, hoping to deflect the conversation away from myself.

"Sure. I was in love once and it got me nothing but a broken heart. For now and maybe forever, I'm a girl looking for the next party. I'll tell you one thing—I knew I wasn't born to stay in Ohio and marry bucktoothed Raymond. He was the boy my father wanted me to marry, so our farms could merge. That's one of the reasons I had to hightail it out of there."

"Were there other reasons?" I couldn't imagine anything worse than marrying a man you didn't love just to merge wealth. Then again, I was lucky not to ever have to entertain such ideas.

"Sure. Aforementioned broken heart. But that's neither here nor there." Sandwich pulled another cigarette from the tin they'd left near the ashtray. "I don't recommend married men, even though the French seem to think it's a fine way to live."

I couldn't help but gasp. "You were in love with a married man?"

"It wasn't on purpose," Sandwich said. "I was young and impressionable." She used Saffron's lighter on the end of her cigarette. The tip flamed red.

"We're all outcasts here in our little group," Saffron said. "I ran away from home when I was only sixteen. Do you know I was a stowaway on a ship?"

"No. It can't be." I couldn't imagine anyone actually doing such a thing. "I thought that was only something that happened in books."

"Yes, it's true. Desperate people must do desperate things," Saffron said.

"I understand," I said. I was starting to, anyway. Perhaps they would sympathize about my feelings for Li. After all, they'd been through difficulties and felt outside of societal expectations.

"What is it, little mountain girl?" Saffron asked. "What's your secret? We all have them, you know."

I said, hesitantly, "It was a secret. Now people know. Some, anyway. Including James."

"Ah, so there *is* something." Sandwich's eyes gleamed in the light from the sitting room. She waved her hand around, making the red end of her cigarette write in the air. As if to punctuate her question, a horn blared from one street over, followed by men shouting.

"I'm in love with a man," I said. "But it's all hopeless. I have a broken heart right at the moment, if you want to know the truth."

"Why's it hopeless?" Saffron asked.

"He doesn't love me," I said.

"I find that hard to believe." Saffron's gaze flickered to Sandwich and back to me. "You're pretty and smart. Kind, too."

"None of those things matter to Li," I said. "He sees me only as a child. I think, anyway. I thought it was his natural reticence that had kept him from confessing his feelings, but it turned out there were none. I read everything wrong." I explained about our musical partnership and how we'd essentially grown up together.

"What else? There's something more," Saffron said.

I nodded. "Yes, there is. He's of Chinese descent." I didn't know how to explain bigotry and hatred. However, my new friends understood without me having to go into detail.

"He's seen as unequal to all the fine white folks," Saffron said.

"Not that it matters to me or the rest of my family." Without going into too much detail, I shared with them the plight of the Wus and how Papa had found them near death and brought them home. "Li went away to college to study music and things were hard for him in Chicago."

"I'm sure they were," Saffron said drily.

"Papa asked Li to be my companion here in Paris but he said no, mostly because I told him my feelings."

"You told him?" Sandwich asked. "Brave."

"Stupid." I sighed and looked out to the building across the street from us. Through one of the windows, I could see a couple dancing together. What a fine picture they made, twirling about that way. "I ruined everything, including our friendship. But then, last month, in a moment of weakness, I sent him a letter and told him about Mr. Basset's behavior."

"Behavior?" Sandwich draped an arm over her concave middle. "What did he do?"

"The thing he does with all the women he teaches," I said. "He wanted that from me too. Or, at least I think so."

"Right, of course," Sandwich said.

"I wrote it all to Li and now he's on his way here." I waved a waft of smoke from Sandwich's cigarette away from my face.

"On his way here? To rescue you?" Sandwich asked.

"You don't need rescuing. You've got us." Saffron uncrossed one leg only to cross the other, exposing her ankles. In men's socks? I was learning something new every day.

"I might not need rescuing," I said. "But I'll be happy to see him." Or would I? Would it be better if I continued here alone? Would all the feelings rush back to me the moment I saw him? It wasn't as if they'd left. Not really. He was still in my dreams every night.

"Men like Basset respond well to other men," Saffron said. "He'll behave himself if he thinks there are consequences." The bitterness in her voice made me wonder about her past. Did she know about this personally?

"It's true," Sandwich said. "Rich and powerful men think they can take whatever they want until another man steps in."

"Li's experience in Chicago wasn't good. There were many cruel people there. He was denied a position in the symphony because he's of Chinese descent. As if all Americans hadn't originated somewhere else."

"Not the natives," Saffron said.

I nodded, ashamed. It was true. The white people had systematically removed them from their own land. Papa had wept while telling us what he'd learned only recently about the government's involvement in ridding the new territory of the native people.

"Li will like Paris," Saffron said. "It's different here than in America. This is where anyone can come and express who they are."

"Look at Josephine Baker," Sandwich said, speaking of her as if they were friends.

A terrible thought occurred to me. What if Li liked it so much he refused to come home? I'd not thought of that until now.

"I'm looking forward to meeting this man who has stolen our Fiona's heart," Saffron said.

"He's quiet." They might think him too reserved, I thought. "He's expressive only through his music until he becomes more familiar with a person."

"I don't know if I can like someone who hurt you," Sandwich said.

"It's not his fault," I said. "You can't make yourself love someone. If I were a little older, perhaps he would have been able to see me that way. Six years is a lot."

"Not really," Saffron said. "When you're ten and he's sixteen, but not now."

"Will you welcome him?" I asked.

"Of course we will," Sandwich said. "If he's your friend, then he's ours too."

The night had cooled, and we went inside to join the others. I'd learned more than my share that night. I couldn't wait for everyone to leave so I could think about it all and then write to Cym. Reynaldo and Saffron were not in love with each other because they preferred their own gender. Sandwich had come over as someone's mistress.

What would Cym think? Would she be surprised? Or would she say something about how sheltered we'd been? What would Li think of my new friends?

James gave me a big smile and held out his hand. I took it briefly and gave it a squeeze. Was James like Reynaldo? Is that why he didn't like me? Is that why I felt nothing with him? I didn't think so. He and I were just not meant to fall in love with each other.

Paris culture was unfolding before me. This city and her people were like a complicated woman who bit by bit revealed herself to me, much like my new friends. To my surprise, it wasn't taking me long to acclimate to a new, more progressive way of thinking. Would I be changed forever?

13

LI

IT WAS THE END OF JUNE BY THE TIME I ARRIVED IN PARIS. MY journey had been arduous and took many weeks. Because I wasn't certain exactly how long it would be until I arrived in Paris, I'd given Fiona a rough estimate. When I'd arrived in port, I sent a telegram to her in Paris.

Arrived in Normandy. Stop. Will arrive tomorrow on the four o'clock train. Stop

When the train pulled into the station in Paris, I didn't know what to expect. Would Fiona be there to greet me? Perhaps she'd changed her mind by now, realizing she didn't need me or any chaperone? Had I interfered in her life when I wasn't wanted? During the weeks it had taken for me to arrive in Europe, I'd had a lot of time to think. Too much time. I'd gone over the different scenarios over and over again. Would I find Fiona in love with this James West? Would she have successfully thwarted the advances of Mr. Basset? What of these new friends she'd met?

With my trunk in hand, I looked up and down the platform. No Fiona. Disappointment swelled in my stomach. I would have to get to her apartment somehow, and I was in no mood to figure out yet another mode of transportation. Then I heard my name. I turned in the direction of the voice. Fiona waved with both hands and then darted toward me. Wearing a white summer dress and a straw hat with a short yellow feather, she seemed smaller than at home. She hurled herself into my arms, almost knocking me over, despite her tiny frame. I had no choice but to drop my valise and hug her in return. She smelled of flowers and honey. The feather on her hat tickled my chin.

"I'm so very glad to see you." Her small chest heaved as she took in a deep breath. "I've missed you more than I can say. I'm sorry for all the trouble I've caused you." Too soon, she pulled away to look up at me.

"You've not caused me any trouble," I said. "I should have come with you in the first place. It was a stupid error not to. Grandmother told me as much."

"Did she make you come?" The space between her brows wrinkled.

"No, no. I meant only that she gave me her blessing to come."

"She won't mind being back at the big house? I feel terrible for dragging you here."

"Honestly, I think she prefers her old room at the house. She misses the camaraderie with the other staff, especially Lizzie. Grandmother might not be the type to retire."

"I'm relieved to hear you say that. You look wonderful but tired." She cocked her head to the right, looking at me with the same expression she'd had as a child when given a treat by Lizzie, almost rapturous in her delight. She still looked at me with eyes filled with love. Months away had not changed that. Why did it make me giddy to see? I was supposed to be stronger and better than this. "Was the journey terrible?" Fiona asked.

"Long," I said, smiling down at her. "But worth it to see you." I'd keep the trials of my travels to myself.

"I've been fretting over it, wishing I hadn't told you about Mr. Basset."

"Why?"

"It was selfish of me. I'm perfectly fine." That silly feather in her hat fluttered, as if in agreement with her assessment of herself. "When I wrote to you, I was low. I shouldn't have burdened you. I was homesick, and I missed all of you so very much. I'm a terribly weak person."

"You're not. You've been here in a strange city all alone. One of us should have come with you. Now I'm here and won't let anything happen to you from here on out."

"Look at you, here now standing before me." She took both my hands, the silky texture of her gloves soft against my skin. "Did you bring your violin?"

"Yes, it's in my case."

"The piano isn't as good as our one at home, but it's not bad." Fiona drew in a breath as if to tell me more but seemed to change her mind. "Enough about music. You must be exhausted, and we have loads of time to discuss all that. James is waiting outside for us. We thought about a cab but decided the subway was better. He's on a strict allowance, and I've been helping him a bit by feeding him. I'd rather do that than take a taxi."

"You've been giving him money?" A bell like the one that rang on Sundays clanged between my ears. What had we done, sending compassionate Fiona over here alone? This was my fault. I was here now. I would fix all of it.

"Not money, but taking him to dinner or feeding him at home. The poor dear needs food to think. He's hoping to find more clients and can't very well do that with an empty stomach, can he? We want to take you to dinner later, but we'll go back to the apartment first. You can have a bath and even a nap if you need one. I cannot wait to show you Paris."

James was indeed waiting outside for us. If not for Fiona, I might have been tempted to curse at the sight of him. Even as a man, I could see the appeal of his high cheekbones, full mouth, and lively eyes. Tall, too. Skin as lily white as Fiona's. I could already see her walking down the aisle of a church with him, wearing an heirloom ring passed down from James's relatives. Poor as church mice, perhaps, but with closets full of jewels and clothes.

My heart thudded. What if she never returned to Emerson Pass?

She introduced us, beaming and completely oblivious to my angst. "This is James West. And this is Li Wu."

We shook hands. His was a firm handshake but there were no calluses, no sign of a man who knew how to work or build anything. I flashed upon the boys at home, how we'd all helped one another build our cottages. We'd sweated and made calluses and been useful to one another. But this man? He was raised in some drafty, cold castle with nothing to show for it.

I hated him.

Why had it been necessary for him to come to pick me up? He didn't appear to have a car. Was he simply here to escort us into a cab or subway? We could do that by ourselves, thank you very much.

Was Fiona in love with him?

She chirped away in her melodic voice. "James has been such a good friend to me here. I don't know what I would have done without him these first few months. He comes with a bevy of friends, all characters. Did I write to you about them? You wouldn't believe all the things I've learned about since I've been here. I'm quite scandalized and may never see the world the same way again."

"Splendid," I said, without conviction. "I look forward to hearing all about it." I really hoped she hadn't learned about the contours of James's lips. *They're nice and full*, I thought, begrudgingly. God, if they'd kissed already I really might not make it through the rest of my time here. I'd jump into the Seine and end it all, dying for love or lack thereof. I chased away those thoughts and took another look at dapper James.

That thick hair of his was remarkable in color and texture—light brown with coppery tones. The kind of hair women liked. Or, I guessed they did. I didn't know about any women but Fiona. I knew Fiona almost as well as I knew myself. Given everything, she was the only woman I would ever know. I'd have to stand aside and watch her fall in love and marry, probably a man like James if not him exactly.

She'd not needed me to come. I knew it the moment I walked off the train. But I was here now. I had to get my jealousy under control. *Remember how you love her*, I said to myself. *By letting her go, you give her what she needs.*

"Li, what do you feel like eating? There's every kind of food you can imagine here," Fiona said. "All of it delicious. Except for the chewy snails and the raw meat. Those two things I cannot stomach. James loves them, though. Don't you, darling James?"

Darling James. How about *dead James*.

My fists clenched. With force, I separated my fingers and folded my hands in my lap, as if I hadn't been entertaining murderous thoughts.

We walked to the underground subway entrance. "It'll take us all the way to our district," Fiona said. "So quickly. You won't believe it. You'll hardly blink and there you are. It's perfectly perfect."

"Outstanding." My face could have been carved from stone just then, as it was impossible to smile. Or perhaps it was ceramic, which would crack if I lifted the corners of my mouth?

We traveled down a considerable number of stairs until we arrived at our underground stop.

"This is the Métro," Fiona said. "It runs all over Paris. Some tracks are underground and some above."

How had they made this train that ran underground?

As if he heard my silent question, James began to describe the building of the Métro and its introduction at the World's Fair. Despite hating him, I enjoyed hearing about the construction of this public transit system that ran under all of Paris. A metaphor, I thought, for all that which we think but don't share. All the secrets we keep under the surface of things.

We waited with dozens of others. When the subway train arrived, the crowd moved slowly, almost as one into the passenger car. There were only two seats left by the time we were safely inside. James insisted on holding on to my suitcase and standing while Fiona and I took the last seats. He wrapped a hand around the metal pole as the car lurched forward. I pushed my heels into the floor to keep from sliding off the chair.

With his wide shoulders and long legs, he was built like a farm boy, this James West, but his accent was identical to Lord Barnes's. Was this what book editors looked like? Had Fiona fallen for him because he was like her father? Was he a good man as Lord Barnes was? If I couldn't have her myself I would make sure whoever it was would be a good man. I owed Lord Barnes that much, not to mention my concern for Fiona.

"Do I seem different to you?" Fiona asked, shifting to get a better look at me. "Older? A woman of the world?"

I smiled, absorbing every inch of her small face that fit perfectly between my hands. Or so I imagined, anyway. How I wished I could cup both sides of her face and kiss her. "You seem like the same Fiona to me."

She stuck out her bottom lip, pretending to pout. "Here I thought you'd hardly know me. I'm a *sophistiquée* now, aren't I, James?"

"Yes, absolutely." James grinned down at us. "She's been very excited to show you Paris."

Who was he to tell me anything about Fiona? I knew her as well as I knew myself. Who did he think he was? Out loud, I said, "I've been looking forward to seeing Paris as well." I turned to look into her deep blue eyes for a moment, falling in for an indulgent second as if she were my favorite swimming spot on the river. If I were a better musician, I would write a song that reflected the exact color of those eyes. However, I was not good enough to create something as magnificent as Fiona Barnes's eyes.

"Our friends are all coming over tonight in your honor," Fiona said.

Our friends? As in, hers and James's?

"I've promised we'll play music for them at some point, but it doesn't have to be tonight," Fiona continued. "They like jazz and blues, nothing too stuffy. They'll talk and talk and drink and drink, even the women. Everyone will be drunk by the end of the night. You might be shocked."

I chuckled. She was still Fiona. "Thank you for preparing me."

"No one cares one bit about things like race or religion," Fiona said. "Not here in Paris."

"Not our nearly corrupt friends anyway," James said.

James. Apparently he was able to participate in the conversation whenever he chose.

Yes, I hated him. Intensely.

"They're *not* corrupt," Fiona said. "Unconventional. Colorful. One of them lives with a man she's not married to." She leaned closer to whisper in my ear. "Also, sorry about the subway smell."

"It *is* a bit pungent." The subway car, packed with humanity, smelled of body odor, dirty hair, and urine. I leaned close to take in her flowered honey scent. "You smell fine though," I whispered back to her.

Her breath caught as her eyes found mine. "Thank you."

After a second, Fiona went on in the same excited tone of voice. "The woman wears only trousers and curses like a man. Somehow, I don't mind, even though she makes me blush. Her name's Saffron and her man is Reynaldo."

Part delight and part shock ran through me. She'd not been exaggerating about the colorful nature of her new friends. Was she right about Paris? Were people allowed to be whatever they were? Would I be welcome here?

Fiona chirped away, her voice soothing me as nothing could. "And there's Sandwich, of course, and the Coopers. Sebastian's a novelist. James is his editor. They worked together on a book that's now being published in New York. Sebastian knows Hemingway. They used to meet in this one café and they'd all drink too much—all these artistic people—and talk about books and philosophy and writing. The Hemingways are no longer here in Paris or maybe we could meet them. Wouldn't Mama and Papa be over the moon? Although, from what Sebastian said, Mr. Hemingway's left his wife Hadley and taken up with a woman named Pauline. People get divorced and remarry all the time here." She giggled. "Have I confused you babbling on this way?"

"A little," I said, truthfully.

"Everything will become clear when you meet them," Fiona said, sounding happy.

Where had all these new friends been when Fiona's virtue had been threatened by this Basset fellow?

"How did you become an editor so young?" I asked James, hoping he'd tell me how old he was.

"He's clever," Fiona said.

"I'm nothing special, believe me," James said. "I met Sebastian through my friends I grew up with in England. Sebastian needed eyes on his manuscript, and I offered to help."

"You're not an editor who works for a publishing company?" My mood brightened considerably to learn this fact about our friend James West.

"No, not yet, anyway." James frowned. "I'm hoping to secure a position after Sebastian's book comes out and he tells everyone how instrumental I was in helping him with the story."

James didn't actually have a job? No wonder he was penniless. Calling oneself an editor for reading early versions of a novel didn't make one so. Surely Fiona could see that? Or was she too dazzled by his smile?

"This is our stop," James said, pointing toward the doors of our subway car.

I helped Fiona stand and the two of us followed after James, who still carried my suitcase in his large hand.

We traipsed up the stairs and into the light of day, emerging like moles. Cars and trucks blared horns and swiped in and out of traffic, reminding me of toy cars in the hands of Flynn Barnes when we were young. I caught a whiff of smoked meat and then another of cinnamon sweet rolls before the exhaust from a car erased both.

The temperatures were hot and the air muggy. Sweat pooled at the base of my spine. I longed to take off my jacket. However, as I inspected the swarm of people on the sidewalks, I decided to keep it on. Parisians seemed to be dressed in their finest clothes, as if they were going to church.

"That way is Notre Dame, which we can visit anytime you wish," Fiona was saying. "You can't see the Seine from here, but we can walk down to see it later. All these boats sail down the river every night and people wave to those of us on the shore."

We made our way around a clump of schoolchildren dressed in red-and-blue uniforms and turned down a small street made of cobblestone. "My apartment's here—third window from the top. And that's my balcony with my friends waiting for us. They were supposed to come later but it seems they've invited themselves in already. Do you see?"

My gaze traveled up the side of the white building decorated with ornate designs and sculptures carved into the stone. Two young women sat on a small terrace. When they saw us, they stood and leaned over the railing. Good God, I hope it was built sturdily. One of the women had platinum-blond hair, obviously fake. She wore it in a bob that curled around her face. I could see her red lipstick from here, stark against her alabaster skin. Pretty, if one didn't mind the face paint and fake hair. The other one must be Saffron. She wore a man's suit and held a cigarette in one hand. Her hair hung just below her ears and was pushed back from her forehead with a bright orange scarf.

"Hello down there." The blond leaned even further over the railing.

"That's Sandwich," Fiona said to me as she waved and called up to them. "We have Li. We'll be up in a second."

"Hello, Li," Sandwich called down.

James was already at the door, holding it for us to pass through. He smelled a bit like the spicy mulled wine Lizzie made at Christmas. The lobby contained a small desk with a petite woman behind it, writing in a ledger. She looked up as we entered and brushed dark curls away from her face. She wore an indistinct dress in the off-white color of the side of the building. "Miss Barnes, is this your visitor?"

"Yes, Miss Lupine. Li Wu, meet our building manager."

A flicker of surprise had come to her eyes at the sight of me. She'd not expected me to look this way. Would she cause trouble? Throw me out of the building?

In a thick French accent, she said, "Mr. Wu, it's a pleasure to meet you. Welcome to Paris."

"Thank you, Miss Lupine."

Her eyes widened. She hadn't expected me to sound like an American.

Fiona had noticed it too. She said, rather sharply, "Mr. Wu is a dear family friend. He grew up with me in Colorado."

"I see." Miss Lupine nodded, clearly done with us for now. She would probably have quite the story to tell her friends tonight. *You won't believe who my tenant brought home.*

James led us up skinny stairs, up one flight and then another, and finally another. "How did you get all your bags up here?" I mumbled under my breath.

"Papa hired someone to do it," Fiona said. Her keen hearing never missed anything. "They were here for quite some time and helped me get settled."

We entered a short hallway and James, once again in the lead, opened the door for us. Did he have a key? He seemed very familiar with the building.

The women from the terrace came into the sitting room, bringing the smell of cigarette smoke. In addition, there was a small dark man sitting on the sofa dressed in a summer suit the color of cream and a bright purple tie. He'd been reading but set the book aside to stand and greet us. A mustache covered most of his top lip, and his black hair was subdued into submission with a thick coating of pomade.

I learned quickly that Reynaldo was the man who lived with Saffron out of wedlock. They rented a room to Sandwich, who had an accent very much like the people I'd met in Chicago. She might look the part of a showgirl, but the American Midwest was stamped on her forehead nonetheless.

"The Coopers will be here later," Fiona said. "When we go downstairs for dinner."

What would they all think of me? Would they see me as an interloper who would keep them from Fiona?

Someone, I'm not sure who, put on a phonograph record. How often were they all here? How did she think with all the noise? I looked longingly at the piano, black and gleaming in the light from the windows.

The next hour flew by. Fiona had James open more wine, and Gabriella brought out a tray with cheese and bread. They all devoured both, making me wonder further about these people. Were they all so poor that they must eat up all of Fiona's cheese?

I shook my head no when James offered me a glass of the dark burgundy wine. Hungry, I took a slab of cheese and a piece of the soft baguette. Nothing had ever tasted as good. I would not tell Lizzie and Grandmother of my immediate betrayal.

The rest of the guests sprawled on the sofa and chairs, as if they lived here. Saffron sat like an uncouth man, legs making the shape of a triangle with the edge of the coffee table. Reynaldo was the opposite of his tall wife, soft-spoken and possessing impeccable manners. When he did speak, Spanish words interspersed with English in a rapid, almost musical pattern. Sandwich, so thin I could practically see through her, perched on an arm of a wide chair and crossed her ankles. She sat upright with her neck elongated and her torso angled toward us while her legs pointed the other way, as if she were posing for a painter or photographer. James West sat in the largest chair, his long legs crossed. The light spilling over him from the windows made him seem almost larger than life. His coppery hair fell into his eyes occasionally, and he flicked it back in a way that made me think it was habitual, this perfectly behaved unruly hair of his. When he smiled, his face went from merely handsome to mesmerizing.

And Fiona? She drifted around the room from person to person, refreshing drinks and offering more cheese and bread. She shone like a star in this new world of hers. The most beautiful of all the women in the room and probably the rest of Paris, too, with her slight figure and rose-petal skin and dark curls cascading around her delicate features. I'd taken her beauty for granted, I thought. Back home, she'd been my Fiona, my best friend and musical partner. The sweetheart of the Barnes clan, with her pure heart and kind ways. Here, she sparkled with life, transcending from the little girl I'd grown up with to this beguiling woman.

More cigarettes were lit. Everyone but Fiona and I partook. The puffing and gesticulating with the cigarettes seemed almost in time with the music. Smoke drifted toward the ceiling and hung there like a fine mist over the river at home. Outside, the sun lowered until it was caught behind the buildings that lined the street. Across from us, the amber light shone through the windows of the apartments like the square eyes of a magical creature. The colors that streaked across the horizon were unlike any I'd seen in the sky before, a dusty rose and not-quite-ripe tangerine.

Fiona's new world. I couldn't help but feel I was indeed an interloper. I'd found her in the middle of a play, and I was an unwanted actor playing a part unsuited for my meager talents.

At dinner downstairs at the café, I was seated next to James. Noisy with laughter, chatter, and the clinking of silverware, I strained to hear the conversation. The chairs were made of wrought iron and pinched my back. Cigarette smoke disappeared into the night.

The Coopers had joined us for dinner. Paula was an athletic, ruddy-cheeked woman with a quality of robustness and pragmatism that reminded me of Cymbeline. However, she lacked the restlessness and physical beauty of our Cym. She seemed satisfied to be her husband's partner without much of the attention on herself. I couldn't imagine her craving attention or adventure. Alternately, Sebastian Cooper seemed hungry for the attention his wife had no need for. He dominated the discussion at dinner, which had veered toward literature. As far as I could tell, Sebastian Cooper was equally insecure and arrogant, a quality many artists possessed. We were self-confident and humble. Without both, we would not produce.

Sebastian had an opinion on many things, including books. My eyes glazed over and I only vaguely listened as he prattled on endlessly about the difference between Hemingway's and Fitzgerald's styles. He, apparently, was more of the Hemingway variety. "The barest minimum of words," Sebastian said as he picked up his wineglass. "I must find the *précis* word, you see. And string it together with the next right word and so on until I have a story. All of which makes my work elegant in its simplicity."

I could understand the concept. Some of the simplest musical arrangements were the most beautiful. I didn't comment on this or anything else said at the table. I'd never been one to participate in chatter. Was it because I was different when I was little, speaking a foreign language only to my grandmother and sister? I don't know. After I learned English and to speak as the Barnes children did, I continued to be more of an observer, commenting only in my mind. It wasn't until later when I heard Fiona practicing her piano upstairs and I went up to investigate did I find my own way to communicate. Music became my language. The vehicle to express the endless swells in my own heart.

But now it was James West who required my attention. The conversations had broken off into groups. With the two of us being on one end of the table, it was mandated that we were to talk to each other. I glanced quickly at Fiona. She was absorbed in whatever it was Saffron was saying. With the ambient noise, I could only see Saffron's lips moving and couldn't make out what she said.

"It's divine to finally meet you," James said, leaning closer so that I had an even better view of his perfect teeth. "Fiona's been excited for your arrival. Good of you to come, mate."

I bristled. Who was this man to act as if he were Fiona's confidant and best friend? That was my position. It *was* good I'd come. Fiona would have slipped away from me forever had I not.

Wait, I chastised myself. *You're the one who sent her away, the one who told her you didn't love her and didn't want her. You pushed her into the very scene before you.*

"What will you do with your time here?" James asked.

"Fiona's encouraged me to take lessons while I'm here," I

said. "Mostly, I'll look after her." *Meaning, you are no longer needed.*

"Yes, she mentioned that to me." He tapped the table with all four of his masculine fingers. "Which reminds me, I have something for you." He reached into the pocket inside his jacket and pulled out a card. "This is a friend of my father's who teaches violin. Fiona asked if I could get you an audition with him. His address is here on the card. He said to come by sometime this week and he'll listen to you play."

I glanced at the name on the card and blinked several times to make sure I'd seen it correctly. "I've heard of him." In musical circles, he was well-known for his master classes. "Thank you."

"It's my pleasure. Fiona's done so much for me."

"Is that right?"

He flushed and looked down at his plate, which now contained only the empty shells of oysters. Prehistoric with scales like an alligator, I'd thought when they brought them out to the table. How could something so ugly have contained such sweet nectar of the sea? "I suppose she mentioned about the loan?"

She had not mentioned any loan, but I nodded as if she had. Loan? She'd told me she was only buying him dinners.

"She was so good to offer it to me, knowing how tight things have been. I'll pay her back once I'm with a publisher. Things will change for me soon."

"Of course."

"I know what you must think." He glanced quickly at me before picking up his glass of the cold, dry white wine the waiter had brought with the oysters.

"I doubt that," I said softly.

His eyes narrowed for a moment. He peered at me, seeking clues to my obtuse comment. If he only knew the complicated web of my thoughts, he would probably run from the table and never return. Perhaps I *should* tell him?

"My father has only homes he cannot afford to keep running," James said. "For generations, we've been useless, without skills of any kind. I'm rectifying that. At least for myself. The editing position is a coveted one, I can assure you. Not a lucrative one at the moment, but once Sebastian's book is out, my circumstances will drastically change. Then I'll pay Fiona back everything I owe her and more."

"I have every confidence you will," I said. I had no confidence.

Fiona's bubbly laugh rose above the noise of the café. She was listening with great attention to whatever it was the old windbag Sebastian was saying.

"Is his book that good?" I asked.

"It is." James smirked and barked out a quick laugh. "I was surprised, too. He doesn't make a great first impression, but there's a talented man under all that bluster."

"What are your intentions with Fiona?" I asked, matching his low volume. "I'm asking on behalf of her family."

"We're good friends." His eyes lifted again briefly to take me in. I felt exposed and vulnerable under his gaze, as if he saw right through me. "What are your intentions?"

"She's my best friend," I said. "She'll never leave Emerson Pass permanently. Not even for Paris."

"We'll see. She just might surprise you." He lifted his glass and peered at me over the rim. "Will you surprise me as well?"

I didn't want surprises. In fact, I hated surprises. "I'm not understanding your question," I said.

"You're here, Mr. Wu," James said. "I believe that speaks volumes about your intentions, whether you're ready to admit to them or not."

14

FIONA

It was nearing midnight by the time we arrived back at the apartment. As I let us in, I put my finger to my mouth. "Gabriella will be asleep," I whispered.

Li nodded. The circles under his eyes had darkened and the whites of his eyes reddened. He stood aside to allow me to go into the room first, then followed behind. I unpinned my hat and hung it on the rack.

"You're exhausted," I said. "We should retire."

"I'm sorry to have to agree," Li said. "It's been a long couple of weeks."

"All right, then, good night." I turned to go but looked back to tell him, "You may use the bathroom first. I'll wait until I hear your bedroom door close before I go in."

He still had his hat in his hands and he lingered by the door. "Are you sorry you invited me?"

"Why would you say such a thing?" I asked.

"Your friends seem to have kept you company, occupied your time and your money." I studied the floorboards. One of the planks had a pattern from a knot in the shape of a half note.

"Gabriella is here to keep you safe at night. What do you need me for?"

"I don't think she's capable of keeping me safe, no matter how good her housekeeping skills are." His tone and words sliced away my joyful mood in one fell swoop. I pressed my fingers into my throat, hoping to dislodge the ache there. Why had he come? He was right. I didn't need him criticizing me or questioning my decisions. But then I remembered Mr. Basset. He would be here tomorrow morning. My friends, as fun as they were, could not be here night and day. Nor could they fully comprehend my fear. They saw it as another demonstration of my provincial upbringing. I could hear Sandwich now, asking me, *Why not take him up on his offer? Let him introduce you to all the right people.*

"How money much did you give James?" Li asked.

I tugged on the fingers of my gloves and yanked them from my hands. "He told you I lent him money?"

"Yes. I think he was embarrassed. He seemed to be under the impression I knew, as if you'd tell me something like that."

I would have. I told him everything. Back home I had, anyway. "Mr. West is a gentleman with a title but no money. He has terrible debt. The creditors were coming for him, expecting payments. He's doing important work, bringing great books to the hands of readers. His financial problems were distracting him from all that. I helped him. It wasn't much to me but everything to him."

"Where did you get the money?"

I didn't appreciate the scowl that seemed to have made permanent residence on his face. "I have my own money. Papa set me up with an account before he left. But I'm frugal. I have few needs. The money won't be missed, even if Mr. West cannot pay me back." I ran one of my gloves through the space made between my thumb and index finger. "He was in danger. I would have done the same for you. For any friend."

"Is that true?"

"Of course it is. What're you saying?"

"Mr. West is a handsome man. I wonder if you might be swayed by that fact?"

So what if I was? It wasn't that, obviously. He'd been good to me. We'd become close friends. But we both knew there was not an attraction. That had been even more evident tonight as I'd stolen glances at Li and James talking together at the end of the table. No one was Li. It wasn't only familiarity as I'd hoped. Seeing him in a different setting had made no difference whatsoever. I longed for him. It might never change, I thought, despairing. The longer he remained close, the more steadfast my affection. Soon, I would return home and there he would be. Was pining away for someone terminal? Would I die a premature death from this unquenched desire?

"Mr. West is a handsome man," I said. "But he's only a friend."

"He has everything you want and need."

I stepped back, smacking into the wall behind me. "You have no idea what you're talking about."

"He's English and fancy with a pedigree and all that. He's the right age for you. He's everything your father could wish for you."

"Have you forgotten his debt already?" I asked, scorn dripping from my mouth. "Or that you were just chastising me for giving him a loan?"

"Lord Barnes has never cared about bringing wealth into the family when it comes to his daughters. Even that will be of no consequence." His cheeks had splotches of red and his eyes snapped with fury.

"Why are you angry? What is it about all of this that makes you speak cruelly to me? After all, you don't want me yourself. Why shouldn't I fall in love with James West?"

He stepped closer. I could smell soap on his skin and the

faint hint of wine on his breath. Stubble peppered his chin. He needed a shave. I'd never seen him without a clean-shaven face. Unfortunately, it suited him. "Because I...because I...don't want you to," he said.

I let out a breath, furious myself now. "You don't get to say anything about my life. I have brothers and a father. I don't need you acting like my older brother. If I didn't know better, I'd think you were jealous of my new friends."

"I couldn't care less about your new friends." His jaw clenched. He stepped backward until he was leaning up against the opposite wall.

"Well, fine then. We've settled it. You shall say nothing about James West or whether or not I allow him to court me."

"There's no courting here, is there? Your friend Saffron and Reynaldo, for example?"

I crossed my arms over my chest. "What about them?"

"They're not a couple. They like people of their own gender."

"I'm very aware of that." Why did everyone think I was stupid? I remembered the way Sandwich and Saffron had looked at each other that day on the terrace—the knowing look between them. Little innocent Fiona who didn't understand anything about the modern world. "How did you know?" I had to ask. How *was* it that he'd known right away?

"It's obvious," Li said. "And then there's that Sandwich woman. She's appropriately nicknamed, since she gives herself away as if she's an ordinary sandwich."

"She's not like that at all," I said, hotter than ever now. "She hasn't been given everything as I have. She's had to make some compromises so that she didn't have to marry her bucktoothed neighbor. You'd know that if you asked any questions instead of assuming things. For someone who claims to feel different from others, you're mighty judgmental."

"I'm merely pointing out the facts." His reasonable tone made me even more furious.

"Sebastian and Paula are married. That should make your provincial mind happy."

"Sebastian has an eye for the ladies. I saw his wandering nature several times at dinner. Trust me, they'll be divorced before you know it."

"Divorced?" I gasped and covered my mouth with my hands. "Impossible. You don't know anything about my friends." Even as I said it, I knew he was right about everything. I wouldn't admit it, though, and give him the satisfaction. "What does any of it matter? None of this changes how much I like them or their worth as human beings. You of all people should understand that."

He glared at me for a moment before deflating like a cake taken too soon from the oven into a cold room. "Fiona." His voice was hoarse and dry. He rubbed his forehead with the fingers of both hands.

"What? What is it? Do you have more to criticize?" My eyes misted. "I thought you'd like them all as much as I. You'd see that here in Paris it doesn't matter if you're different."

"I do see that. I see it clearly. You were right. Things here are different."

"Then why are we arguing? Why are you so angry at me?"

"I'm not angry. I'm…" Again, he trailed off. What was it he wanted to say?

"You're what?" I asked softly, hoping to coax whatever it was out of him.

"I'm tired, that's all. It was a trying journey."

Guilt took away any anger I had left. "You're right. I'm sorry to have kept you out so late."

"It's fine. Good night, Fiona."

"Good night." I nodded. "I'll see you in the morning."

I headed into my room. The small bed had been made up by Gabriella. I could tell by the precise corners of the blankets and sheets. I could never get them as tight. She always changed the sheets on Fridays, whether they needed it or not.

After undressing and donning a light cotton nightgown, I sat on the bed to wait my turn in the bathroom. The sounds of Li washing traveled through the walls. This was too intimate, the two of us here together in such close proximity. Thankfully, Gabriella was on the other side of me. There would be no chance of impropriety. Not that there would be regardless. Li didn't want me.

I wished Cym were here to help me interpret Li's actions. His behavior tonight had flummoxed me. He was always quiet, even at home where he was comfortable. Since his arrival here, he'd seemed out of sorts. Tomorrow, I would give him the opportunity to go home. If he wanted to stay only a week or two and then go, that was fine too. It was better for me here without him. At least I knew it now.

———

THE NEXT MORNING I WENT OUT TO THE SITTING ROOM TO FIND Li there, already dressed and standing by the windows. He slowly turned upon hearing my footsteps. I'd slept appallingly late. It was almost nine.

"Good morning," I said. "I'm afraid I've become French these last few months. Staying out all night and sleeping all day."

"We had a late night," Li said. "Although I've been out already this morning. I took a walk along the river and then stopped at a bakery to pick out a few pastries for our breakfast. Gabriella said she was off to the shops and would return before lunch."

A pot of coffee, two cups, and several pastries waited for us on the coffee table. I went over to pour myself a cup. Despite knowing Li almost all my life, I was suddenly nervous around him. Perhaps that's why I'd felt the need to invite the whole gang over last night.

"Did you sleep well?" I settled in a chair and took a sip of the heavenly coffee. "I don't know why but coffee tastes better in Paris."

"I slept tolerably."

Without being obvious, I inspected him. The smudges under his eyes remained. However, he was shaven and his hair had obviously been washed, as it was damp with the ridges from his comb still evident. All in all, he looked much better than he had the day before.

He joined me, sitting across from me on the sofa. "The apartment is fancier than I thought it would be. I imagined you over here in a hovel, all dark and damp."

"No, Papa made sure he found just the right apartment." With new eyes, I looked around, seeing the intricate carvings in the mantel and in the doorway arches. I'd already grown accustomed to the brightly colored furniture and fussy decorations.

"Mr. Basset comes this morning, isn't that right?" Li asked.

"You remembered?" I asked, pleased. "Yes, he comes at ten two days a week. Usually, I like Gabriella to be here with me, but now you're here so it won't matter." Now, in the light of day, I was vacillating on whether he should stay. He seemed better this morning, less angry. Had he been tired and tipsy last night when he'd lashed out at me?

We talked about my lessons for a few minutes. Unlike my new friends, he understood exactly what I was talking about when I described the work we were doing. "The first few weeks I did nothing but breathe. I never thought breathing could be so hard."

Li scowled. "I remember the voice students at school talking endlessly about breaths."

"Mr. Basset had to train me out of my bad habits. Or that's what he calls them. I had no idea I was doing anything wrong." I set aside my coffee and reached for a plate, then plucked a pastry shaped like a snail and sprinkled with cinnamon and sugar from the basket. "Truth be told, I'm not so keen on all this."

"What? I thought you were getting a lot out of these lessons."

He could have finished the sentence with, *Why else did I come halfway across the world to look after you?*

"I am. It's just that I don't care as much as I should. I can't tell anyone but you. No one else would understand. But I don't want to sing in the opera. All these high, shrill notes—well, I'd rather sing our hillbilly tunes or the blues at the club. As far as jazz goes, there's nothing he can teach me. He knows nothing about it. Too much of a simpleton."

He was staring at me, making me feel like a spoiled brat.

"I should be grateful, I know." I placed my weary head into one hand and pitched my head sideways, peering at him.

"You should be," Li said. "However, I understand perfectly."

"I'm still learning a lot, which I'll use when we get home." I smiled, thinking of playing again at church. "Won't they all be surprised to hear me sing a Mozart piece?"

"They will."

A knock on the door startled me. I'd been so far away in the world of Li and Fiona. "That'll be him," I said, lowering my voice. "He'll seem perfectly charming to you. He always is around men. But he gets nasty the moment we're alone."

Guilt made my chest hurt as I walked across the sitting room to answer the door. Usually, I did my warm-up exercises before Basset arrived, but instead, I'd eaten a buttery pastry. He'd chastise me for it, I could count on it. Dairy was forbidden for serious vocal students.

I yanked open the door to find him standing there, tapping his foot. I'd taken too long to answer. He liked everything at a fast tempo.

I greeted him politely and moved back so he could pass by me. He made sure to brush my bottom under my skirt as he did so. However, when he saw Li standing there, he twitched in surprise. *Good*, I thought. Have him off-kilter for once instead of just me.

"Mr. Basset, may I present to you Mr. Li Wu. He's my best friend and musical partner from home. I've told you about him."

"You didn't tell me he was a Chinaman."

I whipped my head around, hearing the sound of imaginary marbles clanging together between my ears. "Li is a member of the Barnes family, Mr. Basset. While in his presence, I expect you to treat him as such."

Mr. Basset didn't reply as he walked over to the piano. "Shall we get started? I'm on a schedule."

I exchanged a quick glance with Li, in which I hoped I conveyed my apologies for Mr. Basset. He nodded and went back to sit on the couch, preparing to listen. There was a quality to Li that seemed more obvious here in bustling Paris. A stillness that drew me to him. Like a morning after a snowfall or the first freeze when everything is beautiful and precious and there are no sounds but the beating of our hearts. I'd missed his presence more than I could explain, even to myself.

We ran through my scales, which I'd dutifully practiced all week. I expected praise but didn't get it. All he said was, "More practice. You're still too breathy on the low notes. Remember what I said about the nose."

Next, Basset had me sing the piece I was working on for the recital next month. According to him, I was not ready for public performance, but he'd reluctantly agreed that I could participate. From what I could discern from his short explanation, twice a year his students performed at a club. He invited influential men who directed operas and musicals and owned music halls. I'd chosen "What'll I Do," one of Irving Berlins's hits. I loved the lyrics, especially after learning Berlin wrote it for the girl he loved. Her father hadn't approved of Berlin and sent her away to Europe. He wrote it while pining for her, much the same as I'd done for Li over the last few months. I didn't have any trouble connecting to the emotion of the words and music.

I sang through the first verse before Basset interrupted me, giving me notes on my breathing. He had given me so much instruction I couldn't keep it all in mind. I apologized and waited for him to begin playing. The second time he let me run all the way through. As sometimes happened, I got lost in the music, the emotion swelling up in me and coming out of my mouth. He was right about breath. The more I did what he asked, the better I became. I hated to admit it, but it was true. That didn't make his lechery any less disgusting.

When I was done, Basset's lips twitched, as if he were pleased. I stole a glance at Li. He gave me one of his special smiles. I'd pleased him, at least.

"Better, Miss Barnes." He leaned close to my ear. "You didn't have to invite a babysitter, you know. I've quite behaved myself, haven't I?"

I ignored him, asking instead what he wanted me to do next. He got up from the piano bench and drew out a sheet of music. "Here's something new I want you to try."

For the next thirty minutes, we went through the new music. It was a lively tune and challenging for my mouth and tongue. Finally, we were done. I felt exhausted and ready for lunch.

When Basset was gone, I collapsed onto the sofa. Crossing my ankles and clasping my hands together, I waited for Li to say something.

"Your voice has grown," Li said. "We have to admit that."

"Yes. Do you see why I needed you to come? I didn't want to give up everything, but I didn't know how long I could keep pushing off his advances. Of course, he was a peach today."

"Other than the racial slur," Li said.

"I'm sorry about that."

"You didn't say it."

"I know, but I'm still sorry it happened."

He unbuttoned his jacket and adjusted his tie. "It's a good song for you. I want to hear what you sound like with a whole band behind you."

"We could go out to one of the clubs tonight. I heard about an underground jazz club not far from here."

Li brightened. "I'd like that."

"We could go to dinner first. Just you and me. Last night was too much. I see that now."

"Fiona, I don't know about eating out just the two of us. I don't want trouble."

"We won't have any. We'll eat downstairs. They know me there."

He continued to look skeptical but acquiesced. "What do you do in the afternoons?"

"Walk a little. Then come back and work on my vocal exercises. I hate them, you know, but I promised Papa."

We were interrupted by Gabriella asking if we'd like lunch.

"We'd love some," I said. "And then I'm taking Li out for a walk along the river."

"Lovely, Miss Barnes." Gabriella did her customary half curtsy and scuttled back into the kitchen. Shortly after the door closed, I heard a crash and then a flurry of French.

"She's a little clumsy," I said. "I think she's broken five glasses, two plates, and a vase thus far."

Li laughed. "Poor thing."

"But she's so sweet, I can't let her go." I spoke just above a whisper.

"My Fiona." Li smiled as he looked across at me. "Always kind, even to those who don't deserve mercy."

My Fiona? How I wished that were true.

LI

THAT AFTERNOON, FIONA AND I WALKED ALONG THE SEINE. Varied scents drifted toward us along the bank of the river: buttery popcorn, cinnamon, freshly baking bread, grass, urine, stale beer, river water, women's perfume. The weather had cooled, and angry purple clouds threatened a rainstorm. As we strolled, arm in arm, we talked as we always had. She told me more about her exploits over the last few months. I shared my own stories from home, including how her brothers had taken care of the men who attacked me.

"What about the ship?" Fiona asked.

"It was fine." I didn't want to tell her what I'd dealt with. Someday, perhaps, but not this one.

"You don't need to protect me, you know," she said.

"I know."

We walked in silence for a few minutes until we came upon a crowd of people circled around an arena, shouting and cheering. For a moment, I couldn't fathom what I saw. Two boys were in a ring, boxing. Shirtless, wearing fat gloves and dancing around each other in what appeared to be socks on their bare feet. One of the boys had long, floppy hair and the other with hair so short one could see the imperfect shape of his head. A referee was in the ring with them, dancing his own dance as the boys took shots at each other.

Fiona stopped us, just outside of the crowd. Mostly men, wearing bowler hats and suits, sat in chairs all around the ring as if they watched a concert. "What are they doing?" She squeezed my forearm with her hand.

"Fighting," I said, as if she didn't know that in some places men fought each other and people watched. There were gambling bets made on these fights in the States. I'd never gone to one, but I'd heard about them in Chicago.

"They're only children." Fiona's voice trembled with outrage. "Little boys."

"Let's go back." I tried to steer her away but as small as she was, she'd become immovable. This was not good. A Barnes could never walk away from anything they saw as an injustice. "Fiona, come on."

"No, this isn't right. We must do something."

Part of me wanted to laugh; the other wanted to haul her over my shoulder and run. "There's nothing to be done. This must be something they do here."

"Watch children pummel each other? It's barbaric."

The crowd cheered as the bushy-haired boy punched the other one hard enough that he fell to the ground. He wasn't down for long, bouncing up as if the ring were made of rubber.

They danced around for a few more seconds before the long-haired boy hit the other again. The boy with the cropped hair fell. His nose gushed red. The audience shouted, a seething mad crowd enjoying the scent of sweat and blood.

Fiona broke away from me. Before I knew what she was doing, she'd charged through the gathering of men and flung herself against the ropes, shouting for them to stop. For a second, I froze in shock but soon snapped to attention and ran after her. God only knew what could happen to her in a mob of angry men.

The short-haired boy got back on his feet, stumbling as if drunk, a beard of blood covering most of his face. Still, he managed a swipe in the other's direction.

Fiona leaned over the ropes and pulled on the jacket of the referee. "Stop this at once."

The referee swatted her away as if she were nothing more than a fly. The weaker boy went down once more.

Fiona went right back at the referee, this time tugging with both hands on the back of his jacket with enough force that he stumbled backward. He turned away from his duties to look at Fiona. His complexion turned an ugly purple. He pushed her away, shouting something in French, then turned back to watch the boys. The fight appeared to be over as the weaker one remained on the ground.

Thank God, I thought. *It's over and we can go.*

But no. Fiona wasn't done. She started to climb into the ring. I pulled her back by the waist, lifting her off her feet. She struggled to get loose and knocked me off-balance for long enough that she wriggled away and started to climb under the rope and into the ring.

The crowd broke into frenzied jeers, although most appeared delighted at this unusual turn of events. Some hollered in French what I'm sure were obscenities; others threw popcorn at her. One man tossed an empty bottle of beer. It hit her on the head just as I reached her, knocking her hat sideways. Nothing deterred her. She ran to the fallen boy and knelt next to him. He was still. Too still.

"Look what you've done," Fiona shouted to the referee, who shrugged and looked around as if there might be someone to tell him why this unhinged woman was in his ring.

I jumped into the ring. My plan was to haul her out of there and away from this threatening throng of humanity before the crowd turned on us. I sprinted toward her, the floor of the ring soft under my feet. I fell to my knees next to her. "You're going to get yourself killed." Or both of us.

She didn't hear me, too busy using her handkerchief to wipe blood from the boy's face. The men were louder now. Several more bottles of beer flew into the ring. The boy who'd won simply stood there, obviously dumbfounded.

"Fiona, this isn't your concern," I said. "Please, we have to get out of here."

She looked up at me with eyes as wild as a panther. Her curls had fallen from their comb and hung loose around her forehead. "This boy is hurt. We have to take him to the doctor."

The referee was now shouting rapidly in French and gesturing for Fiona to get away. No language barrier could disguise what he wanted. Several of the men from the crowd seemed to have noticed me by then. I heard the word *Chinese* and looked to see two men standing at the side of the ring. Darkness. Hatred. I saw it all there in their eyes.

"Fiona, look at me," I said. "This isn't safe. You're going to get us both hurt or worse. Do you see how they look at me?"

She blinked and then looked around us. The crowd was close now, pressing against the ropes. "What about the boy?"

"He'll be fine. It's not his first time, I'm sure." I got up and offered her my hand. "Please, we have to go."

She allowed me to pull her to her feet. The boy groaned in pain. Frantic, she looked into the crowd. "Where's his mother? He needs his mother."

"No *maman*," the bushy boy said. "*Orphelin*."

"Orphan," I said to Fiona.

"You too?" Fiona asked the standing boy.

He nodded and shrugged, then said something in French.

They spoke the rapid Parisian French that I had trouble understanding. I might have picked up the word *money* but I wasn't
sure. The boys' ribs were evident. They were doing this for the
money. These men were putting them up against each other for
sport, for their own sick enjoyment.

"Where did you find these boys?" Fiona asked, springing to
her feet and lunging toward the referee.

He shook his head and spoke French back to her. I couldn't
tell if he understood her or not.

She turned to the long-haired boy. "Where do you live?"

He looked at her blankly.

"*Où habitez-vous?*" I asked in my slow French.

"*Les rues,*" he said. *The streets.*

For a moment, but not for long because my nerves were
alert to impending danger, I gazed at her with such admiration
and love in my heart that I nearly wept. Fiona Barnes was something. I braced myself for what was coming next. Fiona would
ask me to help her take the boys out of there and back to her
apartment. They would never let the boys go. Or us. The crowd
seemed menacing.

But that never stopped a Barnes. "Li, lift him, please."

I knelt near the boy. His eyes fluttered open and fixed upon
my face. I helped him to his feet. "Can you walk?"

He looked at me with glassy eyes, clearly without compre-
hension.

"Tell him he's coming home with us," Fiona said, nodding
toward the other boy. "And that he'll dine with us."

"*Rentrez à la maison avec nous. Manger.*" I pantomimed eating.

The bushy boy raised his eyebrows. He took another look at
Fiona and then back at me. "*Vous allez me nourrir?*"

"Yes, we will feed you," I said. "*Souper.*"

He pointed to the boy in my arms. "*Mon frère aussi?*"

Brother. They were brothers? What kind of monsters had

arranged a fight between two children? "*Oui.* Your brother too." This made the sordid business seem all the more so. These little boys were made to fight each other for the entertainment of bloodthirsty men.

"They're brothers?" Fiona asked.

I nodded. They were young, probably no older than eight. Despite the misshapen face of the short-haired boy, I saw for the first time they were twins. "*Êtes-vous jumeaux?*" I asked him. Are you twins?

"*Oui.*"

"They're twins, Fi," I said.

Her eyebrows shot up. "Twins. Oh, Li. Twins?"

"Yes." Like her brothers. It didn't take much imagination to see how her mind organized this into the hand of fate. Divine instruction. We would take them home to her apartment and she'd begin making plans to find them a home. I knew it without her ever having to say the words in English or French.

"*Quels sont vos noms?*" I asked the boys their names.

"*Je m'appelle Bleu.*" The one with long hair pointed to himself. "*Mon frère s'appelle Beaumont.*"

"They're called Bleu and Beaumont," I said to Fiona.

Fiona held out her hand to Beaumont. To my surprise, he took it. Eyes downcast, he mumbled something in French I couldn't understand. She smiled at him with that smile that had wrecked many men back in Emerson Pass, then offered her hand to Bleu. He shook damp locks away from his eyes and looked at her. Apparently, her smile had the same effect in Paris as it did at home, because his bloody mouth turned upward into a partly toothless smile. Swollen from fighting, his grin seemed almost ghoulish.

By this time, the referee had wandered away and now stood with a group of men. Bills changed hands. The results of the betting, I guessed.

Bleu spoke urgently while tugging on the hem of my jacket. "*Et notre argent? Ils vont nous payer?*"

"You're owed money?" I asked. "*L'argent dû?*" My American accent destroyed the pronunciations. Somehow, Bleu seemed to understand. He nodded and pointed to the referee. "*Il doit nous payer.*"

"All right, I'll see what I can do." This wouldn't go well, but I had to try. The boys should get their pay after what they'd gone through. I walked over to the referee and asked for the boys' money in French. He argued with me for a moment, saying I was not their keeper and to leave him alone. I persisted, saying as well as I could that they were owed money for what they'd had to do.

The men surrounding the referee pushed closer. I stood my ground. The referee darted toward me, seizing hold of my collar and deluging me with vulgarities and threats.

"Li, let's just go," Fiona called out to me.

I shook off the referee and turned toward her voice. My gaze didn't reach her before he punched me hard on the side of my face. I stumbled backward but remained on my feet. The referee was not a large man, but paunchy, and I was quick. I didn't want to be violent in front of Fiona but it had to be done. I lobbed my fist into the side of his cheek, followed by a solid kick to his chin. He fell against the rope and onto his rear.

The crowd cheered. Did they think this was part of the show?

Bleu was by my side, speaking fast and pointing toward Fiona. It didn't take much to be convinced. I nodded and said to Fiona, "Let's go. We can take the boys with us."

"Yes, come along," Fiona said as if it were nothing.

My jaw stung, but it was nothing I couldn't handle. He hadn't gotten further punches in, thanks to my quick move-ment. I offered my hand to Bleu, and we followed Fiona and Beaumont to the edge of the ring.

Reminding me of the tale of the Pied Piper, the boys docilely went with Fiona. When we reached the ropes of the ring, Bleu lifted the highest one so that Fiona could step through. He waited for me to do the same. I followed, unsteady but managing to make it through with the boy intact.

The crowd, strangely enough, had quieted. Someone called out to Fiona, "*Bonjour beauté.*"

"*Bonjour,*" Fiona said, thrusting back her shoulders and lifting her chin. "Tell them we're taking these boys home," she said to me.

"I think that's obvious," I said, chuckling despite the seriousness of our situation.

"If you think so." Fiona gestured toward the direction of her apartment. "Lead the way, please."

As if I wasn't following her. As if I had any choice at all but to follow her anywhere she wanted. I was at her mercy, now and always.

By the time we reached the apartment, my limited French had run its course. We knew only what we'd learned first, their names and that they lived on the streets.

We'd walked with them between us. The boys held hands the entire way but didn't speak to us or each other. Fiona held her head high and pursed her lips, inviting no questions from me. I stayed quiet and tried not to panic, between looking behind us to see if anyone followed. So far, we were safe.

I unlocked the door and stood aside to let Fiona and the boys enter first. Gabriella, duster in hand, stopped what she was doing and gaped at the sight before her. Two raggedy boys, smelling of the worst of Paris: urine, grease, and perspiration.

Gabriella spoke in rapid Parisian French. I couldn't understand much, other than she wanted to know where we'd found two urchins and could we smell them? I explained this to Fiona, who nodded, and instructed Gabriella to start a bath for them, all said as if it were not at all peculiar that we went out for a walk and returned with two children from the streets.

Gabriella, frowning with obvious disapproval, left the room muttering to herself.

"They'll need new clothes," Fiona said. "Before anything, they need a meal. Let's give them some bread and cheese."

"Before the bath?" I asked, hoping for some relief from their less-than-lovely scents.

"Yes, they were probably fighting for scraps of food," Fiona said. "Look at their rib cages. They're starving."

I nodded and told the boys if they would sit at the table, we would bring them food. Their faces lit up, losing the dull, hopeless appearance for a few seconds. Followed closely by a narrowing of eyes, suspicious. Only desperation would allow them to come with us without questions. A young, pretty woman had asked them back to her apartment. What had they thought would happen? Were they hungry enough to take a chance that we wouldn't do them harm?

A memory jostled awake in my mind.

The day Lord Barnes had come for us had been bright and frigid with temperatures below freezing. We'd been staying in the old office of the mining company, long since abandoned. It had not been built for longevity or insulation. That day, I stared through a crack between boards to the outside. The snow sparkled under the sun. Such beauty brought hard times, I'd thought. We would not make it through the winter. Not unless I could trap and kill something for us to eat, not just today but every day.

I was nine years old. Too young to perish. Too weak and small to know what to do to save us.

I'd heard the bells around Lord Barnes's horses and thought I was imagining the sound. No one came this direction during the winter months. Two men were in the front of a large sleigh. Fear chilled me further. What would the white men want? Was this their property? Would they drive us away? Where would we go?

They would make us leave. I knew they would. The men probably owned this building and all the land around us. A certainty had come over me. We would not make it another day. This was the end. We would die. As cold as the old office was, it provided shelter.

But I'd been wrong. Lord Barnes had appeared, speaking softly and asking if we would like to go home with him for food and warmth. Grandmother had not understood all that he said but had gotten enough that she'd nodded to us that it was all right.

After that day, everything changed for my family. All because of the kindness of one man.

His daughter had inherited the same compassion for the unfortunate.

"Li?" Fiona asked. "Are you listening?"

I looked over at her, meeting her indulgent gaze. "Yes, I'm listening. I'll stay with them if you'd like to put something together for them to eat."

She nodded and gave us each a smile before she headed toward the kitchen. I asked the boys to sit on the sofa, which they did. They perched on the edge of the cushions. Wary expressions and muscles taut, they looked like ragged dogs who had always been shooed away from sitting on the furniture. Their small fists clenched at their sides. Ready to fight or run, depending on what I did. They didn't trust me. How could they?

I sat on the chair across from them, noticing how their hands were nearly black with soot and grime. They smelled of decay, as if they'd taken on the scent of trash.

The bath was now ready. Would they go willingly? How vulnerable would they feel taking off their clothes in front of strangers? I would do my best to reassure them.

I spoke to them in the best French I could muster, telling them I would not hurt them and that we wanted to give them food and shelter. *"Je ne vous ferai pas de mal. Je suis votre ami. Nous voulons vous nourrir et vous donner un bain. Vous pouvez dormir ici ce soir."*

Neither spoke, but Bleu watched me with eyes that suited his name. Beaumont dipped his chin into his neck as if he were a baby bird hoping to stay disguised from the enemy.

Soon, Gabriella returned, telling me that the bath was ready for the first boy. I told her Fiona wanted to feed them first. She frowned in disapproval but nodded. "Yes, all right. We will feed them at the table."

"Will you speak to them in French about what's happening?" I asked, after explaining that I'd tried already but that they didn't seem to understand. "Please, make sure they know we mean them no harm."

"What do I tell them? The mistress of this home is *malade dans la tête*?" Gabriella smiled at her joke.

"Fiona's not sick in the head," I said, biting the inside of my lip to keep from laughing. "Her heart is soft."

"Or her head," Gabriella said.

Gabriella rattled off a few sentences. The boys' eyes widened as they began to understand what we were offering.

"Where should I go to get them new clothes?" I asked her.

Gabriella's gaze swept the boys' bare torsos. "There's a clothing shop around the corner. They will have clothes their size."

"Ask them how old they are," I said.

She did so. Bleu answered, chirping out a few sentences with such rapidity I couldn't follow. He must have slowed his speech for me earlier, I thought.

"They're almost nine," Gabriella said. She asked them about how they came to live on the streets and what had happened to their parents.

Once they answered, she said to me, "Their mother died last year. Bad men came and took all of their belongings and ran them off from the apartment where they were living. They've been living on the streets ever since."

"Ask them about the fight."

"What fight?" Gabriella asked me.

I explained how we'd first seen them and what Fiona had taken it upon herself to do.

"They had them fighting each other?" Gabriella asked. "Mademoiselle couldn't bear it, could she?"

"No, she couldn't," I said.

Gabriella huffed, expanding her narrow chest. "Mademoiselle Fiona will find us trouble."

I didn't answer. She was right. For now, however, we were all safe, and these two little boys needed help.

Gabriella asked them a few more questions, and Bleu answered. "They earn a little from each fight, no matter who wins, and then they buy food," Gabriella said to me.

Fiona beckoned us all to the table in the kitchen. She'd cut up cheese and bread as well as slices of apple. Beaumont made a sound similar to a growl and took his brother's hand. Bleu gave him an assuring nod before they sat next to each other at the table.

Fiona and Gabriella wiped their hands with a damp towel. Unfortunately, it did little to remove the layers of grime. Their fingernails were overlong, with black under them.

"That's good enough for now," Fiona said.

Gabriella made a very French guttural noise and said something about throwing away the towels.

The boys ate with their fingers. Expected, of course, given the food itself. However, unlike the adults we'd had in this apartment thus far, these two attacked the food like starved animals. They were, in fact, starved animals. *These poor mites*, I thought. No one in the world cared for them. I'd had Grandmother, at least. What would have become of Fai and me if Grandmother had perished along with our parents?

The endless ache of hunger. I remembered that too. The emptiness had made us listless and apathetic, too weak to think. However, I knew from experience that with even a little food, their energy would return.

When they had emptied their plates, Fiona whisked them off to the bathroom. Gabriella, with another one of her disapproving sighs, followed.

I gathered the dishes and washed them in the white ceramic sink. Afterward, suddenly fatigued and hungry, I made myself a cup of tea and buttered a chunk of bread, then sat at the table, thinking about money and how it made all the difference between a convenient life and one of hardship. We all loved the same, rich and poor, and grieved and yearned for more or less, but one couldn't deny the significance wealth or lack thereof mattered in life. It's useless to think one way or the other. Philosophies about economics meant nothing. Especially when one was poor.

What would we do about these little boys? God only knew what was in Fiona's mind. She was very much like her father. Her kind heart would decide, without thought to consequences.

After eating, I wandered out to the sitting room, unsure about what to do to help. The day had been warm, so Gabriella had closed the curtains to keep the room cooler. I drew them apart and opened the windows to bring in fresh air. Steam from the bathroom had smudged the glass.

I walked down the narrow hallway to the bathroom and bedrooms. Just outside the bathroom door, I listened to the high-pitched sound of Bleu speaking in French to Gabriella.

I leaned against the wall and looked up at the ceiling. While I agreed they were much too young to be fighting in the streets, what would we do with them? They couldn't stay here. Or could they? What about when we returned home?

The bathroom door opened and Fiona slipped into the hallway. She startled at the sight of me. "You gave me a fright. What are you doing?"

"Nothing really, merely wondering what you think we're to do now," I said gently. "Did Gabriella tell you what they said about their mother?"

Fiona nodded. "They've been living like that for a year. Can you imagine?"

"I can."

She flushed and looked chagrined. "Yes, you can. Stupid me."

"You're not stupid," I said. "Far from it. Does Gabriella know if there are places we could take them? Orphanages?"

"But an orphanage? Think of poor Phillip. He had to live in one and almost didn't make it to adulthood."

I knew Phillip had grown up in an orphanage but didn't know details. Men didn't share that kind of thing with each other.

"We have to do something. They can't go back out there to the streets." Fiona's bottom lip trembled. "I wish Mama and Papa were here. They would know what to do."

"What *would* they do?" I asked. "We must think like them. If we can let that be our guide, perhaps we'll know. For now, I'm going out to buy them new clothes."

"Thank you, Li." She leaned close and to my amazement, stood on her toes to kiss my cheek. "I know I must be an inconvenience to you in every way."

"That's not the way I'd describe it. Or you."

She touched the side of my face with the backs of her knuckles. "I don't know what came over me, but I couldn't leave them there. It's not right, what's happening to them."

"I know. But was it our problem to solve? Is it?"

She scrutinized me with narrowed eyes. "Is it not our duty to care for those who cannot care for themselves?"

I flushed under her gaze, knowing she was thinking of what her father had done for me and my family. "Duty?"

"As Christians?"

"Well, yes." I shuffled my weight from one foot to the other. Our Christian duty was to give to those less fortunate. However, did it mean we were to bring them back to our Parisian apartment for good?

"Papa would tell us to bring them home. Yes, I'm sure that's what he would do."

"Home?" I tilted my head, watching her. Did she mean to Emerson Pass?

"Yes, we will take them home with us to Colorado." Fiona spoke firmly. A new light had come to her eyes. I knew it well. All the Barnes siblings had it when they were just about to propose a preposterous idea. "My family will take them in. We'll give them a new life."

A burst of laughter rumbled out of me before I squelched it. "We can't take them home to America. They'll be unhappy, away from everything they've ever known. Anyway, how would we get them out of the country and onto a boat home?"

One corner of her mouth turned downward. "I know it seems impossible, but I don't care. I'm not leaving them to go back to being abused by those men. They need us."

"Us?"

She trailed her fingers down the lapel of my coat before pulling away and stepping backward. "They need *me*, rather." Her voice wobbled. "Just me."

"I'm sorry," I said softly. I'd hurt her, and for what reason? I was here in Paris. When she'd needed me to come, I had. We were an *us*, whether I could admit to it or not.

She lifted her gaze. The pain in her eyes made me wince.

"For what? What are you sorry for exactly? Not loving me? It's not your fault."

I hesitated before answering, knowing that I could hurt her further if I wasn't careful. "My feelings for you are irrelevant to this situation."

"Are they? Doesn't it all come back to a woman needing a man to solve any problems she might have? Bringing them home without a husband is something most women could not do. But I'm different. I have money of my own, thanks to my trust. I'll do with it what I choose. Your approval, while I'd love to have it, is not necessary."

"I'm quite aware of that." I bristled at the truth of what she said. She didn't need me. She never had and never would. I was the one who had benefited from her father's benevolence. I was the grandson of a servant. "We are not equals, Fiona, and never have been. I'm glad you're starting to understand this."

Her eyes flashed with anger. "Li Wu, that's not what I'm saying at all. I'm merely relieving you of all duty and responsibility in this matter. I will take care of it myself. You may go." She flicked her fingers at me.

Without thinking, I caught her hand and brought it to my chest. "I'm sorry. That's not what I intended."

She jerked away from me. "What is it you want? Why are you here?"

"I'm here because you're my dearest friend." My voice cracked at the end of the sentence. "Maybe I shouldn't have come."

Her eyes glistened. "We're both fooling ourselves if you think I didn't wish it were different. I want you to be by my side. I wish you loved me and wanted to make a life together as a team. But you do not. Thus, I'll do as I please." She swiped under her eyes and lifted her chin. "I want to help these boys and I'm going to do it, with or without your help."

"I'm here to help you, Fi. I always will be. But you must think carefully about this. What will James think?"

"James? What does he have to do with anything?" She glared at me with a mixture of confusion and irritation.

"If you marry him, what will he think about two little boys… in your life?"

"The last time I checked, I wasn't married to James."

"But you could be in the future. Wouldn't it be wise to think about your future when you make decisions like this?"

She flipped a curl from her damp forehead. The hallway had grown even warmer. "Whomever I marry, he will have to understand how I am."

That was the truth if I'd ever heard one.

"Do you not like James?" Fiona asked, continuing to glare at me.

"There's nothing to dislike." Even though I hated him.

"Good. Because he may end up coming home with me too."

Her words thrust me back against the wall, as if she'd shoved me. "Are you planning on marrying him?"

"It's really none of your concern."

I closed my eyes for a second, hoping the waves of pain would subside. It didn't work. I wanted to fall onto my knees and beg her to take back what she said and to tell me she didn't have those kinds of feelings for James. But she was right. It wasn't my concern. She had every right to move on from me. I'd rejected her, after all. "I'm sorry. You must do what you see as best."

"I will."

"I'll go out to the shops and get them some clothes."

She reached into the pocket of her dress and pulled out several French bills. "Take this. If you can't find anything already made, we'll have to take them to a tailor."

"I'll find something." I took the money from her and stuck it into my pocket. "I'll hurry."

She nodded and then stepped back inside the bathroom. I caught a glimpse of Bleu under the mercy of Gabriella's washcloth before Fiona shut the door behind her.

I wasted no more time, gathering my wallet, and went back into the Parisian afternoon looking for clothes for two little boys, hoping that doing something for others would lessen the ache in my chest.

16

FIONA

WHAT HAD I THOUGHT WOULD HAPPEN? I WOULD SIMPLY BRING these children home and all would miraculously fall into place? The truth is, I wasn't thinking. I acted purely on instinct. Two boys were being harmed and I couldn't stand by and watch it happen.

Still stinging from my conversation with Li, I returned to help Gabriella with the boys. We had both of the boys bathed by the time I heard the front door shut behind Li. After Gabriella had dried their scrawny bodies with towels and I'd combed Bleu's hair, I herded them into my bedroom. With towels wrapped around their waists, they stood near the window, shivering despite the warmth of the afternoon.

Gabriella had already told them we were gathering new clothes, and they seemed unconcerned with their lack of dress. Bleu, who spoke for both of them most of the time, yawned. Beaumont followed suit. What did it matter if they had nothing to wear to bed? I would tuck them into my own and let them sleep, safe and warm.

I asked Gabriella to tell them that it was now time for a nap. "And tell them we'll have a meal in the evening if they're good boys and rest." This would give me the opportunity to shop for food. I'd planned on dining out with Li, but we would need to stay in if we had the boys.

I ushered both of them into my double bed. Both kept their towels around their waists but I don't suppose either of them cared much. They were happy for a soft bed.

They curled up together, like kittens in a basket. I could imagine what they looked like during long nights on the streets, huddled together for warmth. By the time I'd drawn the curtains, they were asleep. I gazed down at them for a moment. Although skinny, they were beautiful boys, with high cheekbones and adorable pointy chins. Dark hair and skin bronzed by the sun, they could easily be Emerson Pass's own boys who spent many summer afternoons at the river.

I pulled the sheet over their shoulders but left the covers piled at their feet. The room would continue to warm in the late afternoon, and I didn't want them too hot.

Gabriella was at the kitchen sink scrubbing the boys' filthy clothes. "I don't know, miss, if these will survive the cleaning." She held up a pair of trousers. "Do you see how thin?"

I explained that Li was out finding clothes suitable for the boys.

Gabriella's face clouded. "I do know where there are shops. For my little boy. Lucien. I shopped for him in Paris once."

Little boy? She'd had a child? What about a husband? Where were either of them? "Where is he now?"

"He died," Gabriella said flatly. "A bad fever came to him, and he was too small to fight."

"I'm very sorry." Impulsively, I grabbed her into a hug.

She was stiff at first, obviously surprised, but loosened all at once, as if she were jumping from a cliff, and hugged me back. When we parted, she wiped the corners of her eyes with the back of her hand.

This poor woman, losing her child. A wave of sadness swept

over me. Thinking of losing any member of my family made me want to weep.

My family. What would they think of me taking home two little street urchins? What was I doing? And I'd dragged poor Li into it. As usual, he came along, looking after me. No wonder he wouldn't fall in love with me. I was a pesky gnat.

"You take boys home with you?" Gabriella asked. "Take me too and I will help you?" She smiled, as if she were joking.

Why not, I thought? "Would you be happy in America?"

"I'm not happy anywhere. I simply survive." She looked out the window with a glazed expression. What did she think of when she looked out to the streets of Paris? Did she think of her lost boy? "How old was Lucien?"

"He was only one year old." Gabriella's eyes filled with tears. "My precious baby."

"What about your husband?"

She bowed her head. Dots of red speckled her cheeks. "I have no husband."

No husband. A baby without a husband? The idea was as shocking to me as learning about my new friends and their alternative ways of living. It struck me how naive I'd been—sheltered away as I was in Emerson Pass. Was this why God had led me to Paris? To learn about people who weren't exactly like me and my family?

"Do you think badly of me now?" Gabriella asked.

"Of course not." I didn't think badly of her, but I did see her differently now. I'd assumed things about her without taking into consideration that she might have made mistakes or done things she was ashamed of. But hadn't we all? They might not have as large a consequence as having relations out of wedlock. Or as visible. However, none of us were perfect.

"What happened to the father of your baby?" Was he like Mr. Basset, who preyed on vulnerable women? Had Gabriella fallen for a man like that?

"He died in the war. Before we could marry. The shame followed me everywhere. I was sent away from my village and everyone I've known. My own mother would not even look at me. The priest in our church would not baptize my baby. I left the village with only the clothes on my back and a little money Dimitri had left me. We were planning to marry when he came home for leave, but he never did."

I shook my head, not knowing what to say. "I'm sorry. I didn't know."

"How could you? I don't talk about the past." She wrung the pants over the sink, squeezing as much water out of them as she could. "What will you do with the boys? Please tell me you won't send them away. They'll go back to fighting. We do what we have to—to stay alive. Even when life is miserable, we keep fighting to live. I don't understand why. Every morning I wake and find I'm still here and I wonder why I don't have the courage to smother myself with a pillow."

"Gabriella, I understand the pain must seem unbearable. Losing a child—there's nothing worse. But can you reach inside yourself and find another purpose for living? Another way to have a meaningful life?"

"I've been happier since coming here. With you." She gave me a sad, sweet smile that broke my heart.

"You can stay with me as long as you like. If you truly want to go, I'll pay for you to come to America with Li and me when it is time. You could live in the mountains and learn to ski. Papa and Mama can find a position for you in the big house or once —" I almost said, "once I'm married you could work for me." But I would never marry. Not if it wasn't Li. His arrival here had answered any remaining questions I had. "Or you can work for one of my sisters or brothers." I almost told her about all the babies that had come to us and all the ones I expected we would have. However, I stopped myself beforehand, realizing how painful that might be to Gabriella.

"I would have to leave his grave." Tears tumbled out of her eyes and fell into her dimples.

I handed her my handkerchief. "I imagine it would be hard to leave because of that. But isn't he here?" I tapped my chest. "And in heaven, watching over you?"

She nodded, clutching the handkerchief to her chest. "I know he's there. When I ran away to Paris, I found a vicar willing to baptize him. I told him my husband had died in the war. He didn't check to see if I was telling truth. It is the only thing that allows me to sleep at night, knowing he is with Jesus now."

I led her over to one of the chairs. "Sit for a moment. I'll pour us some tea."

"No, no, I must make tea for you."

"I can do it just this once." I patted her hand and pushed her gently to sit.

She perched on the edge of the chair as if ready to spring away at a moment's notice. Gabriella was unpredictable and tense, ready to run when scared or challenged. I poured us each a cup of tea. "I lost my mother when I was only a baby. She died a terrible death. Papa was left with all five of us. I was only an infant. For three years, we were alone with only Papa, whom we adored. Still, there was something missing. Josephine and the twins remembered our mother enough that they missed her. I was blissfully unaware of her loss. But there was such darkness, Gabriella, in our house. My real mother was sick. Not in her body but here." I tapped the side of my head. "She was confused and depressed. There were incidents of violence against her own children."

Gabriella gasped. "No, how is it possible?"

"We don't understand what could cause such a thing. No one does, really. The doctor was no help. If we had lived in the city, they probably would have sent her to an asylum." I shivered, thinking of such a place. I'd read about them in books and newspaper articles over the years and had felt sick at the thought of anyone being sent to one. "Her episodes had started in earnest after the twins were born. Papa didn't speak of it often, but Josephine remembered a lot from the age of five until ten, when our mother died. My poor Papa. He was all alone, except for Jasper and Lizzie, of course. They'd come with Papa from England when they were all young. They did what they could for him and for us, of course, but nothing could take the place of having a mother. When I was three, our stepmother came to us. She loved us and healed our sadness. The twins and Jo were no longer haunted by the way our mother lived or died." I stopped myself from telling poor Gabriella about my mother's death. To this day, we did not know if she'd walked out of the house with the intent to kill herself or if her madness had caused her to do so. "Cymbeline and I—that's my other sister— learned what it was like to be loved by a mother." I stirred a teaspoon of sugar into my tea. "I'm telling you all this because..." What *was* my reason?

"Because you will take the boys back to America and be their mother and you want me to understand?"

My mouth dropped open. *Be their mother?* I hadn't been thinking of that at all. I'd taken them home to the apartment on an impulse, wanting only to extract them from immediate danger with no thought to their future. But this story I told Gabriella? Was it as a way to remind myself about what Mama had done for us? Welcomed us into her heart without so much as a thought to her own life? "Mama was only twenty-two when she married Papa. I never thought about it then. I was so little. I thought only of how happy I was to have her, not of what she had to give up." Had she had dreams she left to wither away? Did she ever look back and wish she'd chosen differently? No. Not Mama. She and Papa were each other's destiny.

What was my destiny? I'd thought it was Li and our music. I didn't think so any longer.

"She loved your papa," Gabriella said in answer to my question. "That was enough."

"She loved us, too, even separate from him." What is the quality that makes it possible for a woman to love children not born from her own womb? Did I have it in me?

Why was I thinking about all of this now? Was the answer simple? Confronted with these two homeless innocents, I supposed I'd been reminded of the way Mama had become our mother, regardless of blood. But she'd had Papa. They'd become partners and parents together. I had no one. I was too young. Wasn't I?

"I don't know if I can be their mother," I said to Gabriella. "I'm only twenty. I have no husband. My life at home is busy with my music. I'm out late at night. I spend most of my days at the piano composing or practicing. In addition, I don't know anything about raising children. I live at my Papa's house still and probably will for the rest of my life."

"Why rest of life?"

"I won't marry. I'll stay at home and take care of Papa and Mama when they grow old. My younger sisters will marry eventually, and it'll be only me. Perhaps it's what I was born to do." A memory of sitting on Papa's lap came to me. He'd held me tightly and promised I would always be his princess, no matter how much time passed. When had that been? Perhaps when Addie was born? I'd been only six when she'd come. I could remember the joy I'd felt when I saw her little face for the first time. I was a big sister. I'd felt important and necessary. "I'm the person in my family who looks after the others. That's my life's work, perhaps?"

"Music." Gabriella made a gesture toward her throat. "To make beauty with your throat and your fingers. But also, you will marry Li, no?"

I flushed and pushed aside the tears that knocked on the back of my eyeballs. "No, he doesn't love me."

"I do not think you are correct." Gabriella's green eyes darkened. The knitting between her brows deepened. "He has passion for you. I see it in his face. Soft when he looks at you."

I didn't have the energy just then to explain that it was only brotherly affection Li felt for me. It was the same mistake I'd made myself, taking his affectionate ways as romantic love. Anyway, I had the problem of the boys to figure a way through. What *was* I to do with them? I couldn't send them back to their current situation. That was not an option I would consider. I didn't think I could be their mother, either. I didn't know enough and didn't have a home of my own. My best hope was that Papa would allow us to take them in and care for them as if they were members of our family. They could go to school with the other children in our little town. Delphia was around the same age. She would be their friend and show them around. A nagging guilt stopped me, though. Wouldn't they be happier in their own country where they spoke the language? Louisa had needed a family, and the Linds had adopted her. Could we find a couple like that here in Paris? I asked Gabriella about the possibility of a childless couple who wanted to adopt. "Are there orphanages? A place I could take them where they would be looked after and perhaps adopted?"

"There are orphanages here. Run by nuns." She shivered. "One of my friends here grew up in one. They are cold, harsh places. I don't wish the little boys to go there. But it is better than the streets. No one will want them. They're too old. Everyone wants babies. They tried to take my Lucien from me." Her lips twitched into a smile at the memory of her little boy. "He had gold curls. Everyone likes that."

I thought of my brother-in-law Phillip. He'd grown up in an orphanage and longed for a family of his own. A place to belong. People who loved unconditionally, even after terrible mistakes or misjudgments. He had that now, with Jo and their girls and with the rest of us, too. If only Mama and Papa were here, I could ask them what to do. Papa had brought Li and his family back to live with us without a moment's hesitation. Would he do the same for Bleu and Beaumont?

What had I done? Opened up a mess, surely. Would I do it differently? No. I was a Barnes, and this is what we did. Impulsive or not, I had a duty to these sweet urchins, and I would not leave them to waste away on the street.

I returned my gaze to Gabriella. She remained on the edge of the chair, her tea untouched. Did God intend for me to take her back with us too? Had that been one of the reasons I'd come here? I didn't know much, but studying with Mr. Basset was not enough reason for the expense and time. Thus far, that was the only thing truly known. The rest remained a mystery.

"Gabriella, do you have anything keeping you here besides the grave of Lucien?"

She studied her hands, red and chapped from her domestic duties. "Not here. Or anywhere. Dimitri is buried somewhere in northern France without a grave, just one of many bodies." She wiped her eyes. "I would go to America if you would take me."

"We'll talk more about it later. It's a big decision to leave everything you've known."

"America is rich with chances?" Gabriella asked.

"It is, yes," I said. "We can give you a position at the big house or with one of my siblings. My family will help you all we can. Ultimately, it is hard work and fortitude that will make the most difference."

"I will think on it." She tapped her temple. "But I think I would like to go."

"All right, if that's what you wish when the time comes, I'll bring you back with us."

"The boys too? Will they come too?" Gabriella asked.

I didn't answer for a moment. A warmth that started from the top of my head, almost as if the ceiling had opened up and shed sunshine onto me, moved into my face and down the rest of me. I didn't yet know how I would manage to help those boys, only that I would. Just as Papa had done for Li and his family so long ago, I would do the same for Bleu and Beaumont.

"If it is best for them, then they will come with us," I said.

God would guide me.

I give it all to you, Lord. Allow me to be your vessel.

17

LI

I was returning to the apartment loaded with packages from the shop when I ran into James West coming out of a café. Just what I needed to complete this disaster of a day.

"Hello there," James said. It was remarkable how much he sounded like Lord Barnes. "Doing some shopping?"

"Yes, indeed I am." How much should I tell him? Would he think Fiona mad? However, if he did then it simply proved he was the wrong man for her. She needed someone who understood her philanthropic nature. If he was interested in her because of her fortune, his rejection of the idea would be evidence that my suspicions were correct. Should I tell him and watch carefully for clues to his true nature? "In fact, Fiona and I have taken up a bit of a project. We were out this morning and found some adventure."

"Is that right? You must tell me about it. I was just headed your way." He tapped the cover of the book that he held close to his chest. "I've a new novel for her. One I think she'll enjoy."

"What book is it?" Of course he would have the latest and greatest book. This would be impressive to Fiona and the rest of the Barnes clan. They loved their books.

"*The Sun Also Rises*. Ernest Hemingway. He and his wife lived here in Paris when he wrote it." He grinned, facetious. "I say it as if I invented him and Paris, don't I?" He sighed heavily. "I'm discouraged, if you want to know the truth. I'm helping Cooper with his second book and wondering where my life is headed."

We set out together down the sidewalk. I was proud of myself that I hadn't been petty and mentioned that the Hemingway book had been out for a long time and Fiona had already read it.

"How's the new manuscript coming along?" I asked, trying to be polite when I wanted to tell him to turn around and go the other direction.

"Slow. He's yet to get me a new chapter. His wife told me he's belaboring every word, which means there aren't many. Words, that is." He motioned toward the coffee shop he'd just come out of. "I've been in there sitting on the floor next to a shelf of my favorite books and wondering how I'm going to pay the rent on my measly apartment. As loath as I am to admit it, my father is right about me and this ridiculous dream of becoming an editor. This is a fool's errand."

"I can understand why you feel that way but art, in all her forms, is important. You're doing a service, bringing books into the world."

"That's kind of you to say. I'm not bringing them anywhere. Cooper's my only client. I have acquaintances in the literary world but nothing to show them."

"Didn't you say his first book would lead you to a job with a publishing house?"

"I'm hoping so, but thus far it's proven to be futile. Basically, I've been mooching about Paris, using up what little allowance I have and working with Cooper. I need a real job but have no skills. The aristocrats of England have little to offer, I'm afraid. Without money, what are we?"

"In America, there is opportunity no matter your title." Especially if one looked like James West.

"Is that true, though? Don't you need money to begin with? I mean, if I were to go to Emerson Pass with Fiona, what would I do there? Mooch about some more?"

His words turned me cold, despite the warmth of the summer day. Had they talked of James coming home with Fiona?

"I need a wealthy wife," James said. "That would solve all my problems."

The hairs on the back of my neck raised. "Is that your intent with Fiona? Are you hoping she'll marry you and save your family from ruin?"

James had the gall to laugh. "Fiona Barnes is one of the finest women I've ever known. Marrying her would be any man's honor. However, she's intent on marrying for love."

What did that mean? Did he intend to seduce her into falling in love with him? It would be the right answer for him, obviously. But what about my romantic Fiona? Could she love him? What wasn't there to love, I thought, trying to be rational. James West was handsome, kind, funny, and smart. He was a connoisseur of art, music, and literature. Best of all, he belonged to her father's world. Lord Barnes would understand James West, feel comfortable with him and the idea of a marriage to his beloved daughter. Other than West's lack of funds, he was the perfect match for Fiona. However, she didn't need money. Lord Barnes had enough to go around. Therefore, James was, in fact, the perfect match for her. Who was I to say otherwise?

"Listen, West. If it's Fiona you want, then you should make your intentions known to her father. Do this the right way."

He made an annoying clicking sound with his tongue before we separated to allow a smitten couple to walk between us. "It kills me to tell you this, but there's nothing between Fiona and me except a deep and loyal friendship."

I glanced at him. "You're not trying to convince her to marry you? And why does it kill you to say so?"

After an impatient sigh, he halted and pulled me from the sidewalk to stand under the skinny awning of a bakery. "Why do you concern yourself with Fiona and me? It makes me wonder."

"Wonder what?" I nearly growled.

He tugged off his hat and held it in front of him, as if he were worried I might punch him. "If you don't want her your-self, why do you dislike me so much?" He held up his hat in a gesture of self-defense. "I know you don't care for me. It's obvious despite your flawless manners. I may be poor, but people like me anyway. Almost everyone. Fiona says I'm like a golden retriever that way."

"It's nothing to do with you."

"Isn't that what I just said? You're a fool, Wu. An utter fool. You're going to lose her and then what?" He put his hat back on, turned, and continued down the street.

I followed behind, juggling my parcels. "Sometimes love means selflessness, West," I called after him but he appeared not to hear me. If he was a golden retriever then I was one of those small, yapping dogs at his heels. "Do you have a plan to seduce Fiona? Get her to fall in love with you?" I asked, seething.

"You're the chap who would know, aren't you?" For the first time, I caught a hint of hostility in his voice.

I sidestepped a woman pushing a baby carriage. "Pardon me?"

"It's a pity, that's all."

"What's a pity?" I asked through gritted teeth. West's legs were much longer than mine. I was almost panting to keep up with him.

"That you don't return her affection. Is there anything worse than unrequited love?"

"She told you about her feelings?" What else had she told him?

"Indeed. We're confidants. She's shared many things with me, including the unrequited love of her best friend from home. I can't fathom how you could resist her."

"See there, you do want her." I jerked my arm, knocking my face with one of the bags as a sinking feeling washed over me. Would it be better for Fiona if she married James? Was it her destiny to marry James West and raise these street urchins? *Ces enfants des rues?*

And if that were true, then what was to become of me? Where did I belong and with whom? Without Fiona, life stretched before me, empty and dark.

"Let me rephrase that," West said. "It's obvious to me that you feel the same way about her. I don't know why you're making it hard when it should be easy."

"Nothing between us would be easy. She's too young to know that. Too young for me." Even to my own ears, this sounded like a meager excuse.

"She's of marrying age. The women in London have already come out by her age."

"There are other reasons besides that," I said. "You wouldn't understand them."

We reached Fiona's building. He stopped before going inside and turned directly to me. "I might not, but shouldn't it be up to Fiona? Shouldn't you give her enough respect to decide for herself?"

A friendly spaniel stopped to sniff at my feet before his owner shuffled him along with a tug on the leash. "Fiona's naive about such matters. She's lived a sheltered life. Her father doesn't think like most men from his background."

"What's that to do with you?" James spoke mildly, as if we were speaking of some benign pastime. It was infuriating.

I tried to match his tone, but keeping my temper in check

was nearly impossible. "She doesn't know what a couple like us would encounter. America may pretend to be without social or economic or racial inequalities, but that is false. I'm of Chinese descent. That will not ever change. In many places, I'll be spit on in the streets or worse, especially if I have Fiona on my arm. She'll be in danger. Actual danger." I ground my teeth in frustration. James's bland face didn't help matters. "She's not understanding what would happen if I were to marry her. Can't you see that?"

"What I see, with all due respect, is a woman willing to take on all of that for the honor of being by your side. If I were you, that would be enough."

"Enough what?" I asked.

"Enough to know that whatever storms came, she could weather them. You, sir, don't give her enough credit."

"Perhaps." Was that true? Were my views those of an egotistical man? She would be strong enough to withstand whatever shunning came our way. Fiona couldn't care less about all of that. But what about the danger I would put her into? After the attack in my own hometown, the bitter truth had been obvious. I was a liability to whomever I was with. "She's reckless, with no thought to her safety." I blurted out the story of the morning and then held up the packages as evidence. "These are for the boys. We have eight-year-old twins upstairs. Little boys we know nothing about and who quite possibly have put us in danger. I only just arrived in Paris and look what she's done."

"Twins?" James asked, sounding amused. "How interesting. That would make her even more prone to the idea because of her own brothers."

"That's right." My stomach clenched. He really did know Fiona. The months we'd been apart, she'd grown close to James. Who could blame her? He was nearly perfect. Still, I reserved the right to hate him. "Do you understand my fears? There are little boys in the apartment when yesterday we didn't even know they existed. She's already talking about taking them home with us."

"Taking them home to Colorado?"

"That's right. Am I the only one who finds that outlandish?"

"Yes, well, I can see your point." James shook his head. "That *is* reckless and even rash. She wants to take them home? Are you sure?"

"She hasn't said specifically, but I know her. That's where this is headed."

He laughed. "She's unusual, we can agree on that, can't we?"

"Unusual? That's one way to say it." Despite my agitation just moments ago, I laughed too. Tension seemed to melt away as we shared a smile.

For the first time, I felt an ally of sorts. "Do you see why I worry?" I asked. "She's blind to reality at times."

"And too bighearted. Taking on strays like me, for example." James grimaced. "I *do* see your argument."

"Yes, the entire Barnes family has a way of collecting people. Like me, for example."

He nodded before opening the door to the building and allowing me to enter before him. We climbed the stairs in comfortable silence.

We were in front of Fiona's apartment door when I said, "Have you ever loved someone so much that it physically hurts?"

"No, I haven't, but I'm a romantic, so I understand the concept." James clapped my shoulder. "The most wonderful woman in the world loves you and you love her. Can't you simply accept that God's given you a gift? Do not push it aside. Embrace it. Have faith that all will be well."

"It's easy for you to say. You weren't beaten up outside a club that feels like the one place you belong."

His expression softened. "I understand. I truly do. But the

measure of a man is not his vulnerability but what he does despite it. Make this right before you lose her for good."

"Do you really think I should?"

"I do. As far as I'm concerned, you and Fiona have my undying support. Whatever I can do to help, all you have to do is ask."

"How about you take a few of these packages?" I asked. "That would be a good start."

And so we were laughing as we entered the apartment. Something I would not have believed possible only minutes before. Was this a message from God above? Trust in love?

I SUPERVISED THE BOYS AS THEY DRESSED IN THEIR NEW CLOTHES. A bath, a nap, and food had greatly improved their appearance. Fiona had taken the scissors to Bleu's hair and with shorter locks, it was much more obvious they were twins. Although Beaumont's face was still swollen and one eye was practically sealed shut.

When they were properly dressed, I escorted them out to the sitting room where Fiona and James were in deep conversation, heads bent together. They startled when we came into the room and jerkily drew apart, then peered at us with guilty expressions.

They'd been talking about me. What had he told Fiona? West gave me a reassuring smile, putting me at ease. He wouldn't betray my confidence.

"Ah, there are my little gentlemen," Fiona said. "Mr. West, may I present to you Bleu and Beaumont."

The boys nodded. James placed a hand on each of their heads and looked them in the eye. Then he spoke to them in remarkably good French. What couldn't he do?

The boys did as he asked and sat together on the sofa, close enough that their knees touched. Beaumont shook slightly, but Bleu's eyes blazed with fight. If I had to guess, it had been Bleu who had kept them alive.

Through a series of coaxing questions from James, we were able to piece together more details about their background. They'd been orphaned after their mother died of some kind of illness. Neither knew what had killed her, only that she had fallen ill and never recovered. Before her death, they'd lived in a small room in one of the poorest sections of Paris, according to James anyway. When James asked about their father, Bleu lifted his narrow shoulder and said they had never known him. He'd died when they were infants. Their mother had done the best she could, working in a factory during the day while the boys stayed alone. When their mother died, the landlord shoved them out to the street. They wandered, begging for scraps of food, and somehow surviving the winter. When they were approached about fighting, Bleu had not hesitated to say yes. The fights gave them enough to eat for a week if they were careful with the money. *"Des voleurs tout autour de nous,"* Bleu said. Thieves everywhere.

Fiona sat very still while the boys spoke and James translated. Her usually expressive face was set in a stoic mask. For once, I couldn't tell what she was thinking.

I couldn't understand everything the children said, but I understood Bleu when he asked what it was we wanted them to do. What was the payment for the food and clothes? *"Vous voulez quoi en échange de la nourriture et des vêtements? On doit faire quoi pour vous?"*

The frightened glint in his eyes as he waited for our response shattered me. What must he think? What horrible ideas had come to him about what we would take from them in exchange for staving off their starvation for however long we kept them?

James told them that we didn't want anything from them. He

explained that Fiona had a kind heart, especially for children. "She wants you to have food and shelter and go to school," James said to them in French. "*Vous n'aurez plus à vous battre.*" You won't have to fight anymore.

Bleu looked from one of us to another, as if he couldn't quite be sure we were for real.

"*Mais pourquoi?*" Beaumont asked, surprising us by using his voice for the first time. But why?

Why indeed? How would Fiona explain?

"Tell them it makes me sad to see them hungry and without shelter," Fiona said. "I want to help them. Say that, please. Make sure they understand I'll take care of them from now on."

James translated, conveying Fiona's sentiments. When the boys seemed to have reached their limit with all the questions, Gabriella took them into the kitchen for another meal.

Before they left with Gabriella, Fiona smiled at both the boys. Bleu smiled back at her, a tentative one that showed a mouthful of rotten teeth. *These children need so much*, I thought. Was taking them across the ocean to a country where they didn't speak the language or know a soul the correct course? It was such a Barnes thing, believing the answer to everything was in Emerson Pass. But maybe she was right?

After the boys left the room, James poured himself a drink and collapsed into an easy chair. "What a thing you've done, Fiona."

"I don't want to be lectured," Fiona said. "By either one of you."

"Fiona." I spoke as calmly as I could, not wanting to hurt her but worried just the same that she would have her hopes crushed by the realities of government. "We don't know anything about adoption or immigration laws. It might be best to proceed with caution. I don't want you to have your hopes up only to have them come crashing down when we talk to the authorities."

"You have such little faith," Fiona said to me.

My lack of faith seemed to be the theme of today. I filled with even more affection for James when he said, "You know, Fiona, he has a point. Until we know more about immigration and adoption laws, it might be best not to plan too far ahead."

"We don't have influence here like we might at home," I said gently.

Fiona gave us both scathing looks before going to the liquor cabinet and pouring herself a glass of wine. She drank wine before dinner now? Paris had corrupted her. Instead of sitting on her own chair, she perched on the arm of James's. "No, but Papa might. He has powerful connections here. He'll know what to do."

I took one end of the sofa and glanced toward the window, thinking about what she'd said. Would Lord Barnes be able to use his influence to push something like this through? On the other side of the glass, a fat robin perched on the sill.

"If not, we'll just stow them away on the ship," Fiona said. "Like Sandwich did with the old man who brought her here."

"What?" I asked, not following.

"Never mind. You're too provincial to hear about that now," Fiona said. "Once you've been here a few weeks, you'll understand."

I rolled my eyes but had to chuckle. "All right, let me know when you think I'm ready."

"You're barely older than them," I said. "What are you thinking?"

She flushed red. Her slender frame straightened, and she looked for a moment as though she might strike me. I knew she wouldn't, of course, but the way her fists clenched at her sides reminded me of Flynn right before he threw a punch. "I'm old enough to know my own mind, no matter how often you try to change it."

"I'm only pointing out the perils involved here," I said. "We don't know these children. They're French. Taking them to America won't be as easily done as it would be at home where the Barnes family is law."

"We're not law. Papa only does what he thinks is best."

"Regardless, this isn't as easy as deciding to take them home with us," I said. "You're not prepared to raise them on your own."

"Maybe I will." She jutted her chin out and glared at me, reminding me of Cymbeline. "What do you care? It's not as if it will affect your life."

"I don't want you burdened by all this," I said. "You're young. You have your whole life ahead of you. Marriage, a family of your own."

"I didn't say I was adopting them," Fiona said.

"Someone might have to if we're to get them to America," James said.

If we were to get them? "We?" I asked out loud.

"James might come home with us," Fiona said. "As our guest until he gets his publishing job."

I took in a deep breath, knowing I must be careful what I said and how I said it. "You're paying the way of a man who has already borrowed money from you that he'll never be able to pay back?"

She gasped. Her eyes glittered with anger and hurt. I'd gone too far. "You know nothing about James."

"It's all right," James said. "He's right about my prospects."

"He is not," Fiona said, loudly. "Circumstances can change like this." She snapped her fingers. "Especially for clever men like James." She looked me straight in the eye. "As for you, the more you tell me not to do this, the more I want to."

I sighed, knowing I wouldn't win this argument today. Or probably ever.

"This is why we've come to Paris. I know it." Fiona stood and walked to the window. The robin remained, and the two of them seemed to take each other in, two songbirds united in making the world more beautiful. Fiona turned in a dramatic circle, gesturing with her glass of wine in a way that reminded me of a symphony conductor. "I couldn't understand why until today. Studying with Basset is not the reason God brought me here. It was to save these little boys."

"What exactly do you want to do?" I asked, resigned to what she would say next. *Take them home.*

Sure enough, she said exactly that. "I want to take them home. My family will look after them, one way or the other." She didn't say, "like we did you," but she didn't have to. I knew it, and so did she. Her father's legacy lived on in Fiona. There would be no persuading her away from the idea. Not that I would have tried again. I could see that was futile.

James cleared his throat. His eyes had grown tender and sad during the children's tale of woe. But now they glittered with concern, not for the boys but for Fiona. "Darling, he has a good argument. This is a lot to take on. You don't know the children. They could be liars or thieves."

"So what if they are?" Fiona stalked over to the sofa and sat on the other end from me. An emerald ring on her hand sparkled in a spot of sun. "It would change nothing. They're eight-year-old boys who will die on the streets of Paris. It's only by the grace of God the winters haven't already killed them. We'll take them home and my family will raise them one way or the other. They can go to school there. Learn English. Have lives of opportunity instead of this death sentence." She turned to me. "Like we gave you."

I nodded, acquiescing. "Whatever you want, we shall do. How can I be of service?"

She gave me a tight, satisfied smile. "Thank you."

"Fiona Barnes, you're a handful," James said. He looked over at me and raised an eyebrow. "It's going to take quite a man to partner with you."

"There will be no man," Fiona said.

"Darling, you're too beautiful and sweet and smart not to marry," West said. "You'll be depriving your soul mate of his true calling." He gave me a pointed look.

West really knew how to lay it on thick.

"However, about the boys—there's one other idea," James said lightly. "What if we visited an orphanage? There might be a chance of them being adopted by a nice French couple. They passed a law to address the issue of those orphaned after the war. They're encouraging older couples to adopt if they're childless or have lost a child. It's not unfeasible to think they might be better served by staying in their native country, where they speak the language."

"Do you know of such a place?" Fiona asked.

James nodded. "Yes, there's an orphanage not far from here. Run by nuns. Shall we go there and see what they could offer? We could speak to them about the odds of the boys being adopted."

"They won't be," Fiona muttered. "They're too old. My brother-in-law Phillip lived in an orphanage after his parents died. No one comes for older children." Her voice had grown raspy. She pressed a handkerchief against her mouth.

"We'll take a look," I said softly. "But if it's not suitable, then we'll come up with the next idea."

She gave me a grateful smile. "I know you must think I've lost my mind, but I can't let this go. This might be the most important work we ever do."

"If you want, I'll go to the embassy and inquire about adoption," I said.

"I'll join you. First thing tomorrow," West said.

"You will?" Fiona asked, bobbing her gaze from one of us to the other. "Together?"

"We're practically brothers by now," James said. "Both taken into the fold of the Barnes family."

"For heaven's sake, really?" Fiona asked, laughing. "What's changed?"

We both looked at her innocently. "What do you mean?" I asked.

"Never mind, then. Now that we have all that settled, what should we do for dinner?" Fiona asked.

We all looked at one another and burst out laughing.

18

FIONA

James and I were sitting on the patio of the café downstairs waiting for Li to arrive. He'd sent a message with James that he would meet us after an urgent errand. They'd been to the embassy earlier and had asked that I wait until dinner to hear what they'd learned. I feared it would be bad news. Every time I thought of it, my stomach did a nervous flip.

When Henri came to take our orders, Li had not yet arrived. We ordered a first course of fresh oysters and crisp white wine for three. The little boys were upstairs with Gabriella, having their dinner and being put to bed.

James seemed antsy, wriggling around like Flynn had when we were children and been forced to dress nicely for supper.

"What's gotten into you?" I asked. "You're fidgeting."

"Nothing really." He smiled mischievously.

"How come you and Li are suddenly chums?" I stared at him with suspicion, hoping to shame him into giving me answers. They'd both acted differently toward each other since yesterday. I was glad of it, but I had a feeling they were up to something. "Confess, please."

"We had a nice chat, that's all," James said, feigning innocence by raising both eyebrows.

"I told him I needed a wealthy wife. Which is true, of course."

"James, you didn't." I couldn't stop the laughter that bubbled up from my belly.

"I wanted to see what it would do."

"What did he say?" I asked.

"He didn't say much." James buttered a piece of bread and held it aloft as he contemplated my question. "It was more what he didn't say that makes me think jealousy is eating at him. For one thing, he doesn't like me. Everyone likes me."

I laughed. "No one is liked by everyone. For example, as lovely as I am, I would guess that referee from the boxing match doesn't care for me."

"Darling, it's entirely obvious. The man loves you."

I studied my dinner companion, hope rising in me until I was full of it. "Do you really think so? But why would he say otherwise?"

"I told him he was a fool and if he didn't change his ways, he was going to lose you."

"What did he say to that?"

"Something about selflessness," James said.

It seemed as if the floor opened up under me and I went crashing into hard stone. "Do you think he…?"

"I do. That's precisely what I think. He believes you're better off without him, so he told you he doesn't return your feelings. He's a good man, possibly great, sacrificing his own happiness in the hope that you'll find someone who will give you an easy life."

Tears pricked my eyes. I covered my face with one hand, hoping to compose myself.

"It wouldn't be the end of the world if we married, would it?" James asked. "You and me?"

I uncovered my eyes. "What?"

"What if we married? You could take him as a lover later, like so many of the women do here. That solves all our problems."

"James, no. You're not serious, are you?"

He laughed. "I'm only teasing you. However, I could think of worse things than being married to you. It would solve a lot of my problems."

"Well, I'm serious about you coming home with me," I said. Of all the problems in the world for which I had no solutions, this one was clear. "I'll give it to you. Whatever you need. I have plenty in my trust. You can work for Papa in some capacity if need be. My parents will have you as a guest. You can stay as long as you like. Perhaps you'll like small-town life." I spoke as if it were already decided, hoping my confidence would persuade him.

It was his turn to bury his face behind his hands and take in a long, shuddering breath. "Why can't it be simple?"

I studied him, his chiseled features and beautiful eyes. How was it possible that I had not fallen for him? But it wasn't right. There was not the spark of desire or longing that I felt with Li. And anyway, what about James and his needs? He was a romantic like me. He would want to hold out for true love if he possibly could, not marry for money. The woman of his dreams was out there, I felt sure of it. "I adore you, James West."

"And I adore you."

"It's useless to wish for something that simply isn't true. Life doesn't work out the way we want it to sometimes. We must remain fast friends, however, and support each other no matter what comes."

"I agree in theory. However, I have nothing to offer you," James said.

"Your friendship is enough. You're like a brother to me." I touched a finger to my bread knife, surprised to find it warm as if it had just come from the wash. "You deserve love, James, not compromise simply because your father went through all your family money. In addition, what if Li changes his mind? I have to wait, just in case." Saying the words out loud made me feel like a fool. "Hope is a fickle beast, isn't she?"

"Hope is all we have at times. The idea of getting up each morning with no prospects is no way to live. Even if we are delusional, we must believe that better times are ahead."

"Hope is the bravest of all decisions, then?" I asked. "Even in the face of doom?"

"I believe so. As far as that goes—when you have nothing as I have—there's nowhere but upward." He sounded so sad and without hope that my chest ached.

"You have a lot, James. Friends who love you, especially me. You've been my true companion these last few months. Someday, you'll be in the position to repay me. That's how it goes, you know, the ups and downs of life. No one is up forever. Or down, for that matter. Friendship is about being there for all the spaces in between the trials and triumphs."

Unshed tears made James's eyes shine like beautiful glass. "That's a lovely thing to say." He tilted his head to the side and looked down at the table, clearly contemplating something. "My theory about Li, for what it's worth, is that he's more concerned with your welfare than his own. Which is the highest form of love, isn't it? He'd rather have you safe and happy than selfishly take you for himself, knowing it would make your life hard."

I thought about this for a moment. Was it possible James was correct? And if so, what did that mean?

"Anyway, we agreed to be friends for your sake," James said.

"I'm pleased. I'll need all the friends I can get when I show up at home with two little boys."

"I can't say I'm not worried they will make your life difficult and steal your youth."

"It will all be fine," I said.

"And look at what you're doing for me. Taking on a hundred-and-seventy-pound man in need of a home."

I laughed at his self-mocking expression. "I'll have my family to help with the children, whatever is decided about the boys. As far as you go, helping a friend doesn't make me a candidate for sainthood. God wants me to use whatever privilege I have for good. Anyway, I'm never alone, because I'm a Barnes. You'll see once we're home."

James spread butter on a chunk of warm bread. "I can't live off the mercy of my friends forever, but I'm truly grateful."

"Someday you'll be a famous editor and I'll be pleased to think I had a small part in it. Now, if only your perfect match would fall out of the sky," I said.

"Yes, where is she?" He grinned, but his eyes were dull. His future weighed heavily upon him.

I reached for his hand. "Dear James, you will find the girl of your dreams soon enough. I've a feeling she's waiting somewhere, wondering where you are. Until then, you shall become a Barnes, and let us look after you."

"I like the sound of that."

"Hopefully you won't live to regret joining my family," I said, giving his hand one last squeeze.

Out of the corner of my eye, I spotted Li approaching. His scent, permanently tattooed into my consciousness, reached me before he did. I could see right away that he carried a tense energy with him. His cheeks were flushed and his jaw clenched. I'd noticed how tightly people held their mouths now that I'd been studying with Basset. Since I'd conquered breathing, he was on me about my tight jaw.

"Li, there you are," I said, with more gaiety than I felt. My stomach fluttered with nerves once more.

"Good evening." Li sat in the chair next to me and unbuttoned his jacket. He wore a fine heather-gray suit that made his dark eyes seem even brighter than usual. How I longed to trace my finger along the edge of his jawline. Just once. That's all I asked. To know, finally, what his taut skin felt like under the pads of my fingers.

He looked at me and then James. "Is everything all right?"

"Yes, quite right," James said. "We were discussing my future as a Barnes."

Li chuckled as he placed his napkin over his lap. "You'll be a blessed man to have them take you into the fold." He glanced at me. "I know I have been."

Henri brought us plates of fresh oysters on the half shell. After he left, I turned to Li. "Please, tell me what you found out at the embassy," I said. "I can't wait another moment."

"We have a lot of information to tell you." Li dug an oyster from its shell and popped it into his mouth, then chased it with a sip of white wine. He wiped his upper lip with the crisp white napkin. "Unfortunately, what we found out was not entirely encouraging." He looked straight into my eyes.

I braced myself for bad news. "Go ahead."

"There are thousands of orphans, casualties of the war," Li said. "France has set up a foster system to deal with the influx of those who have no parents as well as children who have lost fathers in the war, leaving their mothers without the means to support them. These children are sent to families who can teach them to farm or run other enterprises. Not adopted, mind you, but simply taken in, both as servants and members of the family. It's unclear if we can take them out of the country in the same kind of arrangement. There's a shortage of servants in France, and the children are used to fill the gap. Thus, we may run into some resistance."

"People see them as laborers and servants?" I asked, immediately angered. "They're children."

Li nodded. "In fact, the man at the embassy told me the boys were probably taken in by the fight group under false circumstances. As in, they told the boys they would be sent far away to perform hard labor if they did not come and fight for money. The boys, not knowing any better, went with the men."

"What does that mean?" I asked. "We can't take them home? We have to leave them with the monsters who make them fight each other?"

"Not necessarily," Li said. "When your father comes, he can make a case for fostering them. Although it's unusual that the boys would be taken out of the country, it is possible for it to be done."

"They're living on the streets. No one wants them." I looked down at the plate of ice, seeing it melt in the warm summer air.

"It's not true that no one wants them," Li said. "There are many families who would want to foster two boys who could be trained to help on a farm, for example."

How could this be? Such a ridiculous, unforgiving law, set up to give people free labor. Were most of them interested in children only to use on farms or as domestics? Or, worse, were they sent to cruel and abusive homes? The only way I knew with certainty that they would be well-cared for was to take them home to my family. I fervently wished for my father and his soothing voice here, assuring me that everything would be fine.

"Whatever is the case, we will take them home with us," I said with more confidence than I felt. "Papa will arrange it somehow."

"He has the means," Li said. "And perhaps some influence. We'll have to wait and see. Until then, the embassy advised that we keep it quiet that we have two children living with us. Ones we essentially found on the streets."

"We can't give up." I thumped my fist on top of the table. "There will be a way to give them the future all children deserve." Despite my feisty statement, I'd deflated from the inside out, wishing I could curl into a ball in bed at home in Emerson Pass and forget I had promised the boys a safe future. Was this all a ridiculous notion? Had I gone too far, thinking I had the kind of influence over the world that Papa did? He was a man. A rich man. One who could make things work the way he wanted. Even with him on my side, which I wasn't even sure he would be, I didn't have the kind of influence he had. What if I let everyone down with my impulsive, emotional decisions? I'd made a promise to the boys that I would get them off the streets, but what if I'd made their lives worse? Should I have let well enough alone?

"Fiona, you've set it all in motion," Li said. "Now is not the time for doubt."

"True enough," James said. "We're in it now, and we'll see it all the way through."

"We'll triumph in the end," Li said.

Tears came to my eyes as I gazed from one to the other. These fine men, coming to my service and in fact buoying my spirits. "Thank you, both."

An image of Cymbeline flying off the side of our mountain with her feet attached to skis came to me. She'd not worried about her lack of influence or power. Cym had done what she needed to do to get what she wanted. As outlandish as dressing like a boy was, it had allowed her to compete. She'd won, too. I closed my eyes briefly, imagining her here with us. She would wave her oyster fork like a magic wand and tell me not to worry.

Jo had brought a library to our town when she was my age. We were women who could do extraordinary feats if we wanted them badly enough.

We would figure it out together. Just like the two men next to me, my family would not let me down. They'd see that I was right.

"I had a letter from Mama this afternoon. She wrote to say they'd be here in a month. They'll know what to do. I'm going to write to Cym and Jo as well, so that the family knows what's coming. My sisters are no wallflowers. They know how to get things done. Who knows? They might know of a couple looking to adopt." I stopped, realizing I was babbling.

Li looked over at me. "Until then, we'll take care of the boys and teach them as much English as they can absorb. We don't want to cause trouble with the authorities, so we'll stay quiet and escape attention. All right?"

"Yes, of course," I said. "I'll cause no more trouble." My throat tightened. I scooped the oyster from its shell but still did not eat it. "And now I've gotten you into more of a mess with these boys. We don't even know them. They could be robbing us blind at this very moment."

"I thought you didn't care if they were thieves?" Li asked, a twinkle in his eyes.

I twisted my napkin into a rope. Sweat dampened the end of my nose. I'd said I didn't care, but in truth, I wasn't sure. The light of day brought doubts. "I don't know. That's just it, I can't predict the future."

James grinned and grabbed another piece of bread. "We must have faith in our fellow man. Or boys as the case may be."

"He's right," Li said. "I have utter faith that we're doing the right thing."

"You do?" I asked, surprised. "I thought you were despairing of me."

"Never." Li shook his head. "I shall never despair of you."

We exchanged a smile. For the first time since I'd told him my feelings all those months ago now, it seemed we were back to being Fiona and Li, best friends and muses to each other. "Thank you," I whispered.

Finally, I was able to pay attention to the oysters, displayed beautifully on top of ice and garnished with lemon wedges, shallots, and vinegar.

"Will you want to go home once your parents arrive?" James asked after a moment. "Instead of staying longer?"

"Yes, I'd like to go home," I said. "What about you two? Will you be ready in a month's time?"

"I need to get home to Grandmother," Li said. "But I'm here with you until you're ready."

"As am I," James said.

"You're too kind." Contentment and warmth covered me like a favorite blanket. "Thank you, both, for putting up with my impulsive scheme. I'm humbled by your loyalty."

The men exchanged a glance. "It is we who are humbled by your kind heart," James said.

"An example of how to live well," Li said.

Overcome with emotion, I busied myself with the oysters to hide my stinging eyes. "We'll have Gabriella to help us with the boys on the trip home," I said, changing the subject.

"Has she agreed to come?" Li asked.

I nodded. "There's nothing for her here. Her baby died. She lost her love during the war. A fresh start will be good for her."

"Well, at least she'll look like everyone else," Li said, an edge creeping into his voice. "She won't be hassled on the ship as I was."

We were quiet for a moment until James asked, "What happened?"

"The usual snubs," Li said. "I wasn't allowed in the dining room. They would have refused me the first-class ticket had your brother not called in a favor somehow. The staff asked that I have my meals in my room and not with the rest of the first-class diners."

Nausea made the evening's heat even more cloying. I'd had no idea of his troubles. He'd not shared any details of his journey with me, so it was easy for me to pretend they weren't there. "Theo had to help with a ticket?"

"It was Flynn, actually. He has more ties in the business community."

I picked up my fork but changed my mind and set it back on

the table. Shame had replaced the hunger in my stomach. I'd caused Li a lot of distress. It hadn't occurred to me that he would have trouble on the ship. Why hadn't it? He'd been telling me the truth about the racism he faced, and yet I dismissed it. I didn't want to hear it. Not really. I wanted to pretend it did not exist. Small freedoms and respect I took for granted were not part of his experience. "I'm sorry about the ship. I'm sorry for not understanding the ways of the world and how hard it is for you."

"Fi, don't. It's fine," Li said.

"It's not fine," I said. "I've done you a terrible disservice. Dismissing you instead of fully taking in what you've been telling me. I'm sorry. It is easy for me to pretend that it doesn't exist or isn't as bad as you perceive because of how easy it's all been for me. That said, I remain your loyal friend. Whatever challenges come your way, I will be there with you."

Li hung his head, his glossy hair falling over his eyes. "Fiona, that's just the thing. I do not want you to have to be troubled by my fate. It is not your burden."

My fingers traveled across the tabletop to rest on his arm. "I'm your friend and I love you, which means your troubles are mine. Whatever it is you face, I will be there by your side, just as you've been by mine."

He covered my hand with his and looked into my eyes. "Fi, you're so good. Which is what terrifies me. I'm worried you'll act without thinking in your defense of me." He scooped horseradish and shallots onto an oyster.

"I'll not," I said. "You have my word."

James raised his glass. "Let's toast to you, Fiona. For your big heart and clever mind, for being the sort of friend we all wish we could be. We must believe that all will work out as it should. For now, we go forward with our best intentions and a lot of prayers for all of us."

We clinked our glasses and downed the remainder of the

crisp wine that smelled of green apples and tasted of honey-suckle. I ate the rest of my oysters, enjoying them more than I had anything in a long time. Li was here. He'd forgiven me. James was now part of our family. Soon, we'd have everything sorted about the children.

Henri brought our next course, plates of wide noodles with a ragout gravy. He poured us glasses of Bordeaux. I exclaimed at the delicious aroma. "I smell blackberries, isn't that right, Henri?"

"No, it is not blackberries. Tobacco and chocolate." Henri made one of his haughty sniffs, followed by a remark about our lack of knowledge about French wines. Behind that, however, I could see a genuine affection in his dark eyes. We'd won him over, slowly.

"*Merci*, Henri," I said. "Regardless of my untrained nose, I will enjoy it immensely."

"*Je vous en prie*, Mademoiselle Barnes." He bowed his head.

We clinked glasses again. Then we gave ourselves fully to the savory dishes and fine wine. For the moment, we would enjoy the evening. Tomorrow would bring what it would bring. Regardless, we would be together, and that's all that mattered.

19

LI

OVER THE NEXT FEW WEEKS, A ROUTINE OF SORTS CAME TO OUR unusual household. Our instincts told us to keep the children away from Mr. Basset. He was not our friend. If he learned about our hopes of taking the twins home with us, he was sure to foil it if possible. When he came for Fiona's lessons, either James or I took the boys out to the park where we walked or looked at dogs and people. With each opportunity, I taught the boys new vocabulary until they knew about thirty English words in total. One day, as we were walking toward the park, we passed by a shop with kites hanging in the window.

Beaumont, who spoke only when directly asked a question and never made any kind of fuss, stopped in front of the window. He pointed at a colorful kite hanging in the left corner and spoke to his brother in French. *How pretty it is*, he said to his brother. *So many colors. Could we have it?*

Bleu conveyed all this to me, although at this point in time, I could understand the boys pretty well. They spoke slowly when I was around, which helped considerably.

"Can you ask me for the kite in English?" I asked them.

Beaumont looked up at me from his large eyes framed with dark lashes. "Kite. I want."

"Good," I said. "Yes, you may have the kite, but you must share it with your brother."

I'd lost him with the additional instruction, so I repeated the concept in French. *"Partager avec ton frère."*

"Oui, oui," Beaumont said, bouncing on his toes.

I'd not seen him this excited. Bleu was quick to smile and laugh, especially with Gabriella, with whom he did not have the language barrier. In contrast, his brother was quiet. Often I woke in the night to hear him crying out in his sleep. *"Arrêtez, vous devez arrêter."* Stop, you must stop. It chilled my blood to think of what or whom he was pleading with in his dreams.

We went into the shop and came out with a kite in the shape of a dragon. The boys talked about it all the way to the park. *How would we fly it? Was there enough wind? Would it fly into the Seine if they weren't careful?*

Once there, I put it together, including attaching the string. There was a nice breeze that morning but probably not enough to carry it far. I explained this to them but they were undaunted, asking me to please try.

I ran with it, letting go of the string little by little until, by a miracle, it lifted into the air and sailed high above us in the wind. After I had it flying for a while, I gave each of them a turn. The wind picked up a little by this time and I was afraid they might be lifted from the ground and taken from me. But I needn't have worried. They were fine. Sadly, the wind died down after another fifteen minutes and the kite came tumbling to the ground, smashing into the grass. By then, the boys were hungry for lunch and physically tired so agreed without consternation to ending our outing with a visit to a café for a midday meal.

We stopped at a *boulangerie* that had sandwiches stacked in its display case. I bought three made from prosciutto and a creamy cheese. We sat under an umbrella on the patio to wait. I'd splurged on lemonades for the boys, which they greedily drank while we waited for our sandwiches.

I told them to stop once they'd reached halfway, worried they'd spoil their lunch with all the citrus and sugar. They were obedient children and not yet accustomed to their full stomachs, thus full of gratitude. Fiona had supervised their attire this morning, dressing them in knickers and cotton shirts. She'd made a point to dress them individually instead of in identical clothing. Apparently, her brothers had hated that when growing up. I'd not known this about the twins. How little we noticed about one another, I thought.

We ate our sandwiches in silence, other than appreciative grunts from my young friends. There wasn't a crumb left from any of us when something out of the corner of my eye drew my attention. The boys went rigid and paled, losing all the healthy flush from our exercise in an instant.

It was the referee from the fight, and he was making his way toward us, as red-faced as the boys were pale. Now that I understood more of the way the foster care worked in France, I filled with trepidation. He could legally take them from us, if I guessed correctly.

I'd not had much of a chance to take in his appearance the first time I'd seen him but now I got a full look. He charged up our table and shook his fist at me and then rattled off rapid French that I didn't understand. But in this case, I needed no translation to know what he was saying. The boys slipped out of their chairs and hurled themselves onto my lap, each taking a leg.

"What do you want?" I asked in French. "Speak slowly, please."

The gist of it was this. These were his boys. He'd agreed to foster them and they were to come back to work for him immediately.

I asked him about his wife. "Where is she? Where do you live? I need to know if these boys are safe." At the moment they were trembling on my lap. How could he have pitted these scrawny boys against each other? They weighed no more each than a bag of flour.

The patrons at the other tables were staring at us. Several of the women seemed aggrieved on our behalf. I heard someone call out to the owner to call the police.

"Il n'y a pas de femme." I have no wife. He took care of the boys by himself, he said. They were his to do with as he pleased.

This was a bit of a bluff, but when I'd talked to the people at the embassy, they'd told me only married couples were allowed to foster the children. I mentioned this to my burly friend, followed by a question about whether his fostering of the boys had gone through the formal process?

His fists clenched at his sides. He didn't answer my question, other than to curse at me in French. "I'll be back. This isn't the end."

He stormed away, but not before turning back to give us one more thunderous and frightening scowl.

The boys continued to cling to me. I told them as calmly as I could muster that they were safe. He could not take them. *"C'était contraire à la loi, ce qu'il a fait."* My voice shook. The man had alarmed me as well.

"Do we have to go back to him?" Bleu asked me. "He hit us with his fists. We don't want to return." All of this was in French, but I was able to understand and answer back in their language.

"You're staying with me and Miss Fiona."

"America?" Beaumont asked in English, surprising me.

"Would you like to go to America?"

"Gabriella said there are mountains. Very high ones," Bleu said. "And that it's pretty there and that we could go to school."

"That's all correct."

They'd crawled off my lap by now. The owner brought them each a bowl of gelato, perhaps sympathizing with the traumatic turn our lunch had taken.

"Tell us more," Bleu said before lifting his spoon to his mouth. "Is there gelato there?"

"Not gelato but ice cream. Very similar," I said. *"C'est comme une fête chez les* Barnes." Fiona's family is like a party. *"Ils font de la crème glacée sur leur véranda."* I described how on warm summer days they sometimes made ice cream on the back porch. I described the ice cream maker, how each of the family members took a turn cranking the lever. *"On utilise une manivelle, comme ça."* I moved my hand in a circular motion.

"Will we live with you and Fiona like we do here?" Bleu asked.

"You'll live with someone in Fiona's family. We do not yet know who. Not me, though." I told them about my sister and grandmother, how we lived in our own cottage.

"Mais vous et Fiona êtes mariés?" Beaumont asked. But you and Fiona are married?

I shook my head and left it at that. Explaining the complicated relationship I shared with Fiona was not possible for any eight-year-old to understand, especially given the language barrier.

"We want to live with you and Fiona," Bleu said. "In the mountains. Like a real family."

I didn't know what to say, other than to tell them to eat their gelato before it melted.

"Will she marry James instead?" Bleu asked. These boys didn't miss much, language barrier or not, I thought.

I closed my eyes, pained at the image his question brought to mind. A picture of Fiona in a wedding dress with James by her side made me worry my lunch would come up. The idea of it made me ill. No, I reminded myself. They were not interested in each other. Fiona loved me. I had yet to know what to do about it. I couldn't seem to bring myself to tell her the truth of my feelings. Any time I tried, the words would not come and the feelings of fear and guilt overtook me.

"You must not let her marry James," Bleu said. "She is made for you."

I didn't know if the meaning was lost in translation until Beaumont said, *"Elle est votre âme sœur."* She is your soul mate.

"No, princesse," Bleu said. *"Et vous un prince."*

"How do you know about *âme sœur?*" I asked. "Or *princesse?*"

"We have mother once upon a time," Beau said. "She read to us from a book with fairy tales. We learned about princesses and how they're rescued by their prince."

"I don't think Fiona needs rescuing," I said more to myself than them. "Even if she thinks she does."

"She rescued us," Bleu said. "She's very brave."

We could agree on that, I thought.

"You marry her and we'll be a family," Beaumont said. "In America."

How was this boy talking all of a sudden? The kite flying had loosened his tongue.

"It's not so simple," I said, even though I knew they couldn't possibly understand. They didn't seem to notice that I looked different than Fiona. Growing up in Emerson Pass, no one had noticed either. The other children were accustomed to us. They didn't see any differences. Maybe children were incapable of noticing the distinctions of one race over another. Or, if they noted them, those variances meant nothing to them. Kids were kids. Later, they would learn to see every nuance of race and somehow that would translate into hate.

"J'ai prié pour une famille," Bleu said. *Prayed for a family.* "And then you come." He made a swooping gesture with his hand. It was like the way Fiona had stormed in and taken them from the ring to the apartment.

Beaumont's face lit up into a smile. His cheeks had filled out over the last few weeks. The little street urchin was no longer visible. "We will go America. Be family," he said before taking another lick of his gelato.

How was it possible to resist them or Fiona? For the thousandth time since arriving in Paris, I wondered if I was doing the right thing, resisting love? These boys, even after all they'd experienced, were embracing the love offered them. Why couldn't I?

A WEEK OR SO LATER, WE TOOK THE BOYS OUT TO RIDE THE carousel. By the time we got home, we were all tired from the heat and walking so much. When Fiona suggested a simple supper at home for all of us, I agreed.

Gabriella had the night off. Fiona had convinced her to take a few days off to visit her mother in her village north of Paris in the Champagne region. We'd taken for granted how much she'd done with the boys, given our exhaustion that evening.

"I don't know how Jo does it," Fiona said, stifling a yawn. "Boys, please go wash up for supper."

They didn't need me to translate commonplace phrases. Every day they picked up more.

We gave them their baths and got them into their pajamas. Fiona and I took turns reading to them before bed. One book in French and another in English. We'd gotten a half dozen books from the bookshop on the corner and by now we assumed they had them memorized. I figured it would help with English phrases to see the same story again and again.

I cuddled with Beaumont on one twin bed, and Fiona took the other. Since we'd ordered the beds, I'd slept in the sitting room on one of the couches. It wasn't bad and I didn't complain, because Fiona would have offered up her room to me, which was out of the question. I was her guest. She needed to sleep in her own bed.

Bleu scratched his head. This went on for the length of the storybook. Then I noticed Fiona also itching her head.

Oh dear, I thought. *Nits.* Fai and I had had them the summer before we moved in with the Barnes. Grandmother had used a comb to painstakingly remove them.

"Does your head itch?" I asked Bleu in French.

He nodded, looking ashamed. He knew. They'd had them before, obviously.

"What about you?" I asked Fiona.

"A little." She flushed. "You don't think it's nits, do you?"

"Could be. I'll need to examine you all in a better light." I instructed the boys to head into the living room for inspection.

I sat them down side by side on the sofa and turned on a side table lamp. With the comb, I lifted Bleu's thick hair first. Although the style was now short, the thickness remained. Regardless, right away I saw the tiny insects on the hair at the nape of his neck.

"Yes, there they are," I said.

Beaumont had none. "His hair's too short," I said to Fiona. "Nothing to hold on to."

"Me next," Fiona said, itching the back of her head.

I stood behind the couch and asked her to take out her combs. She did so, letting her curls cascade around her neck and face. I spotted several right away. "Sorry, Fi. You've got them too."

She groaned and covered her face with her hands. "Can we get rid of them?"

"Yes, we need vinegar and oil. I'll have to coat your hair and comb them out." My mouth twitched, wanting badly to break into a grin.

Fiona shot daggers at me with her eyes. "This isn't funny."

Beaumont giggled. His brother spoke sharply to him in

French but seemed to forget the scolding when his head itched again.

I turned back to Bleu. "Would you like me to cut your hair short like Beaumont's? It'll be less hot and all the nits will be gone."

He nodded, explaining that he'd been forced to grow it long so he would look different from his brother.

"We'll need a pair of sharp scissors," Fiona said, despair in her voice. "This is awful. Our friends are headed here tonight. We could infect them."

"Don't worry," I said. "I'll run out to the shops to get proper scissors. Put a note on the door explaining why they shouldn't come in."

"No, call James. Ask him to bring scissors for us," Fiona said. "Anyway, you can't go out. You might have them too. I should check your head."

"We've all been out all day." Even as I said it, I knew it wasn't a good argument. Fiona wouldn't want to take a chance we'd give them to anyone else, especially if we'd already done so.

"We have a problem," I said when James answered the phone. "Nits. Bleu and Fiona both have them."

"Lice?" James asked, sounding scandalized. "Poor Fiona. She's distraught, I suppose?"

I glanced at her. She had both hands in her hair, itching away. "Terribly," I said, trying not to laugh.

"It's still not funny," Fiona said.

"We need scissors to cut Bleu's hair," I said to James. "But I don't know what to do about Fiona's."

She shot me another scathing look.

"You'll need vinegar and oil," James said. "With that combination, you'll be able to get them out. My nephew had them last summer. Nasty little critters."

"Do you think you can find some scissors that will cut hair?" I asked.

"Yes, I have a barber friend. I'll stop by and get them, then head over."

"Tell the others not to visit tonight," I said. "Fiona's request."

"I'm sure they'll all be grateful," James said.

"He'll bring us scissors," I said to Fiona.

From the couch, she said, "Tell him just to leave them by the door. We don't want to infect him. And tell him to tell the others not to come by tonight."

"Come on over here," Fiona said. "I'll look at your head."

"I don't have them," I said after I placed the earpiece back onto the phone. "Nothing itches." Regardless, I sat and told her to look away.

She stood behind me. Her slender fingers riffled through my hair. "It's like silk, this hair," she muttered under her breath.

"And no nits, correct?" I asked.

"I don't see anything."

"Don't sound so disappointed," I said, bubbling over with laughter.

"How is it that I have them and you don't?" Fiona asked.

I didn't know why. I'd held the boys close that very afternoon. "I'm lucky, I guess. Come on, let's mix our concoction."

"Might as well get on with it," Fiona muttered.

I stifled any further laughter. Someday she might find this amusing, but now was not the time.

———

THIRTY MINUTES LATER, BLEU AND FIONA WERE SITTING SIDE BY side in the bathroom. I'd mixed together vinegar and oil in a bowl and planned on spreading it over all the hair, then using the comb section by section to get the nits and their eggs.

We'd left Beaumont in the sitting room to look at a picture book while I worked on his brother's head. I'd stripped Bleu's shirt and had him put on his old knickers. He'd filled out since we'd brought him home with us. I could no longer see his ribs when he breathed, I noticed, as I picked up the scissors James had brought by the apartment. I held them up to the light. "They seem sharp."

Fiona shivered despite the warmth of the small bathroom. "Maybe you should cut mine off, too."

"No, we'll comb yours out." I wasn't physically capable of cutting Fiona's black curls. They were too precious to me. If it took me all night, I would rid her of the unwanted guests.

"You ready?" I asked Bleu.

He nodded and wrapped his arms around his bare stomach, clearly undeterred by this latest drama.

"Here we go then." I gathered a section of Bleu's hair and chopped. The clump fell to the floor, where I'd laid newspapers. I would take them down to the garbage later. "This will rid us of them."

Systematically, I moved around his head, leaving only about an eighth of an inch of hair, and dropped my trimmings onto a newspaper on the floor. His scalp had several scars I hadn't seen before now. "Look at these," I said to Fiona in English.

Her eyes went cold at the sight of what must have been cuts and gashes. "I've never said a curse word in my life, but I really want to now. Ask him where he got them."

"Where did the scars come from?" I asked him in French.

His thin shoulders lifted into a shrug. "Here and there. Before our mother died, there was a man who lived with us. He liked to beat our heads. Then afterward, with the bad man."

I caught Fiona's gaze. "What did he say?" Her brow furrowed.

"He says they came from various places." I snipped another lock of hair. "Including a man who lived with them before they lost their mother."

"There is a place in hell for him," Fiona said, sounding disgusted.

After I finished cutting all of Bleu's hair, I scrutinized him. Even cut short, there was a chance for the bugs to cling to the strands. It would be best to shave his head entirely. I asked Fiona her opinion and she agreed. I explained it all to Bleu, half expecting him to protest a blade that close to his head. Instead, he looked up at me with trusting eyes and asked if it would be like I did in the morning to my face. "Yes, just like that."

"I'll be like you, then?" Bleu asked.

"Yes, a little like me," I said.

Fiona asked me to translate and I did so. She smiled over at Bleu before returning her gaze to me. "He admires you. Do you see the way he looks at you?"

"I hope he understands it's his head I'm shaving and not his face." I went to the cabinet and pulled out my shaving powder and razor. While I mixed it up, Fiona told Bleu to get one of the picture books from the sitting room to look at while I did the deed.

He scampered off, returning just as I'd finished mixing the shaving powder into a cream. "Now, sit here again," I said.

When he was seated, I put cream on the top of his head and as gently as I could, scraped the blade over his scalp. Little by little, I progressed around his head until it was as smooth as a billiard ball. I stood back to gaze at my work. He seemed smaller and thinner without his hair, more like his brother. For the first time, I could see how they were truly identical.

He ran a hand over his head. My stomach clenched, worried he would be upset. Instead, he commented that no bug could cling to him now. "Too, my head's no longer so hot," Bleu added in French as he looked at himself in the mirror and grinned. "*Je suis beau.*"

"You *are* handsome," Fiona said.

"You understood him?" I asked.

She scratched the side of her head. "I'm learning. Catching enough words that I can sometimes piece things together."

Bleu grinned at her. *"Je suis un garçon propre maintenant."*

"Yes, you're a good boy."

"He said he was a clean boy," I said, laughing.

"Clean is a nice thing to be," Fiona said. "But good is better."

"I'm a good boy," Bleu said in English. "And a clean boy."

"Other than the nits," Fiona said, chuckling. "Your English is sounding very good. I'm proud of you."

He looked at her blankly. I translated to him with the French word for *proud*. *"Elle est fière de toi."*

An expression suitable to Fiona's praise drifted over his face, leaving him looking content and happy with himself. I brushed stray hair from his shoulders with a rag.

Fiona went to the tub and turned on the water. "Speaking of clean, you'll need a bath before you go to bed. I'll need to change his sheets, too, won't I?" she said under her breath before looking at me. "Would you watch the water and I'll get clean pajamas for him? Gabriella will do the washing when she returns tomorrow."

"I'll look after teeth brushing and bath," I said. "Send his brother in to do the same?" The twins' teeth had needed a good cleaning when they came to us. They would both lose their baby teeth soon, thankfully, as they were sure to have cavities.

About then Beaumont wandered into the bathroom. He grinned at the sight of his brother's new hairstyle, or lack of one. "Me too," he said. "I want to match my brother."

"It's not a bad idea," Fiona said. "That way we know he's safe from critters."

"All right then," I said to Beaumont. "Come sit."

While Fiona went to strip their cots and put new sheets and pillowcases on, I shaved Beaumont's head, noticing he too had scars, but not as many as his brother. Bleu was the protector of the two of them. I could easily imagine him jumping into danger to save his brother.

A bit later, both twins were bathed and ready for bed. I

offered to tuck them in while Fiona changed into clothes suitable for a possible dousing of vinegar and oil. Once I had them in their cots, which they'd begged to have scooted close together, Beaumont asked for a story. I told them they couldn't have one tonight because it had gotten too late. Lately, I would tell them a story in English about my childhood growing up with Fiona. I don't know how much they understood, but they seemed to love them regardless. They both looked up at me from their cocoons with such disappointment in their eyes that I relented. "A short one," I said.

"*Oui, oui*," they said together.

I closed my eyes for a moment, hoping to conjure up a memory to share with them. "Have I told you about the time Fiona and I started piano lessons?"

They shook their heads as they instinctively moved closer together. My eyes grew scratchy as I took in their small, newly bald heads. They were like two little bald birds in a nest.

"Once upon a time, when Fiona was five years old, she asked her mother and father if she could take piano lessons. At the Barnes estate, which was vast and very beautiful with dark floors and big windows and plush furniture, there was a baby grand piano, like the one in our apartment here. Only this one was never played. Fiona's first mother, who died when Fiona was only a baby, had played. For five whole years, it sat all alone, unplayed. A teacher came to the house and Fiona began her lessons. She was quick to understand and to get better. One day, while I was coming up from the kitchen where my grandmother worked, I heard her playing. The sound was so nice that something inside me changed." I paused, thinking of how to best describe the feeling music gave me, especially when it came from Fiona.

"It was as if I'd heard the sound a home would make. Like nothing else had ever come before, and it was only the music that I needed to make sense of everything. I'd come from nothing, like you two. I lived with my grandmother and my sister Fai in a shack. If we'd not been asked to come live at Lord Barnes's home, I don't know what would have happened to us. We might have died that winter."

"Like us?" Bleu asked. "In the cold winter?"

I blinked, surprised he'd understood that part. "Correct. Since we'd come to the big house and been given beds and warm meals every single day, I'd grown strong and curious. When you have enough to eat and a place to rest your body during the night, it allows you to think about more than the hunger in your stomach. I was able to go to school and I learned English there, just like you're learning now."

They nodded and smiled, obviously pleased with themselves.

"By the time I heard Fiona practicing, I knew English. I was getting good marks on my lessons. At night, I slept in the room with my sister and grandmother. I was happy there. The twins were my friends."

"Fiona's brothers?" Bleu asked.

That's right. I'd told them about Flynn and Theo in some of my other stories.

"But there was something missing. Music was missing." I held up my fingers. "Playing with my own hands. So I asked Lord Barnes if I could take lessons too."

I took a pause to breathe and Beaumont asked, "Did he say yes?"

"He did. I was allowed to take a lesson just after Fiona, and then we learned to play violin. I was especially good at it, so that became my favorite way to make music. When Fiona and I were older and had learned a lot more, we began to play together. Then, when I was grown, Lord Barnes arranged for me to go study music at a university in a big city called Chicago."

"Did Fiona go with you?" Bleu asked.

"No, she was too young to go with me. She was still a child."

"Did you miss her?" Beaumont asked.

"You understand what I'm saying?" I asked.

"Our English is better," Bleu said.

"It's very much better." They were like little sponges, these two. "Yes, I missed her. But I thought of her as a kid back then. She was still growing up. When I came home from Chicago, though, she was all grown up."

I smiled, remembering the first time I'd seen her after I returned home. She'd been in the garden and wore a large-brimmed hat and held a basket of vegetables in her arms. She'd dropped them at the sight of me standing there by the rose-bushes and rushed to hug me. I'd been taken aback at the woman standing before me.

When I'd left, she'd still looked like a girl, but at fifteen she was no longer a child. Still, she'd been too young for me to think of her that way. It wasn't until later that I knew what it was to fall in love with her. Now she was as much a part of me as music. "She was pretty. Just like she is now." In fact, she hadn't changed much since then. If anything, she'd grown lovelier, leaving all hints of a girl behind. "When we were back together again, we started to play music all over town. At church and at dances."

"Then you married and lived happily ever after like the princess and the pea?" Bleu asked in French before yawning.

"Those are only fairy tales," I said. "Not like real life."

"But why?" Beaumont asked. "Can't they be true for someone?"

"We'll see," I said, noncommittally. "For now, you two must get your rest. We've had a big day."

I placed a hand on each of their foreheads before turning off the lamp. "Sweet dreams, little princes," I whispered.

"*Bonne nuit,*" one of them said.

FIONA GROANED AS SHE FURIOUSLY SCRATCHED HER HEAD. "I should have known I had these. I woke up this morning with an itchy head. Even after a good scrubbing."

"I had them once, before we came to live with you," I said to her. "Grandmother had to get them out with her old comb. No vinegar or oil, but she managed somehow."

Fiona moved to sit in the hardback chair. "Get it over with as quickly as possible, please."

As best I could, I soaked her hair with my potion, then began the tedious process of combing through strands a dozen at a time.

"This is disgusting," Fiona said. "But a small price to pay to take the boys home."

"I agree." I poured more olive oil into the small bowl where I would dump the bodies.

"You would, you're not the one itching like mad."

I ran the comb through another clump, successfully scraping away one of the bugs and loosening eggs close to her scalp.

"Are they still alive?" Fiona asked, peering into the bowl. "Oh, goodness, is that one moving?"

I squished him or her with the end of my comb. "Not anymore."

"I'm quite undone." Fiona giggled, high-pitched. "Thank you for helping me, even if I am angered by your obvious enjoyment of my predicament."

"I'm not enjoying it," I said.

"You are, you beast." She glared at me, but her eyes twinkled now.

My stomach fluttered. I was not accustomed to being physically close to her. The curve of her slender neck beckoned to me. Not that I'd ever done such a thing, but I longed to brush my lips against the skin under her ear, regardless of critters. How was a woman this beautiful with her hair slathered in oil and vinegar?

"I feel like a salad's on top of my head," Fiona said, and giggled again. "Why *is* this so amusing to you?"

I continued to comb through another strand but met her gaze in the mirror. "It's not. I simply love having you at my mercy."

"I never thought you had it in you to be so terrible," Fiona said, laughing. "I shall remember this."

20

FIONA

The next few weeks seemed to roll by at a fast pace. I'd gotten a letter from my parents telling me they were extending their time in England by fourteen days. I couldn't decide if I was relieved or disappointed by this news. Between the boys, my lessons, and preparing for the recital, I fell into bed each night exhausted. At least twice a week, our friends joined us for late-night discussions and wine drinking. One night I fell asleep in one of the chairs, coming to only when Li gently shook me awake after they'd all gone home.

Gabriella was a big help and a natural with little children, thank goodness. Without her there, even with Li's assistance, I wouldn't have been able to look after them and do my work. I was beginning to understand what a large undertaking it was to take children into one's home and heart. Every time I thought of my family's reaction, my stomach turned over. What would they think? Would they allow me to keep them?

A letter had arrived from Mama just that morning, prompting me to take action.

Dearest Fiona,

We will be leaving here in a week's time to return to Paris. I can hardly wait to see you and hear about your adventures. Given the date of your recital, we should safely be there in time for it. To say I'm excited to hear you sing would be rather an understatement.

In your last letter, you hinted that you might like to cut your trip short and return home with us. If that's still your inclination, then I will not stop you. If you're enjoying your time and studies, then we have no problem leaving you the rest of the year. However, if you're homesick, there's no harm in coming home early. No one will think less of you, my darling.

I was never one to crave adventure like Flynn and Cymbeline. I'm more like you—all my joys come from my family. This trip has been extraordinary, but I have been left with the distinct feeling that this may be the last one overseas. Your father has enjoyed himself but has found he's adjusted thoroughly to America. He and his brother argued at dinner last night about the class structure in England. As I'm sure you can imagine, your father had strong opinions about all that, given his life in America.

Being away has made me even more sentimental than usual. I've been thinking a lot about those first months when I came to know you children. You were still so little, so precious and sweet. I can remember the first time you wrapped your arms around my neck and snuggled on my lap. In that moment, I knew exactly who I was. Motherhood does that—tells you who you are, all your weaknesses and strengths, all the ways in which you are flawed but also the deep and unselfish love we're all capable of but do not always need. Mothers, well, we need it all.

I should close to get this in the post. We leave tomorrow and will spend the last of our time on the coast before heading across the Channel to France, arriving to you on the last week of July. If you should need to write before then, send a letter to the inn where we'll spend our last few days before heading to France. I've included the address below. Otherwise, we'll see you in Paris! Much love and see you soon.

Mama

I set the letter on the desk and smoothed it with both hands. What should I do? Write to her about the boys or wait until she and Papa arrived? I'd not told them Li had joined me, either. Would they be angered by both choices or neither?

I had no idea how she or Papa would respond to my desire to take the boys back to America. What I'd done was so outlandish that I was without experience to guide me. I could only hope that they would see my benevolent act as such and not foolhardy or impulsive. Regardless, I must prepare them for what waited here in Paris.

Dear Mama,

I'm sorry it's been so long since my last letter. I've been monstrously busy the last few weeks.

I raised my pen from the paper, thinking. How exactly would I explain all of it? A pity James wasn't here to act as my editor, I thought, mildly amused at the idea before sobering to my current dilemma. How should I tell them what I'd done? I dipped my pen back in the inkwell and continued.

I'm dashing this off so that it will be at the inn when you arrive. Perhaps you should sit down before you read the rest of this, as I have something surprising to tell you.

Firstly, Li is here with me. The reasons for this are complicated and best told in person. It's nothing to worry over. I'm fine. Li is well too.

Secondly, I've done something out of the ordinary.

I paused to dip my pen once more. *Out of the ordinary* wasn't quite the right phrase for what I'd done, now was it? Regardless, I must continue.

One day when Li and I were out walking along the river, we witnessed a fight between two little boys. Not a scuffle like Flynn and Theo might have done when they were young (or Cymbeline for that matter), but a professional fight. They were in a boxing ring and people were sitting around to watch. They'd asked the boys to fight each other and made bets on who would win. A spectator sport, if you can imagine!

I couldn't stand it. I extricated the boys from the situation and brought them home to my apartment. They're orphans and had been living on the streets, supporting themselves with these boxing matches. I didn't realize it at first, but they're twins. They remind me a little of Theo and Flynn in that Bleu does most of the talking while Beaumont is quiet, always observing. Their mother died of some kind of illness last year. Their father was killed during the war, dying before they ever had the chance to meet him. For many months they've been living on the streets. It sickens me to think of what they've endured.

Thus, I cannot send them back to life on the streets. We have to help them somehow. The longer they've been here with us at the apartment, the more attached we all become to one another. Given their circumstances, Li has a special place in his heart for them. I'm sure you can understand why that would be. They're sweet and innocent and deserve better than what life has given them.

Li and I have been researching what would be best for them. By law, they're not allowed to be adopted except by married couples, one of whom has to be over the of age twenty-eight. However, we're allowed to offer a temporary solution called fostering. As long as the boys are safe and taken care of, the government is satisfied. Taking them home with us to Colorado may be another matter. I'm hoping Papa can do something to help with that. They need to be with our family. That is what I know without reservation. Exactly what that looks like remains to be seen.

You and Papa may be angry at what I've done. I wouldn't blame you, even as it pains me to think so. However, I couldn't leave them there to be at the mercy of those terrible men who treated them like animals. As I've lain awake at night worried about the future, it occurred to me that sometimes decisions have to be made that no one will understand. This was one of them. I'll do whatever it takes to make this right. For them, mostly, but also for me. This is the singular most important thing I will ever do with my life. That much is clear to me. Whatever comes, I shall take responsibility for them. I know I'm young, but what else is there in this life more important than generosity and sacrifice for the sake of a child?

I remember Louisa—how she came to be with the Linds—what you did for her and how that act of kindness rippled so far. Not just for the Linds and Louisa but eventually for Theo. Also, Papa brought Mrs. Wu and two little children home for many of the reasons I chose to bring Bleu and Beaumont back to my apartment. I hope you'll think of both these events when you're deciding my punishment for making such a reckless decision.

I must go now. I long to see you and count the days until you arrive. Love to Papa. XX

Fiona

I quickly put it in an envelope and copied the address of the inn where my parents would be staying, then called out to Gabriella to let her know I was headed to the post. She came out to the sitting room, wiping her hands on her apron. "Would you be able to stop to buy a quart of milk? These boys drank all of it already. They drink so much milk."

I'd noticed that too.

"Will do. I'll return shortly." I reminded Gabriella that the boys and Li had gone out to play in the park and wouldn't be home for at least an hour.

Smiling, she lifted a hand to her flushed cheeks. "Thank goodness Li took them away. They are nuisances, and I am very hot."

As I walked to the post, sweating in the heat of the afternoon, I tried to predict my parents' reaction to my strange news. I didn't want them to be angry with me. They'd never been so. However, they very well could be, and I must be prepared to defend my position as well as present a plan.

I was twenty, I told myself. An adult. I could be their mother. Of course I could. However, what would people think? It would be tolerable if I were a widow raising children alone, but a young single woman? I could probably say goodbye to any chance of a man falling in love with me.

What did I care? It was Li I wanted. As hopeful as I'd been a few weeks ago, all that had been dashed of late. Li had made no mention of any feelings for me whatsoever. I wouldn't care. Soon, it would be a distant longing instead of one that consumed me. When I returned home, I would throw myself into raising the boys and making a life of my own. My sisters and Mama were near should I need help. With our large extended family, I could do this. Plus, I had my trust. What better to use it for than to build a little cottage for the boys and me? A single parent wasn't ideal, but it was a lot better than what they had before I brought them home.

I would have to be enough for them. And for myself.

21

LI

FOR WEEKS, I'D DEBATED THE BEST COURSE OF ACTION FOR MY life. On one hand, my feelings for Fiona were clear, as they'd always been. However, she'd complicated things by bringing the boys into the equation. Raising two little boys would be hard enough for a young woman, but what about one married to a man like me? Would the boys be in danger if I were their guardian?

Their life couldn't be any worse than if they'd stayed here and lived on the streets. But what about a life with Fiona and me? What would that be like for them, better or worse?

I was contemplating all this when Fiona hustled into the room. "I've gotten a telegram from Papa. They'll be here tomorrow."

"So soon?" My stomach hollowed at the thought. Our time as we'd known it was coming to an end.

"Yes, and they're fully aware of what's happening here. You and the boys, that is. I wrote to Mama a few weeks ago and told her about the boys. And of your presence here." She handed me the telegram from her pocket.

Be there tomorrow morning. Stop. Will discuss future plans then. Stop.

"You told her I was here and about the boys?" I asked, not because I didn't know the answer but as an expression of surprise. "Why are you only telling me now?"

"I don't know. I didn't want you to be alarmed." She looked directly at me before smoothing her dress and walking to the windows, where she stood in a sliver of shade. "And run away from me."

"Run away? Where would I go?" I smiled until I realized she was not saying it in jest.

"There's a whole world of places." She glared at me before flexing her fingers as she sometimes did before she played the piano. Did she want to shove me? I couldn't blame her if she did. We'd been skirting the subject of the future for weeks now.

I rubbed the corner of one eye, perplexed. What did that mean? "Are you all right?" Did the prospect of facing her parents make her upset, or had I done something?

"Telling them—it had to be done," Fiona said. She wiped her hands in a discarding motion. "She and Papa should know what to expect when they arrive."

"What did you tell them about me?" I asked. "About why I'm here."

"I told them it was complicated and that I would explain when they arrived."

I studied her. In the silky pastel morning light through the windows, she was as beautiful as she'd always been. Even more strength and determination had seeped into her visage. She was still delicate to look at, but more than ever her exterior belied her interior. Caring for the boys had brought a new aspect of womanhood to her. She was no longer a child. The morning we took the boys home with us, any lasting immaturity had vanished.

"I'm afraid they'll be angry with me," Fiona said. "Not about you—that will perplex them, of course."

"Perplex them?"

"They thought you didn't want to leave your grandmother alone. They'll find it strange that you changed your mind."

I looked away from her steady gaze. She didn't have to say it. My actions perplexed her as well.

"But the boys? They'll think I've lost my mind. Their disapproval used to be one of the worst things I could imagine. Now, however, I have the boys to think of. I have to put all that aside and do what I believe is best. Even if it angers them. They'll come around, eventually."

At great sacrifice to her own life, I thought, but didn't say. I wanted to ask her if she was sure about all of this, but I already knew the answer. Words meant nothing in this scenario. Only actions mattered. She'd made her stand, and she would not back down from it.

I gazed at her, full of admiration and more love than I'd ever thought possible. That was the thing with Fiona. I thought I loved her yesterday, only to wake to another day with even more love in my heart.

"Still, as brave as that sounds," Fiona said, "I'm scared of what they will do. Ultimately, Papa has the power to take away my trust if he wants. Or to forbid the passage of the boys across the seas. I am at the mercy of a man, as I will always be." She peeked up at me from under her lashes.

She did not have to say it; I knew she meant me as well. I'd denied her my love, leaving her no other choice but to continue forth, broken heart be damned.

I should do the same. Leave her be.

The last few nights as I lay awake, restless and hot, I'd thought a lot about what I should do next. My conversation with West was heavy on my mind. To him, it seemed an easy choice. If I loved her, let her know. Give her everything I was capable of giving.

But there lay the rub. How much was there to give? I was not penniless but not rich. I would never be able to give her the kind of lifestyle her father gave her stepmother. A musician's fees were limited. We would live comfortably with full bellies, playing our music as we'd always done as a way to fortify our souls. So, then, what was the problem?

"Are you sure you want to leave Paris early?" I asked. "What about your recital?"

"I don't care about it. I never did. I came here to…" She seemed to think better of what she was about to say and instead walked over to the piano and sat.

I joined her, standing to the side of the bench. She plucked a listless tune on the piano. From the kitchen came the sounds of the boys and Gabriella talking in French about breakfast. She was asking them if they wanted crepes or eggs, and Bleu had answered asking if they could have both.

Basset was due to the apartment any minute. When I'd been able to, I'd stayed in the living room while they had their lesson. He'd predictably behaved himself in my presence.

"I just want to go home," Fiona said. "And see my sisters. Figure out what is next for me and the boys."

I motioned for her to scoot over so I could sit beside her. Her eyes widened in surprise at my request. I'd not sat next to her since she'd told me her feelings all those months ago. The words that came out of my mouth astounded me. I'd not planned them. "What if we were to stay here with the boys?"

"Stay here? In Paris?"

"I'm tolerated here much more than I am in America."

She scooted off the other end of the bench to stand and look down at me. "And by we, how do you mean exactly? Continue to live as we are?"

"Would it be the worst thing for the boys?" I asked.

"Perhaps not." She crossed her arms over her chest, obviously thinking through what I'd said. "What about your grandmother and Fai? But what about us?"

The question hung there for a moment. If indecision and self-doubt were sins, then I was surely doomed to hell.

"What would we do here? Carry on as we have been?" Fiona asked.

I opened my mouth to speak, but nothing came forth. Seconds passed. Too many of them. She took my lack of communication as negative reaction. "Li, this decision to take care of the boys is mine alone. You should feel no obligation. While I've appreciated your help, it is not necessary. When I return home, I shall have my family."

"Fiona, that's not what I meant." Her words cut as painfully as if she'd wounded me with a dull knife.

She was quiet for a moment, before asking softly, "Is there anything you want to say to me before my parents arrive?"

Before I could answer her, the boys came rushing in from the kitchen, chattering away and asking if it was time for them to go to buy new boots.

"Can we speak about this later?" I asked. "Basset will be here any minute."

"As you wish." She shook her head, as if I'd disappointed her once more.

LATER THAT DAY, THE BOYS PLAYED AT THE PARK FOR AN HOUR, running along the paths between flower beds until they were warm and tired. I fed them a lunch from the basket Gabriella had packed of sandwiches and cold water. When we were finished, the three of us, with each of them holding one of my hands, strolled along the busy sidewalks until we reached a shoemaker's shop recommended by Gabriella as a good place to have new boots made for the boys.

While the shoemaker's wife measured and fitted the boys, I sat near the window, grateful for the coolness of the shop after the heat of the day. I could kick myself with or without a pair of boots on for the way the conversation had gone with Fiona. Over the last few weeks, I'd contemplated many times the right course for the next period of my life. It was not myself I thought of, as it hadn't been all along. But now it was not only Fiona that I worried about but the boys as well.

We had become a unit, the four of us, along with Gabriella. The boys had fallen into the habit of our daily lives. Taking me out of the situation would be confusing to them. For that matter, I didn't want to be out of the situation.

The shoemaker's wife, a pleasant woman with a flat face and kind eyes, looked at me for a moment.

"Are you the caregiver of these two?" she asked me in excellent English.

I nodded, unsure how best to answer that question.

"Do you work for their parents?" she asked as she pushed back stray hair from her face. "Are you their tutor?"

"No, I'm a friend of their family," I said, figuring this was the best way to describe it. As if it were any of her business.

"I see. Well, they are lucky to have such an exotic friend."

Exotic? Was that the word for me now?

I gave her a look that I hoped conveyed my sudden dislike for her.

The door of the shop opened and Sandwich and Saffron appeared. "Li, we saw you here and thought we'd come say hello."

They were flushed from the heat but looked well otherwise. I stood to greet them. "We're having the boys fitted for new boots."

"We've just come from lunching with James. Is it true that

you'll be leaving us and taking him with you?" Sandwich asked. She wore a white dress that hung loosely over her hips. A bit of her red lipstick has smeared above her upper lip, making her seem less perfect and thus more likable.

"Fiona believes it's best for us to go," I said. "If we can get everything put together for the boys, that is."

Saffron gave her hair a good flounce to show her displeasure. "I hate that you're going. But our Fiona isn't like most of us, is she?" She lowered her voice, obviously aware the boys were within earshot. "Will she really take them home and care for them forever? Act as their mother?"

"I think that's what she wants," I said, before explaining that her father's opinion would have to be considered before anything was finalized.

"And what about you?" Sandwich asked. "Are you going home with her or will you stay? It seems you belong here with us."

No, I thought. *I belong wherever Fiona is.*

"Yes, you're a freak like us," Saffron said. "You should stay in Paris. Let her go home with the boys without you. We'll have such fun and never let the party end." She stared at me, as if she'd just presented a riddle for me to solve. "Well, what will it be? Stay or go? You must choose one way or the other."

"Indecision is no man's friend," Sandwich said. "Or woman's."

"Why do I feel you're giving me a test?" I asked, without humor.

"Because we are," Saffron said.

"We're thoroughly disgusted with you, if you must know." Sandwich's mouth curved into a smirk. Her eyes drilled a hole through me.

"Running from love should be a crime," Saffron said.

"Especially when one loves as you love Fiona," Sandwich said.

They swept out of the shop without another word. I stood there, flabbergasted. Was it obvious to everyone how I felt about Fiona?

I took in a deep breath and then gathered up the boys. "Time to go home," I said. "Fiona's waiting."

22

FIONA

GABRIELLA AND I HAD JUST FINISHED PUTTING TOGETHER A shopping list for my parents' arrival when I heard a knock on the door. "Who could that be?"

"Perhaps your friends?" Gabriella said. "They might be out of wine."

I chuckled as I hurried to the door. Gabriella was right. My friends did seem to often show up right about cocktail hour.

To my surprise, it was not my colorful friends but Mama and Papa. I teared up at the sight of them, despite my surprise. "What are you doing here? I didn't expect you until tomorrow."

"We had to change a few things around," Mama said. "Long story."

We embraced, and then I ushered them inside. "Li and the boys are out shopping for boots," I said. "But they should be home shortly."

I spoke as if it were completely ordinary that I now had two little boys and my best friend from home living with me.

"We look forward to meeting them," Mama said. "And it's good they're out. We can talk for a few minutes first."

After saying hello, Gabriella left us for the kitchen where she would put tea together for us. "Where is your luggage?" I asked. They'd come without anything, other than Mama's purse.

"We're staying at an inn down the street," Papa said, in a serious tone. "Figuring you had a full house."

"Yes, about that," I said.

"Sit, both of you," Papa said. "We'd like to hear more details of how this all came to be."

"Spare no details," Mama said as she settled beside my father on the sofa.

For the next thirty minutes, I described everything as best I could, including the choices left to us by the French government. "As far as we can tell, it will take someone like you to sort this all out," I said to Papa. "I'm sorry. I know it must all seem rash to you."

"We'll talk about that in a minute," Papa said. "We want to understand exactly what Li is doing here."

Gabriella brought our tea, leaving the tray on the coffee table before excusing herself. I wished I could do the same.

"He came out of a sense of duty," I said. "You see, I wrote to him about Mr. Basset." I explained all of that as delicately as I could. Papa's face had turned red and Mama's white by the time I finished. "But it's nothing to worry over now. With Li and James here, the poor man's been frightened into good behavior."

Mama picked up her cup of tea and sipped without taking her eyes off me. "And how it is going with Mr. West? You've become quite friendly, I take it?"

"Yes, but not that way. We're only friends. In fact, that's another thing I need to tell you." I explained James's situation and that I'd invited him home. "Also, Gabriella will be coming with me as well. She's a lot of help with the boys."

"Goodness, Fiona," Mama said. "You really know how to gather in the stray cats."

"Yes, I suppose I do." I flushed with embarrassment. It was all true, but I had to remain resolute. I'd made promises and had to keep them.

"It's interesting that Li came all the way here when he said he wanted to stay and look after his grandmother." Papa turned to Mama. "Do you find that interesting?"

"I do." They exchanged a smile. "Fiona, it's time to tell us the truth. What are your feelings for Li?"

A feeling of dread engulfed me. Someone had told them. One of my rat siblings. Which one? Probably Josephine, out of a sense of worry. "What do you know and who told you?"

The front door burst open and the twins tumbled in, with Li right behind them. They all stopped and stared at the sight of my parents sitting and having tea. *Here we go*, I thought.

THE BOYS, BLESS THEM, COULDN'T HAVE LOOKED MORE ADORABLE. Although they both had hardly any hair, their big eyes made up for it.

They stared at my mother and father for a moment, then as if they were of one mind, each slipped a hand into Li's.

"Darlings, look what's happened. My mama and papa are here."

"They don't speak much English yet," I said. "And my French is terrible, but Li speaks enough that we make do."

Mama had stood by then and come nearer, wary, knowing what it was to be a stray herself, and knelt near them. "*Bonjour.*"

"*Bonjour,*" the boys said in tandem.

Li explained to them that my parents had come and they were to use their best English to answer questions.

But it seemed the conversation between a former teacher and two boys was simpler than the division of the Atlantic Ocean and two complicated languages. Soon, all three were sitting on the love seat in the corner of the living room, the boys showing Mama their books and speaking to her in French with a little English thrown in every sentence or so.

I had a bit of a moment then, a flashback of one of my earliest memories, sitting next to Mama on the sofa, with Cymbeline on the other side. She'd read to us from one of our favorite books, *The Five Little Peppers*. They'd been like us, I remembered thinking. Five little Barneses.

I sat next to Papa on the couch. He put his arm around me. "Tell me, love, what other trouble have you gotten yourself into since I saw you last?"

I laid my head against his shoulder and sighed. Everything would be all right. Papa and Mama were here, and they still loved me. I caught Li watching me. We exchanged a stiff smile. When would we have the chance to talk? Not anytime soon.

LATER, AFTER THE BOYS WERE TUCKED INTO BED AND FAST ASLEEP, Papa asked us to come sit. Gabriella had disappeared into her room. Lucky girl. I'd have liked to have escaped to mine as well.

"This is quite an entanglement you've come to us with," Mama said. "Mired in complications."

"Legal and otherwise," Papa said.

"Darling, why don't you tell us what you're thinking," Mama said to me. "Other than bringing them home with us, what is your plan? And Li, I'd like to hear from you as well."

"Yes, ma'am," Li said.

"Bringing them home here was my idea," I said. "As is bringing them back to Colorado with us. Li's only gone along with it because I forced him to."

"Is that true?" Mama asked Li.

"While it wouldn't have occurred to me to pluck the boys from their precarious situation," Li said, "I've not been a prisoner to Fiona's whims. She and I have partnered in all of this together. We're both fond of the boys. In fact, I can't imagine leaving here without them. I didn't mean for it to happen, but I feel rather fatherly about them."

Papa crossed one leg over the other. "I see."

"Papa, what made you bring Fai, Li, and Mrs. Wu home?" I asked. "Surely it was the same instinct?"

Papa made eye contact with Mama in a way that made me think she'd brought up this very argument while speaking of the matter. I didn't know if this was good or bad. I held my breath, waiting for the answer.

"Yes, this is a similar thing you've done." Papa smiled kindly at me. "Which I guess means I have only myself to blame."

"Only there is no Mrs. Wu," Mama said. "No one to be their mother, even though they're under our care."

"I'll take care of them," I blurted out. "I've got my trust money. I can build a little house on our property. With the funds I get for performing, I can make a nice living for us. They can go to school and grow up with the rest of the kids in Emerson Pass, just as we did."

Papa took a long look at me. Embarrassed, I shifted my gaze to my lap. I'd acted impulsively and dragged all three of them into this ridiculous scheme of mine. But the boys, I reminded myself. I mustn't forget why I'd done this. "They have no one but me."

"You're prepared to come home and become their mother?" Mama asked. "Do you understand the freedom you'd be giving up? There will be no more nights playing at the club with Li."

I didn't want to be impertinent, but I had to make my argument. "Gabriella will come with me and help me with cooking and cleaning. She can stay with them at night."

"I suppose she could," Mama said, conceding. "There's no reason why that couldn't work quite nicely."

"What about you, Li?" Papa asked. "What are you prepared to give up to take on this fatherly role?"

"Me, sir?" Li looked back at him with eyes like an animal hoping to remain still enough not to be seen.

Papa's expression darkened. His usual laughing eyes deepened in hue as he continued to look at Li. "Tell me something—both of you." His voice had deepened in a way that sent a shiver up my spine.

"Yes, Papa?"

"While you've been playing house here, has it not occurred to you that these boys would be better off having a father and mother?" In all my life, Papa had never raised his voice to me or said a cross word. This is what it was like to be in trouble, I thought. I would have to tell Cym and Flynn I finally understood.

"It's occurred to me," I said. "But I have only myself to offer them." Nervousness made my underarms prickle with heat. How could they think I would be that much of a nitwit? "However, respectfully, Papa, I am better than nothing at all. Even alone, I am better than the boys living on the streets of Paris."

"If I could work it out with the authorities for us to take them home," Papa said, "and that's a big if—we're asking them to give two young boys to a twenty-year-old-girl—is this what you truly want?"

I looked into his eyes. They were not angry or unkind, merely inquisitive. "Papa, as I said in my letter, this might be the most important thing I ever do. What better could I do with my life than take care of two little boys who have no one?"

"What about your future? Your music?" Mama asked. "You'll have to give up so much. Children change everything. All your choices will be made for you because it will only be about what's best for the children. You might never have another good night's sleep for worrying about one or the other of them."

"Yes, I'm young, but Mama, you weren't much older when you married Papa." I cringed at the squeaky tone in my voice.

"This is true." Mama's brow knit as she appeared to think

through what I said. "What if you meet a young man and fall in love? Are you willing to give up a future with him for these boys?"

"If they wished to be with me and didn't understand why I had to do this, then they are not the man for me." My voice cracked. Tears flooded my eyes. The man I wanted was sitting next to me, and yet I could do nothing to change his mind.

Next to me, Li shifted, as if his pants were suddenly uncomfortable. He handed me a handkerchief, which I used while holding my breath. The last thing I needed was to smell his scent. The smell of the man who had held my happiness in his hand. He'd crushed me. Were these boys a substitute for the love I felt for him? Love that would never be returned. *What have I done?* I thought. I've messed with everyone's lives now. The boys would not survive if they were rejected by us. Not after the safety and comfort we'd provided them the last few weeks. I stifled a sob by pressing the handkerchief to my mouth. They'd learned so many English words and phrases. Was it all for naught?

"You said you didn't regret your decision," I said to Mama. "Didn't you?"

"I did and I do not," Mama said. "However, I'm only pointing out the ways in which this will alter your life."

"What about you, Papa? Was raising five children all on your own overwhelming? Were you sorry you had us?"

"Darling, you and your sisters and brothers are my whole life." Papa placed his hand on Mama's knee. "As is this woman right here. Nothing else matters as much to me. Which is why it's hard for us to imagine you giving up all your freedom when you're so young. That said, if it's what you want, then we will help you. You'll have all of us. Barneses stick together. We always have and always will."

I glanced back up at Papa. He was staring at Li, as if he were a stranger instead of the boy he brought home all those years ago.

"Li, you've been quiet," Papa said.

"Yes, sir?" Li asked, raising his gaze.

"Why did you come all the way over here?" Papa asked.

Li glanced at me. "Fiona needed someone here to keep her safe from Basset. When I realized what he was like, I decided to come look after her."

"Yes, I understand. You came all the way here because you thought Fiona needed you. But *why* did you do that? Simply because of friendship? Or a trip to Paris? Whatever the reasons, I want to hear them."

Li cleared his throat and glanced nervously at me before answering. "I can deny Fiona nothing. Any little thing or big thing, I'll do for her if she asks."

"Now we're getting somewhere," Papa muttered under his breath.

"That isn't entirely true, is it?" Mama asked. "The one thing she truly wants from you—you've denied her that."

"Wha-what do you mean?" Li asked, sounding a bit like a frog.

My hands numbed. It seemed as if I rose above the couch, no longer part of my body. Where was she going with this?

"I mean that Fiona has told you her feelings for you," Mama said. "She's in love with you. But you already know that, don't you?"

"Yes, ma'am." Li had turned ghostly pale.

Bells crashed between my ears. What were they doing? How could they ask Li these things? *Please, let the floor drop and me with it,* I prayed silently.

"You stopped everything to come to her," Papa said to Li. "Which is not the move of a man indifferent to a woman's charms." He uncrossed his legs and leaned forward slightly. "Is it?"

"No, sir?" Li asked.

"Is it truly a question to you?" Papa asked, his voice deep and threatening, as was his posture. He seemed ready to pounce. "After all this, you have the nerve to act the innocent?"

"I don't follow." Li's voice shook.

I instinctively moved closer to him.

"Taking a coward's way out," Mama said softly. "It wasn't the way you were raised. You didn't learn it from your grandmother or anyone else in the household, either."

"Coward?" Li seemed as if he too were going to burst into tears. I moved even closer to him, my instinct to protect him.

"Li has nothing to do with this," I said. "This was all me. I've told you that."

Papa shook his head. "Li has everything to do with this. You've come here on false pretenses, haven't you, son? You've not been honest with Fiona."

"What are you talking about?" I asked, so shocked my tears had stopped.

I turned to look at Li. His eyes were downcast and the tips of his ears red. "You haven't lied to me about anything. Tell them, Li." I looked back at Mama. "He's been nothing but good to me. A true friend. He came because Mr. Basset had scared me. I didn't even have to ask him."

Papa's eyes sharpened. "We'll talk about Basset and why you chose to keep that from everyone but Li in a minute. I'd like to stay focused on Li for now. Why don't you tell Fiona how you truly feel about her?"

"What good would it do?" Li spat out the words, as if he'd stifled them for years. "It will only make it worse. My way is better. I'm protecting her. Do you think it hasn't been at great sacrifice to myself? To my sleep? My well-being? I can't sleep, can't eat. Why aren't you happy I've chosen what's best for her? Why would you want me to burden her for the rest of her life? You know what we'd face. You're a benevolent man, Lord

Barnes. I know this better than anyone. But can you sit there and tell me you'd give your blessing to a marriage that will make your precious daughter miserable? Do you really want to watch as her soul slowly gets chipped away until she's nothing but a bitter old woman who gave up everything to marry an outcast?"

My heart beat so fast I thought it might explode from my chest. Dare I hope that he loved me? Was James right? He'd denied his love because of a misguided attempt to protect me?

"I know my daughter," Papa said. "And her love will be enough to guard her from the sharpest of blades. She's a Barnes. Perhaps, even, the toughest and strongest of all my children. She may look like only a pink rosebud, but she has the strong, deep roots of the entire bush. Her strength is like those roots, capable of breaking through rock and clay to find water. If you do not understand that, perhaps I'm wrong about you. Perhaps you don't love her as I believe you do. Maybe you don't deserve her as I've thought you did."

"There's no need to be angry with him because he believes a marriage would put me in harm's way." I spoke through tears, barely able to get the words out. How could they be so cruel? So threatening? Li didn't deserve this.

"We're not angry with him, darling," Mama said. "We simply want him to know that we support you both. If he were brave enough to claim you for his own, that is."

I tilted my head to look at him while tugging on both ends of the handkerchief so hard I thought the fine material might pull apart. "Are they right?" I whispered to him.

Tears dampened Li's eyes. He shifted to face me. "For God's sake, why else would I come halfway across the world after getting your letter? I do love you. Enough that setting you free has felt like the only option." He turned back to Papa. "Lord Barnes, if anything were to happen to her because of me, I would not be able to live with myself. All I want is for her to be safe and happy. This is how I actively love her."

"You must trust and respect her enough to let her choose for herself whether the risk is worth it," Papa said.

"I choose you," I said softly. "You know that."

"How could a man spend any time at all with you and not fall madly and hopelessly in love? All those years when we were younger, you were just a kid, my musical partner but nothing else. Then, something happened. You grew up and suddenly I saw you in a whole different way. You're everything to me. Everything." He lifted his gaze toward my father. "But what are you doing? How could you give your precious daughter to the likes of me?" He swiped at the tears spilling from his eyes, obviously embarrassed to break down in front of us all.

Papa's eyes misted. "Your selfless love is more than I could wish for any of my children. This is one of the reasons I know she will be well taken care of by you. And she will take good care of you. I have every faith in you. Both of you. If you truly love each other—you'll make compromises and work through hardships together. Will it be perfect? No. Nothing ever is."

A strange sense of calm came over me. Li loved me. He actually loved me. I wanted to dance like Cymbeline, kicking my legs and shaking my hips. He'd been torturing himself all this time, thinking it was best for me. "Li, I'm strong enough to withstand anything, as long as you're with me."

"I'm afraid," Li said. "Afraid of letting you go, afraid of keeping you close."

"You're not the first person to be afraid of love," Mama said. "Loving someone opens you to pain and loss, but what's the alternative? Watching Fiona make a life with someone else when you know it's you she wants?"

Papa stood and held out his hand to help Mama to her feet. "We'll leave the two of you and go back to our inn. We'll come by in the morning to figure out how in the world we're going to get those boys home with us."

I stood and hurled myself into Papa's arms. "Thank you."

"I'm proud of you," he whispered in my ear.

I laid my cheek next to the rough material of his summer jacket. "I thought you'd be angry with me."

He stepped back to look me in the eyes. "How could I be when you're only behaving as I've taught you?"

"Do you mean who I love or that I've brought two little strangers into my home?" I asked softly.

"Both. I've realized of late that you're the most like me of all my children. Cym and Flynn take after me—with their desire for adventure and natural leanings toward rebellion, especially those set by society. But I can see that your heart is like mine in many ways." With that, he turned to Mama and offered his arm. "Shall we, my lady?"

Mama giggled as a flush crept up her neck. "That's what they called me at the Barnes estate. I quite like it." She grinned cheekily. She had my father by her side. He was enough. They could speak of love with authority, for they lived in the middle of it every day. All the compromises and grace they made for each other, day in and day out, were the recipe for a happy marriage.

ALONE WITH LI, I DIDN'T KNOW WHAT TO DO OR SAY. THE muscles of my stomach clenched as hard as a fist ready for a fight.

I heard the floor creak behind me. Li came to stand next to me. Still, no words could come from my mouth. Could I truly let myself believe that he'd come through for me finally? That he would tell me the truth at last?

"Fiona, I'm sorry," Li said.

I drew away from the window and turned to him. "Don't be sorry." *Just love me*, I thought. *Tell me you're willing to fight for us.*

His dark eyes flickered with emotion. "I've made a terrible

mess of things. I'm sorry I've hurt you. Everything I've done, I've done for you."

"After everything we've done together, you had so little trust in me?"

"It's not you. It's the world."

"How better to fight prejudice and hatred than through love? Or do you still think that's naive?" I spoke softly, afraid to scare him away.

"Perhaps you are." He reached out to wrap one of my curls around his finger. "But maybe that's exactly what I need. What we both need."

"I can't be the only one who believes in us," I said. "You have to find it in your heart to take a chance that all will be well. That it's better for us to be together than apart, despite all the dangers."

"I want to. I truly do."

"Then let go," I said. "Let go of all that and grab on to me."

"And believe that despite all evidence to the contrary, the world's more good than bad?" Li asked.

"The world *is* almost all good with very little bad. Good people are going about their business, loving their families and doing the best work they can with the gifts God gave them. The power-hungry and the fearful make it seem otherwise. They're doing their best to destroy faith and love with their wars and their violence. The two of us—the way we feel—means it's our responsibility to fight for love. Every time people choose love instead of hatred, we make a small change that gets us closer to where we all want to be."

A smile lifted the corners of his mouth. He stroked my cheek with one knuckle and gazed at me with such tenderness my breath was temporarily stolen from me. "If anything happened to you because of me, I would not want to live. Furthermore, if you grew resentful and even came to hate me for all the ways I changed your life, it would be as good as death." His expression darkened. I could feel him slipping away, wanting to run.

"What is it?" I asked. "Tell me."

"When I was in Chicago, I almost died. I've never told you or anyone about what happened to me. I've wanted to shield you from the truth but perhaps you're right, I've done you a disservice by keeping parts of my life from you.

"It was late at night and I was headed back to my room after rehearsal. Three men jumped out of the shadows. I didn't know them, but apparently, they'd seen me around. They taunted me and then beat me and left me for dead. I thought I'd die of either my wounds or the cold there on the street. People would walk by and no one would even stop to help me. No one would even know for weeks and weeks, if ever, because the street cleaners would dispose of me into the bin."

"Is that what happened?" I asked. "Did no one stop to help you?"

He shook his head. "No, someone stopped. A young couple. They walked me home and helped me clean my wounds and put me to bed. The next day, he brought a pan of soup she'd made." He blinked, staring down at me. "Is that what you're going to take from this story? That someone helped me?"

"And brought you soup. Was it good soup?"

He laughed, raspy. "Yes, it was good. Not as good as Lizzie's or Grandmother's but decent enough."

"And what does that tell you?"

"That there are good people," Li said.

"Many more good people than bad."

"Yes, but the ones who are bad could hurt you. I can't have that. I'd rather be dead than have anyone lay a finger on you."

"I know you're scared for my safety." I put my arms around his neck and looked into his eyes. He did not flinch or turn away but seemed to relax under my touch. "I'm sorry you went through that. But you can't let it defeat you. I need you. Your family needs you. We all want you around for a long time. We all love you. You're our family. Especially mine."

"What if you'd been with me? It would have angered them even more to see a white girl beside me."

"Or would it have been the opposite? Maybe they'd have stopped, thinking of their mother or sister or even wife. We can't predict what would or would not happen. We can only put our trust in God and pray for the best." I stroked just under his ear with my thumb. The muscles in his neck were strong under my touch. "It's time to give up and let me in. All the way. What we have will not be ruined by anyone. I refuse to allow it. And now, you must kiss me. Finally."

He hesitated, and for a moment, I thought he would run from me, but he didn't. "I've never kissed anyone before."

"Me either," I said. "But it can't be harder than playing an instrument."

"True." He leaned closer and dipped his head, and then his mouth was on mine, soft and warm. His arms tightened around my waist and mine around his neck. We kissed until it became obvious that this was not at all like playing an instrument. It was easy. No practice required. Just in case, however, we went in for another kiss.

23

LI

By a miracle that I could only believe was divinely guided, the next day Lord Barnes was able to make arrangements for the twins to come home with us. Technically, he and Mrs. Barnes would have to adopt them, as I was not old enough, even if Fiona and I were already married.

"It'll be on paper only," Lord Barnes said as he helped himself to a drink. "You'll be their parents in every other way."

Fiona screamed with joy and hurled herself into my arms and to my mortification, placed her mouth on mine right there in front of her parents.

We jumped apart as the boys came running in from the kitchen. They abruptly stopped at the sight of the two of us in an embrace. A slow dawning of what that meant played out across Bleu's adorable features. "*Avez-vous embrassé? Oui, ils se sont embrassés.*" He turned to his brother. "Beaumont, *nos souhaits se sont réalisés.*"

"Did he say something about wishing?" Fiona asked me.

"Yes, he says this is what they wished for," I said.

Fiona withdrew from me to kneel by the boys. "What did you wish for?"

"*Vous savez ce qu'ils sont.*" You know my wishes. "*Nous avons besoin d'une mère et d'un père.*"

"He says we know their wishes. They need a mother and a father," I said. "They want us to be their parents."

"Is it true? Is that what you want? Do you want us to be your mother and father?" Fiona asked, searching their faces for the answer.

"*Oui, nous voulons que vous soyez notre mère et notre père.*" Beaumont pointed at Fiona. "*Vous serez ma maman.*"

"Succinctly speaking, that means yes," I said to Fiona.

She tented her hands under her chin, looking from one of them to the other. "I know the word *maman*."

"*Oui, nous voulons tous être ensemble pour toujours,*" Bleu said.

"They want us all to be together forever," I said.

Next to us, Mrs. Barnes sighed sentimentally. "How sweet they are."

Lord Barnes nodded. "It's not hard to see how the kids fell in love with them, is it?"

Bleu and Beaumont turned their attention to Lord Barnes with an inquisitive wrinkle between their eyebrows.

"We will be your grandparents," Lord Barnes said to them.

"*Qu'est-ce qu'il a dit?*" Bleu asked. What did he say?

I told them in French that Lord Barnes and Mrs. Barnes would be their grandparents.

"*Oui, oui,*" Bleu said. "Very good."

"Tell them what to call us," Mrs. Barnes said. "Grandmother and grandfather."

"*Grand-mère et grand-père,*" I said.

"I can't wait for them to meet their new family members," Mrs. Barnes said under her breath. To her husband, she said, "We're blessed with a growing family, are we not?"

"We are." Lord Barnes put his arm around his wife's shoulder.

Beaumont smiled and said in halting English, "We go to America. We will be family."

"Is that what you want?" Fiona asked, falling to her knees and holding out her arms to the boys. "Do you want to come to Colorado?"

Beaumont put his hand on Fiona's shoulder. "*Oui, nous voulons aller au Colorado voir les fleurs sauvages et votre folle de sœur sauter avec ses bottes et ses skis.*"

I translated. "They want to see the wildflowers and watch Cymbeline jump off the mountain. Fiona has told them all the stories of home, as have I. We weren't sure how much they understood with my poor French, but apparently quite a bit."

"*Et faire partie de votre grande famille désordonnée,*" Beaumont said.

"He wants to be part of our big, messy family," I said, laughing.

"They obviously understood you well, if that's what they think of the Barnes clan," Lord Barnes said.

I helped Fiona to her feet. "It will be my pleasure to be part of your big, messy family." I turned to Lord Barnes. "Whether it's been legal or not, you've all been family to Grandmother, Fai, and me and never asked for anything in return. It would be my great honor to be Fiona's husband. Asking for the hand of your precious daughter is not anything I take lightly. I promise to do my very best to take care of her, to give her a life where she can thrive and be her kind, generous loving self. Do I have permission to marry your daughter, Lord Barnes? Mrs. Barnes?"

"Li, you're taking on three instead of just one?" Mrs. Barnes asked, gesturing toward the boys. "Are you sure?"

"I am, Mrs. Barnes."

"He's picked nits out of our heads," Fiona said. "What more could I ask for?"

"Oh, dear, well, in that case, my love, you must give them

permission posthaste." Mrs. Barnes laughed and looked at me with shining eyes. "That's almost a marriage license in itself."

Lord Barnes glanced at his wife and then back to me. "Yes, you may marry my daughter."

"One moment," Fiona said, beaming. "Li, shouldn't you formally propose? I should be allowed to say yes or no."

"Yes, yes, of course." I fell to one knee and looked up at her. Out of the corner of my eye, I saw the boys clasp hands. "Fiona, will you marry me and be by my side through the good and bad for all the days of our lives?"

"Do you know how good it is to hear you say this?" She fell back to her knees before me and cupped my face with her hands.

"It feels good to say it." My knees weakened at the sight of her pretty eyes filled with tears.

"You've made all my dreams come true. I would very much like to be your wife. In fact, it's perfectly perfect."

"You are my everything. My muse, my inspiration, my best friend, and soon my wife." We kissed, chaste and quick. The boys cheered.

It turns out that cheering sounds the same in French as it does in English.

"ARE YOU SURE ABOUT THIS?" I ASKED FIONA THE NEXT DAY AS WE waited outside a French church. We had agreed to marry before we left for home, wishing to be able to share a cabin on our long trip back to America.

"Josephine will be angry with me," Fiona said. "But we can always do another ceremony at home if the sisters insist upon it."

Instead of her sisters and brothers, Fiona's friends had come to witness our vows. Her parents were there too. Mr. Basset was not invited.

We were married in a small ceremony in a Lutheran church not far from the apartment. It all flew by so fast that later I had trouble remembering the details. Afterward, we all went out to a festive meal at our café. Even Henri seemed happy for us, cracking a few smiles as he brought out decadent courses of oysters, fennel salads, pasta with chanterelle mushrooms, and roasted lamb, and finishing with a plate of fruit and cheese. Each course was paired with a lovely bottle of wine. By the end of the evening, after many toasts and congratulations, we were all warm and slightly tipsy. I'd almost forgotten our wedding night was still to come by the end of the evening.

Fiona's parents had arranged for us to have a night at an upscale hotel and had offered to stay with the boys, even though Gabriella was fine on her own.

Later, I stood by the window and looked out at the lights of the Eiffel Tower while Fiona changed into her wedding-night attire. Mrs. Barnes had insisted the hotel have a view of the famous tower, saying it was romantic and noteworthy. I agreed, although, at this point in the night, I was too nervous to enjoy the view.

Finally, Fiona emerged from the bathroom. She wore a lacy nightgown that clung to the curves of her hips and small breasts. I swallowed and took a deep breath at the same time, making me light-headed. I held on to the back of a chair to keep from toppling over and giving myself a head injury before we were able to consummate our marriage.

I was dressed in only an undershirt and a soft pair of pajama bottoms. Her hands went to her mouth. "Is it really you?" Fiona whispered. "Is this truly happening?"

"Yes, it's all real."

"Are you as nervous as I?" Fiona moved to the end of the bed and sat, as if her legs were suddenly unable to hold her upright.

"Do you remember the first night we played at the club?" I asked.

"Very well, yes. If I recall, we were both scared witless."

"I'm more nervous than that night."

She covered her mouth with her hands, giggling. "Me too."

I went to sit next to her on the end of the bed. "Whatever happens, we can try again."

"Cymbeline and Josephine have assured me it's very fun," Fiona said. "But I'm having trouble understanding how it all works."

I chuckled and smoothed a stray curl from her eyes. She had her hair completely down, and without combs or barrettes to hold her thick curls in place, they were as unruly as sweet pea bushes in the late spring. "We're novices," I said. "But perhaps after a time, we'll become experts at playing these new instruments?"

We both giggled, sounding like schoolchildren.

"What happens first?" Fiona asked.

I ran my thumb over her rosy bottom lip. "We kiss, I think. After that, we'll have to feel our way through it."

"Like a new piece of music." She sounded more confident thinking of it that way.

"Yes, practice makes perfect."

"Perfectly perfect," she whispered before I silenced her with a kiss.

THE NEXT MORNING I WOKE TO A SLANT OF SUN IN MY EYES. IT took me a moment to remember where I was. I grinned, remembering the night, and rolled over to take a look at my bride. She was asleep on her side with one pink cheek pressed against the pillow.

We needn't have worried about making this new kind of

music together. After a few tries, we were quite good at it. In fact, learning to love Fiona wasn't nearly as difficult as the violin or piano.

Her eyes fluttered open, and a smile spread over her pretty face. "Hello, husband."

"Hi, wife."

"It's still all real, correct?" Fiona asked. "You and me?"

"You and me and the boys."

"We've gotten ourselves into a fine mess, haven't we?" She smiled and reached for me.

"The best kind of mess, if you ask me," I said against her mouth.

"I still can't believe you love me. I'm pinching myself fifty times a day to make sure it's not a dream."

I looked into her eyes as I tangled my fingers into her curls. "I wrote you a letter confessing my love. Ages ago now, after everything that's happened since then. I didn't think I could say the words out loud, so I'd written them in a letter."

"When?"

"I planned on giving it to you the day the men attacked me." My chest tightened thinking of it all, the beating and the spiral of despair that had nearly drowned me. "What they did—it made me believe that I was selfish and wrong to tell you how I felt. Honestly, even though I've hurt you, everything I did was for you."

"I know. I can see that now," Fiona said. "You were so strong not to tell me when I was pouring my heart out to you."

We didn't have breakfast until quite a while later.

24

FIONA

WE ARRIVED HOME SAFELY AFTER WEEKS AT SEA AND THEN AN arduous train journey from New York City to Denver and then finally to Emerson Pass. As so many times before when one of us had come or gone, the entire family was waiting for us at the platform. Both my little sisters were crying by the time Mama reached them and took them into her arms.

"I shall never leave you for such a long time again," Mama said to Addie.

"I was perfectly fine. Quite brave, actually," Delphia said.

"I'm sure you were, my brave girl," Papa said, hauling her into his arms. "But we missed you more than we can say."

After we introduced James to the family, we all went home to spend the afternoon in the backyard, eating, playing croquet, and listening to music.

We introduced James and our little boys to the family. Bleu and Beaumont clung to Li and me. "Don't worry," I said to them. "After a while, all this chaos will be completely normal."

Cymbeline, with her round belly tucked under a linen shirt-dress, held me so tightly I could hardly take in a breath. "Don't ever leave me again," she whispered into my ear. "I can't bear it."

"I see. It's all right for you to leave but not me?" I asked, teasing.

"And look what you've brought home," Cym said. "A whole family. Isn't it just like you to have two boys before I could even give birth to my baby."

Later, we were all gathered together in the yard watching Delphia teach the twins how to play croquet. Although she was only a year older and much smaller than her new twin family members, that didn't stop her from bossing them around and acting superior. They didn't seem to notice, as they hung on her every word. Although I doubted they could understand half of what she was saying. Mama and James were playing croquet with the children while comparing thoughts on several new books.

Papa, Phillip, and Flynn had disappeared into his study to talk about business. Shannon and Louisa were sitting together speaking with their heads close, perhaps giving each other advice about how to put up with a Barnes twin. The smallest of our clan were upstairs taking afternoon naps, giving their mothers a break. Even Louisa's infant son had cooperated and gone down at the same time as his older cousins. Since I'd been gone, we had another Barnes to add to our messy family. Louisa had given birth to a little boy they'd named Simon, after her father. I'd never seen her as happy, and for that I was thankful. Shannon was back to her joyful self as well, now that Flynn was behaving himself. Well, as much as Flynn could. There had been talk at lunch about growing Phillip's ski-making shop to include a larger factory. The glint in Flynn's eyes when he talked about expanding into more markets than just our town told me that soon they would have another thriving enterprise.

Gabriella was downstairs with Lizzie probably getting an earful about all things Barnes family lore. She might wish to return to Paris. Li's cottage, which I guess was my cottage now, too, had only three bedrooms. With his grandmother still living with us, we didn't have a room for her. Thus, she would stay in a room here at the big house until we had it all sorted.

Li was inside, playing the piano in the parlor just off the enclosed front porch. The notes drifted out the windows, giving a musical background to the glorious afternoon.

That left Addie, Jo, Cym, and me to sit together in chairs under the shade. Lizzie had sent up lemonade, which refreshed us in the heat of the afternoon. The sky was a color blue I'd not seen anywhere else during my travels. Birds chirped in the trees. A slight breeze brought the scent of the sweet peas that bloomed on the other side of the fence. I let out a happy sigh and stretched my legs out long. "You can't know how happy I am to be home."

"Honestly, I can't believe you brought home two children," Cym said. "Only you could go to Paris and instead of getting into trouble end up bringing home two darling waifs."

"That's our Fiona," Jo said. "From the time she could talk she was rescuing someone with her loving heart."

"Is that true?" I asked. "I don't remember it that way at all."

"It's how I remember it," Josephine said. "And since I'm the eldest, what I say goes."

"Agreed." I squeezed her hand. "I'm glad to see my sisters," I said.

"It was dreadful without you," Cymbeline said. "I thought for sure I'd have this baby with you still in France and the thought made me want to bury my head under the pillows and not come out."

"Viktor would have had something to say about that," I said.

"They're adorable," Jo said, referring to Bleu and Beaumont. "I wish I could understand them better."

Cym had her glass of lemonade perched on top of her baby bump. "Do you see I have a shelf now? Isn't it convenient?" She rolled her eyes. "I don't know why anyone would do this twice. It's a pity I couldn't have ordered twins."

Despite my sister's complaints, she glowed with happiness and good health. Josephine looked well too, juggling her two little ones with such ease that I wished I could take a spoonful of her and have it give me magical mothering powers.

"We're delighted for you," Josephine said, patting my hand that rested on the chair's wide wooden arm.

"We could hardly believe what we were reading," Cym said. "I've never made it over to Jo's house faster than I did that day."

I'd written to them about my marriage and the boys in the same letter, sending it to Cymbeline's address and asking her to share it with Jo.

"You know how to get people talking, that's for certain," Jo said. "Everyone in town knew about the boys before the sun set that day."

"It was Flynn," Cymbeline said. "He told everyone he saw that you and Li were married and if they had anything to say about it they better tell him right then."

"No one had anything to say about it." Josephine laughed and sighed at the same time.

I joined in her laughter, imagining Flynn walking around town threatening the innocent. "He's always been protective of us."

"However misguided," Cym said. "The Barnes girls don't need anyone protecting us."

"Why would we, when we have you?" I asked.

Jo gestured toward James, who was bent over his croquet stick preparing for his shot. "He seems to be fitting right in here with us."

"He's a charmer," I said, noticing how both my little sisters seemed taken with him.

"It's a shame his friend's book hasn't led to more work," Josephine said. "But perhaps it will all happen the way it should."

"We never know what's coming, do we?" Cym asked. "When

our wishes don't come true and we think it's over for us, only to wake to find a new path that's even better."

I glanced over at Addie, who sat slightly apart from us and scribbled away in her notebook. "Adelaide, tell me how you are. You've barely said a word this afternoon."

She blew a strand of blond hair from her eyes. "I'm sorry. I don't mean to be standoffish. It's just that I have a new story idea and want to get it all written down before I forget."

"What kind of story this time?" Jo asked. "Romance or mystery?"

Addie flashed a shy smile. "This will be a story of the romantic nature." Her eyes drifted toward James, who had his head thrown back laughing at something Mama had said. "My hero will have coppery hair and dancing eyes."

I hid an amused smile behind my hand. James had an admirer.

"Someday, he will be your editor," Cymbeline said, sounding drowsy. "And you'll make lots and lots of beautiful books together."

"Why do you say it that way?" Addie asked, holding her pencil aloft. "As a statement instead of a question?"

"I don't know. Often, I feel things deep in my bones. Like premonitions maybe?" Cym swiped her thumb through the condensation on the outside of her glass. "And sometimes I have to dream big enough for all my sisters."

I turned my head to look at Cym directly. "Have I disappointed you? Giving up on Paris and Mr. Basset?"

"What? Goodness no," Cym said. "You're doing exactly what you should be doing. That's the thing about you, dearest. You do life exactly as you want to, without worrying about what others might think."

"That's how you live, Cym," I said. "Especially you."

"Takes one to know one," Jo said.

"I should very much like to write a real book someday."

Addie chewed on the end of her pencil. "Maybe I'll write the story of our family."

"That would be a twisted tale," Cym said, and wriggled her eyebrows. "Full of juicy parts."

"Cymbeline," Jo said. "May I remind you that Addie is still a child?"

"I'm not really," Addie said. "A few more years and I'll be as old as Fiona is now and maybe I'll be married too."

"You're only fifteen," I said. "Don't be in too much of a hurry."

"But how can I write about romantic things without having a love story of my own?" Addie asked, with another glance at James.

A knot of worry disturbed my peaceful state. Addie was a child. She had no business falling in love with a grown man. Although there were about the same number of years between them as there were Li and me. James would not be here in Emerson Pass, however, by the time Addie was old enough for him. He'd said just last night that he would stay long enough to come up with a plan and way to support himself and then be off to New York. I'd put it out of my mind, I decided. Nothing to worry about. Right?

I would make a mental note to discuss this further with Cym and Jo.

"If I guess correctly," Jo said, "our new friend James will have half the girls in town chasing after him."

"New blood," Cym said. "The wish of every small-town girl."

"I must hurry and grow up, then," Addie said, sounding concerned, "if I am to get James to fall in love with me."

"It worked for Fiona and Li," Cymbeline said. "Not that I'm encouraging such a thing. I'd rather see you write a book than marry and lose all ambition."

"How can you say that?" I asked Cym. "When you're so

happy with Viktor? You can't tell me that love isn't the finest thing of all. Even better than jumping off a mountain."

"Yes, love is grand," Cym said. "But so is winning."

"Poor long-suffering Viktor," Jo said, laughing. "Patience was his friend."

"Still is," I said.

"Do you see how mean they are to me?" Cym asked Addie.

We all laughed, our giggles as lovely as the birds that chirped above and the notes coming from the piano. I was right, I decided, feeling rather smug. Love in all its forms was indeed the grandest of all things.

LATER, AS WE SETTLED INTO LI'S COTTAGE AS A MARRIED COUPLE, I found Mrs. Wu in the garden picking tomatoes. I breathed in their delicious scent and held up a hand in greeting. "Can I help?" I asked.

She straightened, a fat tomato in hand. "No, dear. I'm done. But you can carry the basket inside."

We walked together across the small backyard toward the house. I had plans already to make the garden a haven for entertaining. I'd not have time before the cold weather came, but next spring. I shared some of my ideas with Mrs. Wu, pointing out areas where I would plant flowers and put a swing in for the boys.

"Speaking of changes," Mrs. Wu said. "I'd really like to stay at the big house. I sleep better there in the bed I'm accustomed to. And Lizzie's quite frantic without me there. She's too proud to say so but I know she was relieved when I returned."

"Have you spoken to Li about it?" I asked. Did she want to move out for her own sake or ours?

"Yes, we spoke of it earlier. He was in agreement. How else

will you have room for these boys of yours? I think he might be glad to be rid of me."

"Well, I doubt that. However, you're just down the road. We can be together anytime we want."

We reached the back porch. She stopped me from going up the stairs by putting a hand on my arm. "Miss Fiona, I have something to say."

"Yes, ma'am?" I held the basket in front of me, the ripe tomato scent tickling my nose. The evening air had cooled and felt delicious next to my bare arms and face.

"You've made Li happy. I'm glad for it. For you. I understood his reservations, of course. But in the end, we cannot hide. Not from love or from hate. Both have to be faced with courage."

"Yes, I believe so." She smiled up at me, her face etched with wrinkles, yet her beauty shone through. "Thank you for welcoming me into your family."

"Pish posh, you've been family all along," Mrs. Wu said, sounding remarkably similar to Lizzie. They hadn't spent every day together for twenty years and not picked up a few of each other's habits and ways of speaking. "I'm grateful for your family. For your father and mother's kindness and now for you. You've given my boy meaning and purpose."

I thanked her and then held the door for her to go inside. The boys were in the kitchen with Li learning how to take the ends off green beans. There was a mound of beans in front of each of them. They snapped the ends off each one and added it to a new pile while chatting in French with some English tossed in every few sentences.

They beamed at us when we entered the kitchen. Li looked up from where he'd been cutting potatoes for our dinner. This was my life, I thought. Simple and sweet. The stuff of dreams. Mine, anyway.

The boys asked if I would play the piano while they worked

and I obliged, but only after asking Li if he was sure he could spare me.

He nodded. "Best leave this to the experts, right, boys?"

They agreed, so I went out to the other room and sat at the piano to play a Gershwin tune I was supposed to have performed at the nightclub in Paris. This was a better audience, I decided. Where else could the scent of sweet peas mingle with tomatoes in the dry mountain air?

Home. This is where I belonged.

I looked up when Li entered the room with a glass of sherry for me. He sat down on the bench and kissed me lightly. "Welcome home, bride."

"Thank you, groom." I took the glass from him and took a sip before placing it on top of the piano. "What shall I play next?"

"I'll play one for you. One I wrote for you when you were away and I was miserable. Music saved me, Fiona. It always has."

I rested my cheek against his warm shoulder. "And brought us together."

He brushed his thumb along my cheekbone. "Are you sure you won't regret leaving Paris before the recital?"

"I'm quite sure. This is what I've wanted all along. We'll make music together here and if that's all we ever do, it will please God. I feel certain of it. Our music brings people joy, right here in Emerson Pass."

"We couldn't ask for a better life," Li said.

"We could not."

His slender fingers poised over the keys for a second before he began to play a tune sweet and elegant at once. The notes sent goose bumps up my arms. They were the story of our love, of our life, of our families. Of our two lives merging into one. As it was destined to be.

A NOTE FROM TESS...I HOPE YOU ENJOYED FIONA AND LI'S STORY. For more Emerson Pass tales, be sure to pre-order Addie's story, The Wordsmith, which comes out September 20, 2022

Join my newsletter and never miss a release or sale! Also, get a copy of Emerson Pass Contemporaries, Book One, The Sugar Queen just for signing up! https://tesswrites.com/

MORE EMERSON PASS!

Josephine's story opens ten years later in The Spinster of Emerson Pass. Get it here: The Spinster

The rest of the historical series….
The School Mistress
The Spinster
The Scholar
The Problem Child
The Seven Days of Christmas (a novella)
The Musician
The Wordsmith (coming September 2022 so pre-order now!)

The first of the Emerson Pass Contemporaries , The Sugar Queen , starring the descendants of the Barnes family is available at your favorite retailer.
The second in the contemporary stories, The Patron is also available. Will Garth and Crystal ever find a way to leave the past behind to embrace each other and the future?

For more Emerson Pass, download the historical books in the

series. Travel back in time to meet the original residents of Emerson Pass, starring the Barnes family.

The School Mistress

The Spinster

The Scholar

Sign up for Tess's newsletter and never miss a release or sale! www.tesswrites.com. You'll get a free ebook copy of The Santa Trial for your subscription.

The Spinster

Her love died on a battlefield. He carries a torch for a woman he's never met. Can the tragic death of a soldier entwine the souls of two strangers?

Colorado, 1919. Josephine Barnes wrote every day to her beloved fiancé battling in the trenches of the Great War. Devastated when he's killed in action, she vows never to marry and buries her grief in the construction of the town's first library. But she's left breathless when she receives a request from a gracious gentleman to visit and return the letters containing her declarations of desire.

Philip Baker survived the war but returned home burdened with a distressing secret. Though he knows it's wrong, he can't stop reading through the beautiful sentiments left among his slain comrade's possessions. Plagued by guilt, he's unable to resist connecting with the extraordinary woman who captured his heart with her words.

When Josephine invites Philip to join her gregarious family for the holidays, she's torn by her loyalty to a ghost and her growing feelings for the gallant man. And as Philip prepares to risk everything by telling her the truth about her dead fiancé, he fears he could crush Josephine's blossoming happiness forever.

Will they break free from their painful pasts to embrace a passion meant to be?

The Spinster is the second book in the heartwarming Emerson Pass historical romance series. If you like staunch heroines, emotional backdrops, and sweeping family sagas, then you'll adore Tess Thompson's wholesome tale.

Buy *The Spinster* to read between the lines of destiny today!

The Sugar Queen

The first in the contemporary Emerson Pass Series , The Sugar Queen features the descendants from the Barnes family. Get ready for some sweet second chances! To read the first chapter, simply turn the page or download a copy here: The Sugar Queen.

True love requires commitment, and many times unending sacrifice. . .
At the tender age of eighteen, Brandi Vargas watched the love of her life drive out of Emerson Pass, presumably for good. Though she and Trapper Barnes dreamed of attending college and starting their lives together, she was sure she would only get in the way of Trapper's future as a hockey star. Breaking his heart, and her own in the process, was the only way to ensure he pursued his destiny. Her fate was the small town life she'd always known, her own bakery, and an endless stream of regret. After a decade of playing hockey, a single injury ended Trapper Barnes' career. And while the past he left behind always haunted

him, he still returns to Emerson Pass to start the next chapter of his life in the place his ancestors built more than a century before. But when he discovers that the woman who owns the local bakery is the girl who once shattered his dreams, the painful secret she's been harboring all these years threatens to turn Trapper's idyllic small town future into a disaster. Will it take a forest fire threatening the mountain village to force Trapper and Brandi to confront their history? And in the wake of such a significant loss, will the process of rebuilding their beloved town help them find each other, and true happiness, once again?

Fast forward to the present day and enjoy this contemporary second chance romance set in the small town of Emerson Pass, featuring the descendants of the characters you loved from *USA Today* bestselling author Tess Thompson's The School Mistress.

The Patron of Emerson Pass
She's afraid to take risks. He's an incurable daredevil. When tragedy throws them together, will it spark a lasting devotion?

Crystal Whalen isn't sure why she should go on. Two years after her husband's death on a ski trip, she's devastated when a fire destroys her quiet Colorado mountain home. And when she can't keep her hands off the gorgeous divorcé who's become her new temporary housemate, it only feeds her grief and growing guilt.

Garth Welty won't be burned again. After his ex-wife took most of his money, the downhill-skiing Olympic medalist is deter-mined to keep things casual with the sexy woman he can't resist. But the more time they spend with each other, the harder it is to deny his burgeoning feelings.

As Crystal's longing for the rugged man's embrace grows, she worries that his dangerous lifestyle will steal him away. And although Garth believes she's his perfect girl, the specter of betrayal keeps a tight grip on his heart.

Will the thrill-seeker and the wary woman succumb to the power of love?

The Patron of Emerson Pass is the emotional second book in the Emerson Pass Contemporaries small-town romance series. If you like lyrical prose, unexpected chances at happiness, and uplifting stories, then you'll adore Tess Thompson's sweet tale. Buy *The Patron of Emerson Pass* to rebuild broken hope today!

ALSO BY TESS THOMPSON

ABOUT THE AUTHOR

Tess Thompson is the USA Today Bestselling and award-winning author of contemporary and historical Romantic Women's Fiction with over 40 published titles. When asked to describe her books, she could never figure out what to say that would perfectly sum them up until she landed on...Hometowns and Heartstrings.

She's married to her prince, Best Husband Ever, and is the mother of their blended family of four kids and five cats. Best Husband Ever is seventeen months younger, which qualifies Tess as a Cougar, a title she wears proudly. Her Bonus Sons are young adults with pretty hair and big brains like their dad. Daughters, better known as Princess One and Two, are teenagers who make their mama proud because they're kind. They're also smart, but a mother shouldn't brag.

Tess loves lazy afternoons watching football, hanging out on the back patio with Best Husband Ever, reading in bed, binge-watching television series, red wine, strong coffee and walks on crisp autumn days. She laughs a little too loudly, never knows what to make for dinner, looks ridiculous kickboxing in an attempt to combat her muffin top, and always complains about the rain even though she *chose* to live in Seattle.

She's proud to have grown up in a small town like the ones in her novels. After graduating from the University of Southern

California Drama School, she had hopes of becoming an actress but was called instead to writing fiction. She's grateful to spend most days in her office matchmaking her characters while her favorite cat Mittens (shhh…don't tell the others) sleeps on the desk.

She adores hearing from readers, so don't hesitate to say hello or sign up for her newsletter: http://tesswrites.com/. You'll receive an ebook copy of her novella, The Santa Trial, for your efforts.

Made in the USA
Las Vegas, NV
18 March 2023